Threads of Gold

Christine Pope

Dark Valentine Press

THREADS OF GOLD

ISBN: 978-0692526057
Copyright © 2015 by Christine Pope
Published by Dark Valentine Press

Cover design and book layout by Indie Author Services.

To learn more about this author, go to
www.christinepope.com.

THREADS OF GOLD

CHAPTER ONE

My father was late coming home the evening before. Since this had become something of a regular occurrence, I hadn't thought more than once or twice on his tardiness during the night in question, besides making sure that Cordell, the household's man-of-all-trades, kept a lamp burning so there was no danger of my father stumbling in the dark when he finally did find his way home.

Perhaps a lamp should not be necessary, not when a man would normally know his house as well as his own face, but let us just say that my father was often quite impaired by the time he made his way home in the small hours of the morning.

Now he sat at his place at breakfast, blinking irritably at the warm morning light streaming in through the many-paned windows of our dining chamber. "Cordell, shut those damnable curtains!" he snapped, and of course Cordell rushed to comply.

My sister Iselda shot me a troubled glance, but she knew better than to speak. No, she kept her head bent over her bowl of porridge with honey, her hair almost the same color as the golden liquid poured on top of the cereal to make it a bit more palatable.

For myself, I could only force my features into an outward aspect of serenity I most certainly did not feel. Affecting not to have noticed my father's brusque tone, I said calmly, "Cordell, would you mind very much bringing in some more tea? The pot is empty, I fear."

He hurried over and took up the empty teapot, even while he shot me a quick glance, dark eyes worried, as if attempting to gauge my mood. Most of the time I did not bother to engage with my father—what would be the point?—but on occasion I would decide I'd had enough of his intemperate ways, summoning the courage to rebuke him for his behavior, even though I knew I would likely regret it later. Cordell was far too well-mannered to ever interfere in these arguments, even though I knew they troubled him. I could not say I enjoyed the quarrels, either, but sometimes I found it impossible to hold my tongue.

What made matters worse was that I had discovered some months earlier a certain tenderness in Cordell's attitude toward me that would have been unthinkable even a few years ago. He was not so very old—thirty, perhaps, or thereabouts—and, if not precisely handsome, certainly not ill-favored. Once upon a time, our relative positions would have been so very different that he would never have contemplated even thinking of me as anything except his master's daughter.

Unfortunately, we had fallen quite a great distance over the past three years.

But we had not fallen quite so far yet that Cordell would not do as any of us bade him. He took up the empty teapot and hastened off to the kitchen, while I squinted through the now-darkened room at my father. The gloom could not entirely conceal the pouchy darkness under his eyes, the bleariness of his gaze.

And even though I knew I should have left it alone, said nothing, I could not prevent myself from asking, "How was the gaming last night? You were at Lord Selwyn's, I believe?"

For that was how my father had been consoling himself the last few years, with cards and drink at the home of any petty nobleman who did not mind lowering himself to gamble with a member of the merchant class, as long as said merchant had enough ready coin to bring to the table. Whether my father would continue to have said coin for much longer was up for debate, but at the moment he considered it a better use of his funds to game with the lower ranks of the nobility than to make sure there was bacon on the table at breakfast, or that his daughters had new winter boots.

Ah, well, I was done growing. I could make do with my boots for another year. Iselda, on the other hand, seemed to grow half an inch each month, and could barely fit into the slippers she wore day in and day out. At least I was more than handy with a needle, and could keep our clothing mended, our stockings darned. Indeed, my embroidery had been deemed so fine that it was good enough for court. Of late, I'd begun to plot in the back of my mind, attempting to come up with some way of offering my services to the fine ladies of the realm so I might bring in some extra money for the household. The only problem with that plan was that my father would most likely go into a flying rage if he ever learned I had attempted to lower myself in such a fashion.

Now he scowled and reached for his mug of cider. He was not one for tea, and the mildly alcoholic pear drink probably did more to restore him than anything else would. I knew he had to have been drinking something far stronger while gambling at Lord Selwyn's home.

"The gaming was well enough," he said, although I noted how he would not look at me.

That was a sure sign that he had lost, and lost badly. I tried not to sigh. It would have been so much better if my father had entrusted me with the household accounts, for at least then I would have known how close we were to ruin. As it was, it seemed as if our family was a ship driven onto a rock, foundering there and teetering with every wave, but not yet so precarious that the next influx of the tide would drive us on a reef and break us forever. And all I could do was guess, and attempt to calculate the worth of the few pieces of jewelry I owned, as well as the grander items my mother had left behind, and wonder if it would be enough to keep us afloat.

How long any such funds might last, I did not know. I was the eldest child, and therefore my father's heir, for at least here in Purth a young woman could inherit land and money, if not a title. But all that would count for very little if it was all gone by the time my father left this world.

I knew I should not be thinking such things. My father was not so very old—some five and forty—and therefore should have had many years left to him. But the loss of his wife, and the dwindling of his fortunes, had taken their toll on him. True, the first set of disasters were none of his doing. First, there was my mother's death in childbed, and the much-longed-for son with her, when Iselda had just turned nine. Almost immediately after that, most of the continent suffered a poor harvest, following a hot, dry summer of little rain. The shortfall left my father little enough to load on his small fleet of ships, or to send off with one of the overland caravans that traveled between our homeland of Purth and neighboring kingdoms such as Farendon, and, to a lesser extent, Seldd. Then there was the loss of one of his precious ships in a violent squall off the coast of South Eredor, followed by the realization that he did not have the capital to replace it. And so on.

I decided to try another tack. "Will you be going to your offices this morning?" I inquired. Lately, it seemed as if he had been spending just as much time at home as the small storefront he maintained on Larksheath Street, in a district of mixed shops and warehouses and merchants' offices. I knew he disliked going to the office, as it was only a further reminder of the distance between him and the men he rubbed elbows with every night, but even as depleted as our fortunes might be, there was still day-to-day business that must be handled.

Another scowl. "If I am, it will be on my own time, Annora, and so do not bother to poke and prod to get me out the door."

My hackles went up—mostly because he was correct. It was too wearying to have him underfoot all day, and yet he was the master of the house. I certainly did not have the right to order him to go to his office so that Iselda and I might have some peace and quiet for a few hours.

"I am not poking and prodding," I replied calmly, as Cordell returned with a fresh pot of tea. He poured for me, perhaps lingering longer at my elbow than was strictly required, and then moved around to refill my sister's cup as well. After that, he set the red stoneware teapot down on its trivet and went back to keep watch in one corner, in case any of us should need something further. "It is only that I thought I would beat the rugs today, and you know how that gives you sneezing fits."

That would be Cordell's and my task, along with Darinne, our one and only housemaid. Once upon a time, we had had five maids, and a footman, and...well, suffice it to say that those days were long gone.

Since I had fairly cornered my father, his brow only looked that much more furrowed. Of course, he could always command me to put off that one particular bit of housekeeping until later in the week, but, untidy as he might be in his personal life, he was house-proud. It would never do for us to have a chance visitor who might note some dust on a mantel, or a rug long overdue for a good cleaning.

"Very well," he said at last, then drained his mug of cider. "If you must. But make sure it is all done by the middle of the afternoon, for I will be coming home early to prepare for Baron Lesender's birthday dinner."

"Oh," I replied, my tone flat. Baron Lesender's gatherings were legendary. I only wondered at my father being invited to one, especially an event as auspicious as a birthday celebration. But I supposed that word had long ago gone around that my father had a tempting combination of poor luck and an open purse, a sure way of getting invitations to households he truly had no reason to be visiting.

There was no point in my protesting that he should not attend such a gathering. I would only be scolded for my impertinence, and I had had quite enough of confrontations with my father that morning. Nothing I could do or say would prevent him from going, and if I was silent and meek now, then at least I might gain a few precious hours of solitude.

"Well, I hope you have a lovely time," I told him, and left it at that. From the way he arched an eyebrow at me, I could see that he hadn't been fooled by my overly sweet tone.

But at least he said nothing else, and got up from the table soon afterward, making his ponderous way down the hall and up the staircase to his room. Over the past few years he had begun to put on a good deal of weight, blurring the lines of a face that had once been handsome, a figure that once had been strong and broad-shouldered. Now it cost him some effort to go up and down those stairs.

I could do little about that, however. He would not cease his drinking, nor deny himself the rich foods he loved. Perhaps that was why he dined out at the homes of these so-called "friends" of his so often. At their tables he could get the dishes we had been deprived of in our own house. Just as well for me,

I supposed. After all, a meager household budget was one way of ensuring a slender waistline.

"My lady, you should not be doing this," Cordell protested as I picked up the broom and swung it against the rug he and Darinne held with grim determination.

"Who else?" I replied, fighting back a cough, for the rag I had tied over my mouth and nose had slipped down to my chin during my exertions. "I cannot ask Grimsby, for his domain is the kitchen, and if I offend him, then I will have to bake all our bread and prepare all our roasts as well."

Cordell's mouth tightened, but he did not immediately reply. Grimsby was our cook, and although he had complained lately and often about the lack of variety in our meals, I could tell that his innate stubbornness prevented him from leaving the Kelsden household for a better situation. At any rate, asking a cook to do a housemaid's work was quite beyond the pale. Better for the daughter of the house to perform the messy task, especially if such unladylike doings were well hidden from the outside world. No one could peer into our courtyard to see me standing there with my hair bound up in a rag as I wore my oldest and most threadbare gown. Our house was the last one on the street, and was bordered on the one side by a row of stately oaks. In the winter they did not afford us much privacy, but now, in the late days of Sevendre, their luxuriant foliage had just begun to turn golden but had not yet started to fall, and so I thought myself hidden enough from prying eyes.

"He's right, my lady," Darinne put in. "That is, you should not be doing such work, but since it's the work of three people...." She let the words trail off, and shrugged her plump shoulders. It made sense for her and Cordell to be holding the rug while I hit it with the broom, since they were both stronger than I. And, unlike our manservant, Darinne didn't see any need to coddle me. She'd only come to the household some two years ago, a good span of time after my mother's death. By then I was eighteen, quite old enough to be thinking of marriage, and certainly not anyone in need of sheltering. Iselda she did cosset, and I did nothing to stop her. Perhaps between the two of us, we could be, if not precisely a replacement for the mother my little sister needed, at least someone to watch over her and make sure she came to no harm.

"Since it's the work of three people, we might as well get on with it," I said, then swung the broom against the rug again, watching as another puff of dust emerged from the fine weave. The silk carpet had come from Keshiaar, part of my mother's dowry, and still wasn't the slightest bit threadbare, even after more than twenty years of use.

Not bothering to reply, Cordell only tightened his grip on the rug and hung on doggedly as I beat it again and again. Perhaps someone passing by and witnessing the spectacle would have said I was hitting that rug just a bit harder than was strictly necessary. It did feel good to swing the broom and watch as more dust was propelled outward by the force of my blows. And if I was thinking of my father and how much money he was going to lose tonight, and therefore swung a little harder each time, who could blame me?

"Enough," Cordell said at last. "My lady, it is as clean as it is going to be."

"All right," I replied, lowering the broom. To be sure, my arms ached from the effort, and I wouldn't have been able to keep on for much longer anyway. "You may put the rug back in the drawing room. After that, Darinne, please make sure everything is dusted in there. You know how annoyed Master Kelsden becomes if everything isn't just so."

She nodded, and she and Cordell then shouldered the rug and began to march it back into the house. I lingered in the courtyard, slapping the dust from my skirts. Out of the corner of my eye, I could see movement in the upper story of the house. Iselda's window.

I smiled up at her and waved, and she waved back. No doubt she'd been sitting on the window seat and watching our antics, rather than attending to her sums. A tutor came to see her twice a week, but today was not one of his days to visit. Not so long ago, that same tutor had come every day. As the household's finances had dwindled, however, those visits had become more and more widely spaced, and I feared that soon my father would decide to dispense with his services altogether. At any rate, my sister should have been doing the work her tutor had left for her, but no doubt it was far more entertaining for her to watch me beat the drawing room rug half to death.

Affecting a mock frown, I mimicked scribbling on a piece of paper in the air, and she grinned and shook her head, then disappeared. I was sure if I had hurried up the stairs right then, I would have found her at her desk, busily at work. Poor Iselda. She had a very quick mind but was easily distracted, and being trapped in the house all day couldn't have been easy for her.

Actually, it wasn't all that easy for me, either.

Frowning, I tugged the rag from my hair as I went into the house. Subjected to this rough treatment, my heavy brown locks fell to my shoulders, pins scattering on the polished wooden floor. I'd just bent to gather them up when I heard footsteps.

"Is everything all right, my lady?"

I scooped the fugitive hairpins into my palm and then straightened to see Cordell watching me with a sort of worried admiration. A proper lady of more than sixteen was not supposed to go about with her hair down, but there wasn't much I could do to repair my current disheveled state without seeming too obvious.

Instead, I managed a smile and attempted to ignore the wayward locks falling over my shoulders. "Quite all right, Cordell. Is the rug back in place?"

"Yes, my lady." He paused then, giving a wary glance around us. "But if—if I could speak to you alone?"

Oh, dear. I prayed he was not going to make some entirely inappropriate declaration of love. That was the sort of display which could send him packing, and yet our meager little household needed him so very badly. I knew we would never be able to afford someone else who was even half as capable. Why he'd taken such a paltry wage, when he could have done better for himself in a grander household, I did not know. I only hoped his choice had not stemmed from some misplaced affection for me.

"Very well," I replied, my tone resigned. "Since Darinne is in the drawing room at present, perhaps my father's study?"

That seemed safe enough. He wouldn't be home for several hours, and there was no risk of anyone overhearing us in there.

Cordell's dark eyes lit up. "That would be excellent, my lady."

I nodded at him and headed on down the hallway, with him a few steps behind. As I went, I couldn't help wondering what had prompted him to speak to me now. Was it the tense scene at the breakfast table this morning? But really, that hadn't been so very different from a hundred other similar episodes. Unfortunately, my father and I didn't need much encouragement to begin sparring with one another.

Although I had suggested it, something did feel slightly wrong about entering his study with Cordell. Because it was my father's room, all was neat and orderly—the ledger sitting on top of the desk had been lined up neatly with the inkwell, while a feather pen lay precisely perpendicular to the ledger.

The curtains were open, probably because Darinne had been dusting in here earlier and needed the light. Outside the window, the oak trees' golden leaves waved in the breeze. Something about the sight of them made my heart give an odd little lurch. Perhaps it was only that I wished I could be outside and free like those leaves, rather than little more than a prisoner in this stuffy house. It had been so very long since I'd escaped the narrow streets of Bodenskell, the city where I had been born.

And where you will most likely die, I thought, then wanted to shake my head at myself. What on earth was I doing, thinking about death on a bright autumn day such as this?

I drew in a breath. "What is it you wished to speak to me about, Cordell?"

His gaze shifted to the door, almost as if he expected my father to appear there, even though he was a good ten-minute walk away. Yet another reason why it was a good thing for him to visit his office; we did not have a horse or carriage, not anymore, and so he was forced to get a small amount of exercise when going to and from his place of business.

Then Cordell looked back at me, and I wanted to cringe. That tenderness I had noted was back, his dark eyes seeming to focus on me and nothing else. I had never been the object of such attention before, and I was not sure what I should do about it.

"My lady," he said. One hand lifted briefly, as if he wanted to reach out toward me but didn't quite dare. "I know I must seem very forward, speaking to you like this, but I fear I cannot stay silent any longer."

Not knowing what else I should do, I nodded. In a way, it was rather thrilling to have a man gazing at me the way Cordell was now. My father did not allow me out in company, and I had never had any suitors. What his intention was, in keeping me so isolated, I had no idea. Surely with our finances in such ruin, the intelligent thing would have been to find me a rich husband. The mirror told me I was comely enough that such an arrangement might have been possible, if I had been given the opportunity, and yet I was still left severely alone.

Cordell hesitated then, as if sifting through the words in his mind so he would be assured of choosing the right ones. Then, to my surprise, he seemed to gather himself and took both my hands in his. Something about the way he did so seemed to indicate that he had moved swiftly in order not to lose his nerve.

His fingers were warm and strong, and not unpleasant, even callused as they were. Somewhere in the back of my mind I thought that perhaps I should be pulling my hands away, but for some reason I did not. Perhaps I was so startled that I didn't know quite what to do.

He appeared to take my lack of protest as encouragement, for he moved closer. His gaze flickered over my face, and for the first time I noted that he had quite long lashes, heavy and dark like his hair. Some might say his nose was too long, or his mouth too wide, but he was still attractive enough even so.

"My lady, I have had some news. My brother has passed away—"

"Oh, I am so very sorry," I broke in, somewhat startled, for this was not the sort of thing I had been expecting him to say. "Do you need to take your leave for a while, to be with your family? We will have to ask for my father's permission, but—"

"No, that is not it." His hands tightened on mine. "My brother and I were estranged. That is why I have been working here in your household. He seized the part of my father's inheritance that should have been mine, leaving me with nothing. But now I have had word that he is gone. A fall from his horse, I was told. And so the inheritance has come to me."

To my utter shock, Cordell sank to his knees then, gripping my fingers the entire time. "I know this must seem very sudden, my lady, but it was not my place to speak before I could offer you a future that would include the comforts you are used to. The estate is small, but it is mine, and comes with a fine vineyard and a good sturdy house. I would very much like it if you would consider sharing it with me."

All I could do was gape at him. Yes, I'd known that he admired me on some level, but it was quite a leap to go from that flicker of interest to an offer of marriage. At least, I assumed that was what he'd just asked of me.

Best to be sure, I supposed. Voice small, I said, "Cordell, are you asking me to be your wife?"

He blinked. "Yes—oh, that was stupid of me, wasn't it? All this time thinking how I would say those words to you, and I couldn't even ask you properly!"

His expression of consternation was so intense it might have been comical, under different circumstances. "It's quite all right," I said gently.

"Is it?" His eyes were staring into mine, that same question burning in them.

For a long moment, I didn't reply. I could only stand there, feeling his hands on mine and the roughness of the calluses on his fingers, and gaze back down at him. Cordell as my husband? Could my mind even encompass such a thing? I'd certainly never thought of him in such a way. And yet he was certainly not ill-favored. I could do much worse. He was a man of property now, with a home in the country. If I told him I would become his wife, I could escape Bodenskell. I could breathe in fresh air and see the sky, and know that I would never have to suffer my father's petty tyrannies again.

But...I did not love Cordell. How could I? He had been a servant in our house, quiet, unobtrusive. I had never thought of him that way. Could I allow myself to open my heart to him? I had spent the last few years closing myself in, not allowing myself to be intimate with anyone. I had no close friends, and my sister was someone I had to watch over, not confide in.

At the same time, I did not wish to hurt the man who knelt before me. His dark eyes were pleading with me to make the leap, to trust him, and yet I wasn't sure if I could. Not even if going with him meant I would at last be able to escape my father's household.

My lips parted. I had intended to tell him that this was so sudden that I wasn't sure how to respond, but I was not given that opportunity. Even as I drew breath to reply, I heard my father roar, "What the devil is all this?"

At once Cordell pulled his hands from mine and scrambled to his feet. "S-sir, it is not what you think—"

My father's impressive bulk filled the doorway. Cordell was of a height with him, but slender. Right then I could not say that my father appeared so much overweight as fully capable of breaking the younger man over his knee.

Even though my heart raced so quickly that I could feel it beating against my stays, I raised a hand, saying, "Father, truly nothing happened. Cordell was only—"

"Only what?" my father snapped. "The two of you alone together, your hair down in a most unseemly fashion…what do you think it looks like you were up to?"

Somehow I kept myself from reaching up to push my hair back over my shoulders so it would be less conspicuous. "We were up to nothing at all."

"It is true, sir," Cordell added. "That is, I was asking your daughter to be my wife."

Far from mollifying him, Cordell's statement only appeared to intensify my father's ire that much more. "You what? *What?* A servant asking a daughter of this house to be his wife?"

At the word "servant," Cordell straightened further. No, I did not love him, but I couldn't help admiring him in that moment, the way he met my father stare for stare and did not back down. "Reduced circumstances forced me to take a position here, Master Kelsden, but those circumstances have now changed. I have inherited land and a home in the country, and—"

"And what?" my father roared. Cordell's explanation did not seem to have mollified him at all, but rather inflamed him even further. "So you thought you would make my daughter— my daughter, whose beauty surpasses that of all the ladies at court—a farmer's wife? Insolence!"

Truly, I had never thought my father paid any particular attention to my looks. I had the notion right then he was exaggerating for effect, but even so, I couldn't prevent a small flush of pride from passing over me. That came and went quickly, however, replaced by a need to defend Cordell.

"Indeed?" I broke in, making no effort to keep the skepticism from my tone. "If I truly am such a jewel, why am I so hidden away? If it were not for Cordell's presence, I doubt I would know what a man even looks like!"

He reddened slightly at my words, and seemed as if he was about to speak. My father gave him no opportunity, however, saying,

"You think this a man?" He made a dismissive gesture toward Cordell, then shook his head. "Clearly, you are quite lacking in discernment." Shifting toward the unfortunate man-servant, my father went on, "And you, fool, will have no further chances at her. Pack your things and go from this house."

To my surprise, Cordell stood his ground and said calmly, "I had already intended to give my notice and depart, for I must leave this place to go claim my inheritance. But I had not yet had the lady's reply before you interrupted us." His gaze moved from my father to me. In that moment I could see the strain in his face, the worry in his eyes, but he spoke in steady tones as he continued, "My lady Annora, what is your will?"

My will? I stood there, mouth dry as the answer seemed to elude me. Oh, how I wanted to be gone from my father's house! But that would have meant leaving Iselda behind, and how could I ever abandon her in such a way?

"Her will is to do as her father wills," my father said. He appeared calmer now; perhaps my lack of immediate response to Cordell's question had convinced him that I had no true desire to abandon my family to live with a servant. "Is that not correct, Annora?"

Somehow I managed to unstick my tongue from the roof of my mouth. "Your offer honors me, Cordell. But—"

"But you would rather stay here with this tyrant than marry me." The warmth had left his tone, and now he sounded cold, detached, as if that was the only way he could manage the rejection he had just suffered.

"No, that is not it," I protested. "I cannot leave my sister—"

"I understand," he said, then bowed slightly, with more grace in the movement than I might have expected. It did seem as if he was more than the servant he had always claimed to be. "May the blessings of the gods be with you, good lady." Dark eyes shifted to my father, and held. "If I may pass?"

"Yes, pass," my father growled. "And be gone from this house."

Chin high, Cordell walked past my father, then down the hallway toward the back of the house, where he slept in a small room off the kitchen. For a long moment, quiet reigned in the study. I fancied I could almost hear the thudding of my heart within my breast, although that was most likely only my imagination.

Then my father gave me a cruel smile. "Really, Annora, could you do no better than that?"

Something inside me seemed to give way, and I burst out, "Oh, let me be!", before I pushed past him and ran up the stairs.

It was a good thing I could have made my way anywhere in the house blindfolded, for in that moment everything before me dissolved into tears, and I stumbled the rest of the way quite without seeing, blinded by my misery.

CHAPTER TWO

I selda came to me as I sat on my bed and sobbed. Of course I did not see her at first, blinded by my tears as I was, but I felt her thin arms go around me, even as she asked,

"Were you truly in love with Cordell?"

I shook my head, then blinked back my tears as best I could. Somewhere in my room was most likely a handkerchief, but in that moment I couldn't be bothered to go searching for it.

"No, dearest, I was not, but he was a good man."

"And if you had gone with him, you would be safely away."

It did not seem right to me, that a girl her age should be saying such things. But Iselda watched and listened and understood. As Darinne had once said, her soul was far older than the body which housed it.

"How could I be safe, if you were not with me?" I asked, hugging her.

"Perhaps." My sister was silent for a moment as she appeared to consider the question. "But perhaps you could have asked Cordell if you could bring me with you."

Which was something I had considered. I had just not been given the chance to ask. I shifted on the bed, and Iselda let go of me and scooted away a bit. Her big green eyes were fastened on me, as if waiting for me to answer her.

I wished I could. Instead, I inquired, "Do you like Cordell?"

She nodded. "He is kind. He would bring cookies upstairs and leave them outside my door when he knew I was studying and didn't want to be disturbed."

This was not news to me, for I had caught him doing that very thing once or twice. But I was heartened that Iselda had liked Cordell as well, had thought him a good-hearted man. At least that meant my judgment in such matters wasn't entirely lacking.

I wiped at my eyes again, and Iselda tilted her head to one side.

"If you did not love him," she asked, "then why are you weeping?"

"I don't know," I replied frankly. "I suppose it is the realization that I could have gotten away, that I could have done something to change my life."

She was silent again. "It is odd," she said after a pause. "That is, you are now twenty. I don't see why Father hasn't tried to find you a husband. Isn't that how it is supposed to work?"

Yes, it was. I should have been betrothed already, to the son of a friend or business acquaintance, or, failing that, a relation distant enough that the health of our children would not be a consideration. Our own parents had been betrothed from a very early age, their match agreed upon by their parents when the two children were both just eight years old. They were from merchant families, and it was thought to be a good match. I sometimes wondered about that, however, for even when I was younger and my mother very much a part of my life, I could tell that she and my father did not get along all that well. His drinking had intensified after she was gone, but he had liked the bottle a little too much long before that.

Indeed, on some days when relations between my father and myself were even more strained than usual, I would begin to wonder if she had died just so she could get away from him....

Of course I could never say such a thing to my younger sister. I patted her on the shoulder and got up from the bed, looking at last for a handkerchief, as it seemed clear by then that my nose had no intention of drying up anytime soon.

"I suppose Father is holding out for some grand match," I said as I rummaged through the top drawer of my bureau, which held odds and ends such as handkerchiefs and scarves and gloves and fans. A worn cotton handkerchief was at the bottom of one stack, and I plucked it out and used it to blot my nose. By then my eyes, fortunately, were more or less dry. "How he intends to accomplish such a thing, when we have little to provide for a dowry save the gown on my back, I am not sure."

My sister raised a skeptical eyebrow. "But you are so very beautiful," she protested. "Surely that is enough."

I wanted to smile at her naïveté, but that would only be mocking her, and I knew she was serious. "That is a lovely compliment, Iselda, and I thank you for it. But it would have to be someone very generous indeed to overlook my regrettable lack of any meaningful wealth."

"Cordell didn't seem to care."

No, he did not. He had already come into money and land he had not been expecting, and so wanted nothing from his bride save affection. Or at least that was how his offer had appeared to me.

"Cordell is not most of the men here in town. His situation was different."

She seemed to think that over, then nodded. "It is too bad that Father was so...intractable." This last word was uttered with some pride; I guessed that she had only recently added it to her vocabulary. Her expression grew somewhat alarmed. "Do you think he will come to scold you?"

That prospect had worried me at first as well, but it had now been at least a half-hour since I had fled up the stairs. If he had intended to come and remonstrate with me, he would have done so immediately.

"No," I replied. "I am sure he thinks he has done well enough in running Cordell off, although he may have regrets in the morning, when we have only Darinne to wait on us."

And little joy either of them would have in that situation. I repressed a sigh, realizing I might have to take up a number of Cordell's former duties. We would hire another manservant in time, I supposed, but that could take a good while, especially considering how little we were able to pay.

"And besides," I went on, "Father will be getting ready for Baron Lesender's dinner, and no doubt will be thinking little of us."

"Is he really going to the house of a baron?" Iselda asked, wide-eyed.

"You were there when he told us of it. That does seem to be his plan for the evening."

"He will lose a great deal of money, won't he?" This question was asked matter-of-factly, as if my sister already judged it a foregone conclusion.

For that matter, it was. Oh, to be sure, every once in a while, my father would have a rare night of good luck and would come home beaming over the change in his fortunes. But these evenings of fair fortune occurred with such rarity that those infrequent windfalls couldn't do much to alter the woeful state of our finances, especially since he would only view his new riches as a sign that his luck had changed permanently for the better...until the next time he went to the gambling table and lost it all over again.

"Most likely," I told my sister. "But we will survive, as we always have."

She was fiddling with the laces on her sleeves, not looking at me. Because she was only thirteen, her hair was loose, falling in warm gold ringlets over her shoulders. Some of the court ladies, I had heard, would spend hours getting their hair to curl just so, but Iselda's did that all on its own.

Then she asked, in a very small voice, "What will we do when it is all gone?"

My heart broke a little, hearing that question. She should not have to worry about such things. Her only cares should be how well she fared in her studies, or the color of her new gown, or whether to purchase her new boots in black or brown. Or possibly, just possibly, to wonder if the boy who lived down the street had given her an admiring glance as she came home from the marketplace.

"That is a very long time off," I said stoutly, even though I truly had no idea how long our money would last. My father did have some income still, even if it was greatly reduced, and so I couldn't say that all our money flowed in only one direction. It might last for some time.

"Even so. What will we do?"

"Then I suppose we will go to live with our Aunt Lyselle." She was our mother's younger sister, a great beauty in her time, who had married a baron and who lived on a grand estate in the mountainous mining province of Daleskeld, many miles to the north. We had a letter and a basket of extravagant gifts from her every midwinter, but otherwise we did not hear much from her. I knew that she disapproved of my father and his behavior, but would not interfere unless it became painfully obvious that we had been left with no recourse.

Or perhaps were about to be put out on the street.

"I haven't even met her," Iselda said, her tone morose.

"Yes, you have, but you were only four at the time, and so perhaps do not recall. And she was at Mother's funeral, but…." I stopped there, realizing too late that I should not have brought up such a painful subject. For after our mother passed away, Iselda became so deathly ill that we feared we would lose her as well. Because she had been confined to her sickbed, she had not attended the funeral, and so had not seen Aunt Lyselle. "Anyway," I went on, my voice brisk, "she is a very great lady, and lives in a castle of stone, where I am sure there would be plenty of room for us, should matters come to such a pass."

"I would wager that *she* would be able to find you a husband," Iselda said, somewhat trenchantly.

"I suppose she would," I replied, my tone light. "But that is not currently her concern, as she has three daughters of her own to marry off." Not that finding her girls husbands would be any great problem, since they were reputed to be as lovely as she, and had their father's wealth and title to recommend them as well.

My sister nodded again, and appeared willing to let the matter go after that. I could not quite sigh in relief, not in her presence, but after I had reminded her of the sums she still had to complete, and the calligraphy exercises that were yet undone, she gave a sigh of her own and went off to her room, leaving me to some much-needed solitude.

I went to my window, which looked out on the street. By that hour, the sun had begun to dip to the west, and people were returning to their homes. Most everyone on our little lane, which dead-ended just past our house, was engaged in trade of some kind, whether they were merchants like my father, or owned a shop or factory, like Master Brelsland, whose business was the weaving of cloth. My father had taken me to his factory once when I was not much older than Iselda was now, and I had been fascinated by the complex machines, which could produce fine fabrics so much more quickly than the small looms some people still kept in back rooms or in storage, even if they were no longer used.

My mother had taught me to weave and to spin, although I had not touched the spinning wheel in years. I much preferred embroidery, and not merely because it was a way to make the gowns Iselda and I wore, made of inexpensive cloth, look so much finer with no additional expense but for a few skeins of embroidery silk. Stitching those patterns onto our gowns, or on a pillow cover, brought a little extra beauty to our lives, something I thought my sister sorely needed.

Movement on the street caught my eye, and I realized that not everyone was coming home for the day. No, there was my father, sallying forth on foot, head topped by a fine hat with crimson plumes, wide torso covered by his best black velvet doublet. If that velvet was beginning to be a little worn at the elbows and along the seams, well, I doubted many would notice in the dim lighting of most of the rooms used for gaming. Or at least I hoped they wouldn't. Ours was not the most amicable of relationships, but that didn't mean I wanted people to laugh at my father's poverty behind his back.

He would return very late, this time in the coach of whoever was feeling charitable enough to give him a ride home. As he disappeared around a corner, I felt a small spurt of fury deep within my breast. All along our street, other fathers were returning to their families to share their evening meals, but mine seemed to care nothing for his daughters. We would eat alone, as we almost always did, Iselda and I at the great expanse of the dining table, which had been built to seat so many more than two.

And tonight there would be no Cordell to bring us our meal. My heart ached at that realization, although I doubted it was because I had suddenly realized my true feelings for him. No, it was more that he had been a part of our lives, someone to provide the illusion that we weren't constantly being left on our own. Now he was gone, and I was sure he would mend his heart with a girl close to his new home, someone who wouldn't care that he had once been a servant in a merchant's house.

Angrily, I pulled the draperies shut and went out of my room, down the stairs, and into the kitchen. Grimsby started in fright at my sudden appearance.

"My lady Annora, what are you doing in here?"

His round red face had always reminded me rather of a tomato, and never more so than in that moment, his cheeks even ruddier from the heat of the cook fire.

"I have come in here to see if the food is ready to bring out. Since Cordell is now gone, we no longer have anyone to serve."

"I'll do it, my lady," said Darinne, emerging from the pantry with the butter dish. "It isn't fitting that you should be in here, nor thinking of bringing the food to the table. I can do it, and don't mind. It's not as if I'm having to serve at a grand dinner party."

"No," I replied. "We have not had one of those for some time."

One of her sparse eyebrows lifted, as if she were attempting to decide whether I was teasing her or not. The sad truth was that we had never had any kind of a dinner party in my home, at least not since I was old enough to remember. Perhaps my parents had entertained when they were newly married, but I somehow doubted it. I was born only eleven months after they were wed, and that probably would have curtailed any efforts at hospitality for a while.

"Well, then," Darinne said, after an awkward pause, and went out to the dining room with the butter.

I followed, mostly because I could see that Grimsby was not pleased with my presence in the sacred confines of his kitchen. Poor man—I knew he wanted to make dishes that were elegant and delicious at the same time, but since he was given only inexpensive cuts of meat and simple vegetables and roots to work with, there was not a great deal he could do to provide much variety. But everything was savory enough in its own way, and I had learned to be content with that, even though I knew my father dined on spiced meats and fine ragouts and all manner of delicacies when he went out in the evening.

Darinne was silent for a moment as she set down the butter and then adjusted the layout of the dinnerware on the table, shifting a plate here, a fork there. Her eyes would not meet mine.

"Did you know something of it?" I asked her then. "Of what Cordell intended?"

At first she said nothing, but only moved a water glass a fraction of an inch to the right. Since she had never before shown any sign of being interested in such niceties, I had to assume she did so now in an attempt to stall me. After a moment, she let out a small sigh. "Not precisely, my lady. But it was easy enough for me to tell that he thought very highly of you. And a few days ago he received a letter, and seemed a little off after that."

"'Off'?" I repeated.

"Not himself. Absent-minded. It seemed clear enough to me that his thoughts were somewhere else." She backed away from the table and smoothed her hands over the front of her apron. "Now I know where his mind was. 'Tis a shame, my lady."

"So you think I should have accepted his offer?"

"It's not my place to remark on that." This time she did look at me, hazel eyes dark with concern. "But it's unfortunate he didn't ask a day sooner. That's all I have to say on it."

I reflected that she might have a point there. For the afternoon before, my father had gone down to the warehouse where he rented space, taking with him his sole assistant to perform inventory. They had not returned until almost dinnertime, at which point my father had changed his garments and gone back out to the party at Lord Selwyn's town house. So if Cordell had come and spoken to me then, with no danger of interruption, his proposal might have had a very different outcome.

However, the past could not be altered, not once it had been set. I lifted my shoulders and told Darinne, "And that is all we should say. For he is gone now, and that is all that has changed." Glancing away from her, I took in the dining room, with the plaster on the walls that should have been refreshed years ago, and the chairs and table that showed scratches and scars from long use. It was all so familiar to me that I barely gave its shabbiness a second thought, but in that moment I realized how neglected it all appeared. There was little I could do about it, though, save to mend a cushion or a curtain here and there as necessary.

Cordell is gone, I thought then. *But I am still here...and likely to remain here.*

Dinner was a quiet meal, both Iselda and I subdued. Afterward, she excused herself to go to her room and read. I could not fault her for that, even though I knew she was not reading any improving works, but rather some hastily printed bundles of rather lurid stories passed on to her by Lysia Devenning, who was a year older than my sister and who liked to indulge an overactive imagination. The stories were not, perhaps, the best reading material for my sister, but I did not try to take them away from her. She had a good enough head on her shoulders that I felt she could distinguish the realities of life from the outlandish exploits described in those packets of stories, and why should I deny her the chance at a little escape?

As for me, I only dragged myself up to my room and took up my embroidery. Lighting two candles to work by was perhaps an extravagance, but I had no other entertainment, and besides, the piece I stitched was a new covering for one of Iselda's worn pillows. The bright colors might cheer her up, or at least make her quite utilitarian room a little prettier.

Although that was my intention as I sat down, my attention seemed inclined to wander. More than once I had to stop and go back to pick out something I had just stitched, and the Selddish knot I was attempting kept falling apart under my impatient fingers. At last I paused and set the embroidery hoop down. I sat at the table by the window, and my gaze strayed there instead, although night had fallen and I could see little but the orderly lines of lamps along the street, each casting a circle of warm yellow light, but not doing much to dispel the dark of a moonless night.

Perhaps I watched for my father's return. However, it was far too early for that; he did not often return home before midnight, and more often than not, I was unable to stay awake until the inevitable coach came along to drop him off.

Right then, in the candlelit warmth of my chamber, I could not help wondering what Cordell might be doing in that very moment. He had not told me how far away his new inheritance lay, and so I did not know if it was a day's ride off, or someplace much farther than that. Perhaps he was on the road, stopping at an inn for the night, or perhaps already home, back in the place where he had grown up. Was he thinking of me, or had he already pushed me out of his thoughts, just another part of an unpleasant chapter in his life, one that he now wished to leave behind?

I wanted to tell myself that it was foolish to let such matters crowd my mind. It was not as if I had a particular attachment to Cordell. But still...what would I have done if he had bent down to me, placed his lips on mine?

No man had ever kissed me, so I could not say. Most likely I would have been so shocked that I wouldn't have reacted at all. And yet, such things were supposed to be pleasant, were they not?

If I had had a friend to discuss such things with, it might have been better. But the only girl close to my age who lived on my street had married three years ago and now lived in the country near Hardismere. At any rate, Janille and I had never been that close, despite our growing up so near one another.

Her family was prosperous, and I feared she thought we Kelsdens were quite beneath her, if not a disgrace to the entire street and its otherwise upstanding inhabitants.

And my mother had died before she could tell me anything except the vaguest of hints as to what it might mean to be married, to be intimate with one's husband.

I allowed myself a weary little sigh, then rebuked myself for being maudlin. It was late enough that I should just go sensibly to bed. Perhaps once I put this strange, long day behind me and got a good night's sleep, I would be better prepared to face whatever might come the next day.

First, though, I went to check on Iselda. As I had thought, she'd fallen asleep with one of the crudely printed little pamphlets still in her hands. I took it gently from her fingers and placed it on her bedside table, then pulled the covers up a little farther over her chest.

She murmured something unintelligible and rolled over on her side.

"Good night, dearest," I whispered.

The snuffer lay next to the candlestick on the table. I picked it up and put out the candle before tiptoeing from the room. Because my sister had learned to take care of herself years before, she had already washed her face and cleaned her teeth before climbing into bed to read her stories, and so I knew I could leave her as she was without having to rouse her.

I had just gone back to my own room to begin my own preparations for sleep when I heard quite a rattle of wheels and hooves on the cobbled street outside. Puzzled, I glanced at the hour candle on the mantel. Only a little past ten in the evening, far too early for my father to be returning home.

But if he had already run out of funds, or met with some other misfortune....

Heart beginning to pound with worry, I went to the window and pushed the curtains aside. Down on the street, I saw a great black carriage with a crest in gold on its side, although in the uncertain light I could not make out precisely what it was. Besides that, there were a dozen men mounted on horseback surrounding that carriage, all wearing livery of blue and gold.

Blue and gold? But those were the colors of the royal house.

My befuddled mind had only grasped that astounding detail when there came a great pounding on the door. At once I hurried out into the corridor and scrambled down the stairs, even as Darinne and Grimsby met me in the entry, their eyes wide with shock.

If Cordell had been there, he would have been the one to open the door. As it was, the three of us stared at one another, not sure who should take up that duty. Yes, I was the eldest daughter of the house, but it was not expected that a young unmarried woman should be the one to put herself out in such a way.

The pounding came again, and I set my jaw and stepped forward, since both my remaining servants seemed too overcome to do anything helpful. Grasping the latch, I lifted it, then swung the door open. On the step outside stood a very grand man indeed, perhaps of an age with my father, but still trim and athletic enough. He wore an embroidered velvet doublet topped by a heavy neck chain ornamented with dark glinting rubies. To either side of him were ranged the soldiers I had spied earlier, now afoot. The helmets they wore cast their faces in shadow, so I could see nothing of their expressions.

As I stood there, mouth agape, the grand man swept off his feathered cap and bowed as low as if we had just been presented at court. Straightening, he flashed me a dazzling smile and said, "Annora Kelsden?"

I could only nod.

Apparently not put off by my lackluster response, he went on, "I am Lord Edmar, Duke of Lerneshall, and advisor to the king."

Dumbfounded, I flashed a quick sideways glance at Darinne and Grimsby, but they still seemed to be rooted in place, incapable of offering any assistance. At any rate, what help could they give me, when we had suddenly been confronted by one of the greatest peers in the land?

From behind me in the foyer, I caught the briefest flash of white. My sister Iselda, come to see what all the commotion was, although she had the good sense to remain on the stairs and not approach the door.

The duke raised an eyebrow then, but his smile did not falter. Still showing those excellent teeth, he went on, "Annora Kelsden, you will come with us. Now."

CHAPTER THREE

How could I refuse a command like that? Again I glanced over at Darinne and the cook, but they appeared far too cowed by the duke's splendor to even speak, let alone offer any sort of protest.

"My cloak—" I began feebly, but the duke raised a hand.

"You have no need of it. The night is fine enough, and there are furs in the carriage. Come now."

He extended a gloved hand. What could I do but take it? I feared I would not be able to do as he asked, that my trembling legs would betray me, but instead I walked serenely enough from my house to the waiting carriage, although I could not prevent myself from casting a quick glance back at my sister, who looked on in mute worry from her perch on the staircase.

A footman stood by the door to the coach and helped me inside. A moment later, the duke followed, and the footman closed the door behind us.

The interior of the coach smelled of fine leather and the faintest traces of something spicy and aromatic. Snuff, or perhaps the pomade in the duke's hair. Whatever it was, I found it pleasant enough, although its perfume was not sufficient to calm me.

I grasped the edge of the tufted leather seat, hoping that clutching it might still some of the trembling in my fingers. "My—my lord, may I ask what this is about?"

It came to me immediately afterward that I should have called him "Your Grace," as that was the proper form of address for one who possessed his title. But perhaps I could be forgiven for not having all my wits about me.

A flash of his teeth in the darkness. "You may ask."

He said nothing after that, though, and I realized he was toying with me, just a little.

Beneath my worry, anger flared, but I pushed it aside as best I could. It would never do for me to lose my temper around a man such as he. I did not pay much attention to the doings of those at court, for their antics and amusements certainly did little enough to affect me, but I knew enough to recall that Lord Edmar was one of the greatest men in the realm, second only to the king and his son, Prince Harlin.

"Am I—am I in some kind of trouble?" As the question left my lips, I realized how foolish it was. Even if I had transgressed in some way...which I most certainly had not...the constable for our district would have been the one knocking on the door, not a man as important as the Duke of Lerneshall.

"'Trouble'?" the duke repeated. Another of those smiles. "I suppose that will depend on you."

Oh, so now he was talking even more in riddles. I resolved not to ask any further questions, for it seemed clear that Lord Edmar had little inclination to enlighten me, or in fact to do anything to ease the worry that had become an ever-tightening band around my throat.

Surprisingly, the duke spoke again. "He was telling the truth about one thing. You are a very beautiful young woman, Annora Kelsden."

My first impulse was to inquire how he could he even see me well enough to make such a statement, considering how dim it was within the confines of the carriage. But then I wondered who this "he" Lord Edmar had spoken of could even be.

After an awkward pause, I said, "Thank you, Your Grace."

A chuckle, warm and sounding a bit too intimate. "You are most welcome. But I am remiss. Are you chilled? Would you like one of these furs for your lap?"

I squinted into the darkness and was just able to make out a pile of something soft on the seat next to him. "No, thank you, Your Grace. I am quite comfortable." Well, comfortable with the temperature, at least. Even though we were almost to Octevre, and should have been experiencing our first frosts, we had just come through a spell of unusually mild weather, and the night air was not that cold at all.

"If you are certain…." The duke appeared to shrug, then pushed the furs away from him and into a corner. "It would not do for you to take a chill."

Whence this solicitude had come from, I couldn't begin to guess. Truthfully, I was having a good deal of trouble attempting to discern his mood at all. Perhaps it was only that I had no experience of great men, of their humors, but he had first seemed quite ominous, and now had changed his tack and was worrying over my comfort. And as for that comment about my looks, I had to confess to myself that I was not sure how to view that at all.

"I am certain, Your Grace. But thank you."

He seemed to take my reply at face value, and said no more. Somehow, though, I could sense his gaze on me in the darkness. Color flooded my cheeks, although I doubted he could see my flush, as the dim lighting would have only allowed him to pick out the contours of my features.

The carriage seemed to tilt slightly as we hurried on through the night. It felt as if we were traveling uphill. And if that were the case, then our destination must be somewhere in the grander districts that clustered around the king's palace at the heart of Bodenskell.

My heart sank somewhat at that realization, for terrible thoughts had begun to race through my mind. Perhaps Lord Edmar had attended the party thrown by Baron Levender as well...and perhaps my father had lost so badly that he had nothing to offer the great man save his own daughter. That might explain the comment the duke had made earlier about my beauty....

I swallowed, and turned to glance out the window. The lampposts were set more closely together here, providing enough light for me to see that we had left the more modest houses and shops of my own district behind, and that to either side were tall structures of three or even four stories, with fanciful edgings of carved stone. Yes, this did seem like the sort of place where a duke might keep his town house, even if he still had a great estate out in the countryside.

Despite my resolution to not ask any more questions, I couldn't prevent myself from inquiring, "Forgive me for asking, Your Grace, but where is it that we are going?"

He, too, had kept watch out the window, only the one opposite me. Shifting away from it, he replied, "Why, to the palace. The king would have discourse with you."

In that instant, I could feel my heart sink to the very soles of my slippers. Why on earth would the king want to speak to someone as lowly as I? Bad enough that I now faced a duke, but the king himself?

My thoughts then grew quite chaotic. The first thing that passed through my mind was gratitude that at least I had changed out of the dreadful gown I had worn to beat the rugs, but the one I wore now, while far newer, was certainly nothing suitable for meeting the king. But oh, what did that matter? Nothing I owned was fit for such an audience, not even the gowns I had embellished with fine embroidery. We could not afford threads of silver and gold and copper, but only humble silks. And I had been quite haphazard in putting my hair back up, as I had only done so to mollify my father, in case he should catch a glimpse of me, and not because I was concerned with the appearance of the end result.

Somehow I managed to draw in a breath. "The king, Your Grace? What—"

"It is not my place to speak of what the king wishes to say to you. In a few minutes, you will find out for yourself."

This last was delivered in such forbidding tones that I quite lost the will to make any further inquiries. Whatever warmth had been in his tone earlier, it seemed that now Lord Edmar was becoming rather weary of me.

It was in an uncomfortable silence that the carriage drew up to the palace walls. The gate stood open, so apparently they were expecting us. Or perhaps it was always open; I did not know the protocols for such things, as I had never been this close to the palace before. The horses' hooves clattered on stone as we entered a large courtyard. Here all was lit by torchlight; I could see grooms hurrying forward to attend to the horses, and a footman in very grand livery opened the door for us.

The duke got out first, then paused by the step and offered his hand. I could do nothing but take it, since refusing his help would have been the height of rudeness. His gloved fingers grasped me tightly as he assisted me out of the carriage, and his hand lingered on mine for longer than was necessary once I reached solid ground.

Bending low, he said in an undertone, "No matter what happens next, I think it has been a very great pleasure meeting you, Annora. If you make your way through all this, I believe I would like to extend our acquaintance."

There was no mistaking his meaning. I wanted to snap at him that he was old enough to be my father—even if he had done a much better job of weathering those same years—but I knew better than to say such a thing out loud. Besides, it was not so uncommon for older men to take an interest in younger women, or at least so I had been told.

I dipped a little curtsey, managing to pull my hand from his at the same time. "I look forward to that, Your Grace."

He smiled, but there was a certain tightness to his expression that seemed to indicate he'd detected my distaste. To my relief, however, he appeared to let the matter go, and instead pointed toward an arched doorway off to one side. "If you will come with me."

When I was very little, I used to take twigs from the oak trees that bordered our property and put them in the fast-running water in my street's gutters following a heavy rainstorm. I felt rather like one of those twigs now, caught up in currents I couldn't control and didn't understand. All I could do was follow the duke as he led me into the castle. A pair of guards fell in behind us, and I startled. And what was their purpose? To make sure I didn't bolt?

Where could I even go? The events of the past half-hour had shown me that my home was certainly no sanctuary.

At first the corridors around me were of unadorned stone, probably because of their proximity to the courtyard. Quite soon, however, the hallway we traversed widened, and was hung with tapestries in rich hues, showing hunting scenes and landscapes. The work was quite fine, and I wished I could have come here under different circumstances so I could examine them up close.

The duke, however, did not seem as if he would have allowed such dawdling. He walked along briskly, and I had to lengthen my strides to keep up with him. So there was no time to inspect the tapestries, or take anything more than the most cursory glance at the runner beneath my feet or the statues of chiseled marble that had been placed along the corridor at regular intervals. Perhaps it was foolish for me to even be concerned with such things, but I doubted I would ever get to see the palace again. Besides, thinking of such trivialities helped to keep my mind away from the far more important topic of why I was here at all.

After several minutes, we mounted a low, wide staircase and came to a set of enormous carved oak doors. They stood open, with no fewer than ten men standing guard on either side. The room beyond was lit by a series of great wrought-iron chandeliers studded with a myriad of candles, which cast a warm light and the scent of beeswax into the chamber.

We entered. That is, the duke strode in, with me a pace or two behind. Ahead of us was a dais, and on that dais sat a man in a throne of carved oak studded with cabochons of gems—garnet and amber and onyx. He was some years older than my father, and wore a simple crown of heavy gold set with an enormous emerald in the center.

My steps faltered somewhat—was I supposed to curtsey now?—but Lord Edmar said under his breath, "Keep going until you reach the bottom of the dais," and so I propelled myself forward, only stopping when I reached the correct spot. Then I did curtsey, so deeply that I feared I might lose my balance. Somehow, though, I managed to keep myself from falling over.

As I began to straighten, I heard the duke say, "Your Majesty, this is the girl the merchant spoke of."

"The merchant"? He could only have meant one person by that, surely. And yes, as I resumed a more or less normal stance,

I spied my father out of the corner of my eye. He stood off to one side, flanked by a pair of guards. His expression was one of mingled terror and shame. At least, that was how it appeared to me, although I had never seen my father display either of those emotions before. Seeing him so cowed, I felt a chill begin to trace its way down my spine, although I did my best to look meek and humble.

Then the king rose from his throne, and I immediately looked back toward him. His eyes were pale blue, shrewd, as he descended the steps of the dais and approached me. He was not quite of a height with Lord Edmar, but the crown made up some of the difference. For a long moment, he said nothing, and only continued his inspection of my person, from my untidy hair to the scuffed slippers on my feet.

Again I could feel blood rise to my cheeks, but I did my best to keep my chin up, even though I knew I could never look my monarch directly in the face. Was that even allowed? My mother had taught me how to address the various members of the peerage, had shown me how to make a fairly passable curtsey, but of course she could never have guessed in any of her wildest dreams that I might one day have an audience with the king.

"So this is the wondrous Annora Kelsden," he said at last, addressing the duke. "I will confess that I was expecting something more, although I suppose she might do well enough if she were cleaned up a bit."

My mind was too busy dissecting his use of the word "wondrous" to take offense at anything else he had just said. All I could do was remain standing there, my gaze carefully focused off somewhere beyond him. For some reason it settled on the throne, taking in the artful carvings of oak leaves and vines, the carefully placed cabochon stones, some of them so large I didn't know whether they would have even fit in the palm of my hand.

The duke only inclined his head. That seemed to be all the reply the king desired, for he turned back toward me and said, "We have the spinning wheel ready for you. There is no natural light at this time of day, of course, but just beyond is a chamber that we have filled with many candlesticks. I assume that will be sufficient?"

For the longest moment, I could do nothing but stare at him, at the thinning chestnut hair the crown couldn't quite conceal, the heavy lines bracketing his mouth. I understood the individual words he had spoken, but combined, they made no sense. Spinning wheel? What manner of nonsense was this?

Of course I could not ask such a thing of the man who ruled my land. I cleared my throat and somehow managed to force out a reply. "I beg your forgiveness, Your Majesty, but I am not quite sure I understand. You wish me to spin some thread for you?"

That innocent question seemed to provide a good deal of amusement for King Elsdon and Lord Edmar, as they both began to chuckle. A glint entered the king's eyes, and he said, "Yes, we would like that very much. If you don't mind, of course."

"No, Your Majesty, I don't mind," I returned in some confusion.

"Excellent. Edmar, if you would show her the way?"

The duke gestured off to our left. I followed his pointing finger and saw that a door stood open at the far side of the throne room, revealing a smaller chamber ablaze with light. I began to move in that direction, and then I heard my father's strangled tones.

"Your Majesty—if I may have a moment to speak with my daughter—"

"You will speak to her afterward, and not before," the king broke in. His brows drew together, and he glanced over at me. "Continue, Annora. You see there the chamber I spoke of?"

I nodded.

"Then go with Lord Edmar."

There was nothing I could do except walk toward the room he had indicated, the duke a few paces ahead of me. I did not quite see the reason for his doing so, since my destination seemed clear enough. But I went where I was directed, and did not dare to look back toward my father. Something very strange was going on here, although I could not begin to guess what it might be.

Entering the chamber, I saw that it was quite empty, save for a spinning wheel of polished walnut, far grander than the one back at my house, and a series of candelabras sitting on carved wooden shelves on the walls. The light they cast was, as the king had said, quite brilliant, and I blinked at the sudden glare.

Next to the spinning wheel sat a chair, also of polished walnut, and on the stone floor immediately next to it was a pile of straw. I stared at it, puzzled, wondering what on earth that untidy mess was doing in such an otherwise spotless room.

Brow puckered, I turned back to the duke, who had stopped just inside the doorway. "I fear I do not understand."

In this light, I could see that his eyes were a clear grey. They crinkled a bit at the corners as he gave me an indulgent smile. "What is there to understand, Annora? There is the spinning wheel."

"But where is the wool? I see only a pile of straw."

The smile didn't fade. Indeed, it broadened, to the point where it caused a faint little chill to run down my back. "That is what you must spin."

"Spin...the straw?" Once again, I had that feeling of nothing in the world making sense, of words being put together in incomprehensible strings of syllables.

"Yes." The duke crossed his arms and gave me a piercing look. "That is what your father swore you could do."

I began to understand then why my father looked so guilty, so frightened. Deep in his cups, he had probably made some outlandish boast. Only this time, it appeared as if that tall tale must have involved me somehow.

Contradicting one of the greatest men in the land was not something that appealed to me, but I knew I must make some protest in my defense. Speaking carefully, I said, "Your Grace, I fear there has been some sort of misunderstanding. I don't know what my father said, but—"

"He said you were so gifted in weavecraft that you could spin straw into gold. Is this not true?"

Suddenly it seemed as if there was not enough air to breathe, as if all the candles in the room had drawn it away to fuel their flames. I wished I could put a hand out to one of the walls to steady myself, but I stood in almost the very center of the chamber, and the promise of their support was too far away.

Was there any way to escape this nightmare? Most likely not, but I had to try.

I clasped my hands together, and prayed that I looked properly meek and beseeching. "Your Grace, it shames me to say such a thing, but when my father has drunk more than he should, he can sometimes say things that are—well, that are perhaps exaggerations."

The smile disappeared as if it had never been there in the first place. "Do you mean to say that he lied?"

"No, no—" I broke off, then shook my head in frustration. "For a lie requires some intent, and I do not believe it is ever his intention to prevaricate. It is more that his tongue can run away from him in the heat of the moment."

"Ah."

That was all Lord Edmar said, but I could see a frown beginning to settle itself on his fine brow. At that unfortunate moment, the king himself appeared at the duke's shoulder. He had been smiling, but as soon as he saw me standing there, and the spinning wheel sitting idle, a scowl to match the one Lord Edmar wore settled on his features.

"What's this?" King Elsdon snapped. "I expected to see you hard at work, my lady."

I opened my mouth to reply—how, I knew not—but the duke spoke first.

"She claims there was some misunderstanding, and that her father misspoke."

"He lied?"

I could not contradict the king. It had taken all my courage to attempt some explanation with Lord Edmar, and I had none left. All I could do was look down at the floor of smooth and polished stone, and wish that it would somehow manage to swallow me up.

But the gods did not see fit to give it that ability, and so I remained where I was, with my king and one of his greatest courtiers staring at me as if I were some kind of particularly loathsome insect that had had the temerity to enter their hallowed halls. Neither of them spoke, and it became clear enough that they expected some sort of reply from me.

Once again, I cleared my throat. "Your Majesty, as I was not there, I don't know what he said. I—"

"Ah, but *I* was there," Lord Edmar broke in. "One of Baron Levender's more tedious gatherings, as it turned out, but there was one man, a rather common sort, who was having the sort of spectacular losses with the dice that one just had to watch. He made all sorts of claims to Levender's man, the one running the table, and at last said that it did not matter how much money he lost, for his daughter was so wondrously talented that she could verily spin straw into gold."

"And you believed it?" I exclaimed, shaken past caring whether I offended him. "Your Grace, you are a man of the world. Surely you must have known his story was nonsense."

Dark brows drew together. "I will admit that was my first instinct, but then I heard the murmurs, how people were saying that must be the explanation, for a man who lost as much at the tables as he did, week after week, must have a secret source of income. Else, my lady," the duke went on, giving me another one of those steely looks, "your family must surely have been on the street some years ago. Or do you have some other explanation?"

Of course I did not, for my father took care that I would never know the details of our finances. Perhaps it did seem strange to the outside observer that we should manage to go on year after year and suffer such astounding losses, and yet not have to endure any material alteration in our circumstances. Yes, there had been some belt-tightening, but not to the extent where we had to move our residence, or do completely without servants.

I shook my head, since I could not trust myself to speak. My legs had begun to tremble, although I hoped my heavy skirts might hide the evidence of my mounting fear.

The two men exchanged an unreadable glance. Or at least I could not begin to decipher it.

Then Lord Edmar said, tone heavy, precise, "Perhaps you do not understand the rules of the gaming table, my lady. But when a man owes his host a goodly sum, and claims he has the means to provide that sum, he must do so within three days, or all is forfeit."

"All is forfeit"? What did he mean by that? Would they take our house, our meager belongings? Would we at last be compelled to seek sanctuary with my Aunt Lyselle?

Since I said nothing, the duke went on, "I see you do not understand. Because your father claimed that his daughter could spin straw into gold, and placed that claim as surety against his bet, then the debt must be repaid with such. Otherwise...." He stopped there, and seemed to shake his head, as if showing for the first time some concern for my welfare.

The king had no such scruples, however. Eyes narrowing, he said harshly, "Otherwise, the debt will be declared forfeit, and you will both pay with your lives."

CHAPTER FOUR

There was no question of my going home. No, immediately after my confrontation with the king and the duke, two pairs of guards appeared to escort me to a cell far below the grand rooms of the palace itself. A short time later, the spinning wheel and the pile of straw were deposited in my cell, along with the chair that accompanied them. Well, at least His Majesty did not expect me to sit on the cold stone floor while attempting to perform the impossible. Why he had not brought me to this cell to begin with, I did not know, but perhaps he had wished to play at courtesy when he had thought everything would go his way. Now, however....

For some reason, I could not even weep. Perhaps it was only that this had all come as such a shock that my mind hadn't quite yet absorbed what was happening. Yes, that had to be it. Sooner or later, understanding would blossom, and then....

I leaned my head against the bars of the cell and took in a breath, then another. This was not the time to panic. I had to think of something. After all, they had given me three days.

Oh, yes, of course, I mocked myself. *Within the space of three days, you will have accomplished something that no alchemist has yet to manage.* For of course men had been attempting to make gold from dross for uncounted centuries. Straw into gold, I had to admit, was a new one, however.

Hopelessly, I turned away from the cell bars to survey my new surroundings. There was a mean little pallet laid on top of a sort of stone shelf protruding from the wall, and a basin of water, but that was all, besides the hated spinning wheel. I already detested the look of it.

At least I appeared to be the only prisoner here. Perhaps there were other levels that had their own occupants, but I was alone. It was possible that the king had shown some mercy and made sure that I, a sheltered young woman, would not be housed next to any male criminals.

Since I didn't know what else to do, I made my way over to the chair and sat down. By then it must have been very late, and yet I had no inclination to lie down on the pallet that had been provided for me. Doing so seemed too much like an admission of defeat. The chill from the stone floor had already begun to penetrate my thin slippers, and I wrapped my arms around myself, trying to will away the sensation of encroaching cold.

I heard footsteps approaching, and my heart began to beat a little faster. Was it possible that the king had already decided his punishment was far too severe, and had sent someone to free me?

But no, the person who appeared then was my father, with a guard to either side. Oh, gods...were they going to put him in a cell down here as well? What would happen to Iselda?

That did not seem to be the plan, however, for the guards backed away, allowing us some privacy even as my father approached the bars of my cell.

"Oh, Annora," he began, but I fastened him with as severe a gaze as I could muster, and interrupted,

"Do not bother with apologies, Father, for I fear there is nothing you can say that would make all this any better! What in the world were you thinking?"

He scowled then, obviously annoyed by my brusque tone, for I had never spoken to him in such a manner before. Then again, he had never given me reason to, even with all our previous disagreements.

"I was thinking they would not be such fools as to believe such a thing! But I was in a tight corner, and needed some way to get out of it. I would have paid my debt."

"How? For I certainly cannot spin straw into gold, and so I fail to see how you could have repaid such a sum, if it truly was as great as Lord Edmar seemed to imply."

My father then had the strangest expression cross his face. Truly, I could not say for sure what exactly it was. Not shame, precisely. It was more as if he had been caught at something, and desperately wished there existed some way of avoiding the consequences.

At last he said, "I would have repaid it with your mother's dowry."

"'My mother's dowry'?" I repeated, certain I must not have heard him correctly. "But it was small, and gone years ago."

His eyes would not meet mine. "That is not precisely the truth. It was actually quite a large sum. Those are the funds that have kept our household going all these years."

I had thought I was angry earlier, but now my rage seemed to come boiling up out of nowhere, like the eruption of one of the geysers in Daleskeld Province, far to the north. Fingers wrapped around the bars of my cell, I spat, "Kept your gambling habits going all these years, more to the point. For I did not see that money going toward better shoes for your daughters, or lamb for the dinner table instead of mutton. How dare you take what was mine and Iselda's, and use it for your own petty weaknesses!"

"You have no right to speak to me that way—"

"I have every right, for not only have you taken that which was not yours, but your ridiculous lies will now cost us both our lives!"

Instead of being shamefaced or worried, my father's expression took on a crafty air. "Perhaps not."

"'Perhaps not'?" I repeated incredulously. "You heard what the king said!"

"Yes, I did, but I also had a chance to speak with Lord Edmar privately afterward. He said that perhaps we might be able to work out some sort of arrangement, once the king's temper has cooled a bit."

I did not like the sound of that overmuch. "'Arrangement'?"

"Yes. He had high praise for your beauty and your spirit, and said that he could never allow such a treasure to be wasted.

After a suitable time has passed, he will speak to the king on your behalf, and will see that you are freed." A pause, and my father added, "At which time you will of course show the duke your gratitude."

My life might have been a sheltered one, but even I understood what he meant by that. "So," I said slowly, "you would prostitute your daughter to save your own hide."

"Must you be so harsh? It is a way for both of us to live through this. And if you would stop to think about this logically, you would see how good this could be for you. Lord Edmar is a widower. Charm him enough, and you could be a great lady."

I couldn't help it. Despite my desperate situation, I found myself laughing, and then shook my head. "Oh, Father, I fear your brain is still befuddled with drink. Why in the world would a man of Lord Edmar's station marry one such as me, when he can have me on his own terms, and still seek a wife who could bring land and riches to the marriage?" Truly, my father's delusions seemed to know no bounds. But then I sobered, thinking of how I might have avoided this nightmare, if only Cordell had spoken to me a few hours earlier. "You would have done better to let me marry Cordell. At least then you would have been guaranteed a place of shelter in your old age, when all your funds had truly been exhausted."

My father's features twisted with rage. "Do you think I would have ever allowed you to waste yourself on someone so common? A servant?"

"A good man," I countered. "One whose worth is probably greater than yours at the moment, if someone were to compare your balance sheets. But of course you never allowed me to see the household accounts, so I cannot say for certain."

"You were destined for better things than that. Better to be a duke's mistress than a farmer's wife."

I could only gape at him after he made that pronouncement. In that moment, I realized he truly did believe what he was saying and was not merely trying to convince me of the advantages of such an arrangement. And as I stared into his face, saw his anger that I would not meekly agree with whatever he proposed for me, I began to understand.

"You wanted this all along," I said slowly. "Oh, perhaps not these very circumstances—I cannot quite believe that level of iniquity, even now—but that is why you kept me so sheltered all this time, made no effort to arrange even an acceptable match. You hoped your path would cross with that of the right nobleman, and you would dangle me before him as a means of paying off your debts, so that you might keep more of the dowry money for yourself."

"That money is mine," he rasped. I could not help but notice that he did not even attempt to deny the rest of what I had just said. "I earned it, from being locked in a loveless marriage, one that gave me no sons. What did you ever do to deserve it?"

Blood going cold, I backed away from the bars. I needed to put some distance between us, even if it was only a few feet. "Get out," I said, my voice twisted with loathing. "I have nothing more to say to you. You are not my father, for no father would ever utter the words you have spoken here this night."

He gave me a mocking little smile. "You are very noble now, Annora, but I think you may change your mind as that third day looms."

"Of course you hope I will," I retorted. "For if I do not, then it is your head on the block as well as mine."

"Would you really do that?" he inquired, expression all false innocence. "For what would happen to Iselda, if she had no parent left to care for her?"

"She would go to Aunt Lyselle, you snake, and far better for her to be with her aunt than with the unnatural creature who calls himself her father!"

That seemed to sting him at last, for I thought I saw his eyes narrow slightly. But he only said, "Think on it, Annora," then turned and walked away toward the stairs. The guards came up to flank him, and the three of them disappeared. Why he had been allowed to walk free, I could not say, but perhaps he had offered Iselda as his excuse, saying that she had no one else to look after her, and the king had agreed. After all, he already had one daughter of Benedic Kelsden locked up. He did not need them both.

That was when my knees failed me, and I stumbled over to the chair and sank down upon it. The flush of anger receded, now that I was all alone, and I began to shiver. Truthfully, I could not say whether the chamber was really all that cold, or whether I shook from reaction. In the end, it probably did not matter one way or another.

So many things made sense to me now. A horrible sense, but in a way I was almost glad that I knew. My father had never been one to show affection to his children, and I had accepted his behavior as what must be usual in such situations, since I had no way of knowing anything different. I had never been able to understand why my father had not contracted a marriage for me early on, for it would have relieved him of at least one mouth to feed. But, ever the gambler, he had waited, thinking that the risk he took might pay off for him one day.

What in the world he would tell Iselda when he got home, I had no idea. Some self-serving lie, I was sure. Whether she would believe him or not was an entirely different matter. My sister had a way of seeing the truth in things, even though she could not have guessed at the depths of our father's iniquity.

Once again, I heard footsteps. This time I would not allow myself to hope that they promised any release, but I did raise my head to see who approached. It was one of the guards, a man probably some ten years older than I, with a pleasant enough face. In his hands he held a bundle of furs, soft and luxurious.

"From His Grace, Lord Edmar," the guard said, pushing them through the bars of my cell. They fell soundlessly to the stone floor, which at least appeared clean. "He did not wish you to take a chill down here."

No, of course not, I thought bitterly. *It would not do for his conquest to have a runny nose or a sore throat.*

Even so, I rose from the chair and went to retrieve the furs. They were warm and softer than anything I had ever imagined. I wondered then if they were the same pelts the duke had with him in the carriage that brought us here.

I could feel the guard's eyes on me, watchful, curious, so I said, "Thank His Grace for his generosity. These will greatly ease my tenure here."

There. That sounded courteous enough. I knew my words would be taken directly to Lord Edmar, and he could think of them what he willed.

The guard nodded and walked away, taking up his post near the stairs. I supposed I should be grateful that he did not intend to loiter too near my cell. The illusion of privacy was spurious at best, but it was better than nothing.

I took the furs to the pallet and settled myself down on it, first taking off my slippers before pulling the threadbare blanket over me and then disposing the furs as best I could. By then, I could tell that it would indeed be quite chilly by the time the night was over, and I found myself glad of their warmth.

And by the third day down here, would I be so grateful to the duke that I would do whatever he wished? I hoped I was stronger than that, but I just could not say.

One day passed, and another. Each morning, I was taken from my cell and guided to a bath chamber, where I could attend to my personal needs. Several changes of clothing had also been provided for me, far grander than anything I owned. Whence all this largesse had come from, no one said, but it did not require too much thought to determine that it must be Lord Edmar, making sure that I would have multiple reasons to show my gratitude to him. The empty hours were enough to drive anyone mad, but I coped as best I could, dozing much of the time, worrying about my sister and wondering what was happening at home during those periods when sleep eluded me.

I must confess that by the evening of the second day, I found myself thinking it could not be so bad as all that. Yes, the duke was much older than I, but he was still a handsome man. Surely giving myself to him would be better than dying because of my father's folly. And although I did not think that wayward man worthy of much consideration, I also did not want my stubbornness to result in Iselda losing the only parent she had left.

All this time, the spinning wheel had still sat in the middle of my cell, seeming to mock me. Once or twice I had even picked up a few pieces of straw and attempted to feed them through the device, but of course all that came out on the other side was the same piece of straw, albeit a bit crumpled-looking. It was utterly mad that anyone should expect me to do such a thing.

That night, I laid myself down on the pallet as calmly as I could, but my heart was racing within. The next day would be my third one here. By the time the sun set on that day, I would have to produce gold for the king...or I would have to send word to Lord Edmar that I was willing to do as he asked, in exchange for having the king pardon me for my supposed crimes.

It was not, I feared, much of a choice. And perhaps I did not even have that choice. I had only my father's word to go on when it came to the duke's intentions, and he had already proved himself less than trustworthy. Perhaps I had misread Lord Edmar's intent in sending me the furs and the gowns. Perhaps even the horrible hope that he might spare my life if I would become his mistress was entirely incorrect.

They had, by that point, realized that having two guards watching over me was foolish. No, there was only one in his usual position by the foot of the stairs. I knew that half the time the man given night watch duty did not stay awake for all of it. What was the point? I certainly did not possess the means to escape, and neither would there be anyone likely to come in and attempt to rescue me. I could only wait and worry as my doom approached.

The shadow of sleep was just beginning to steal over me when I heard a voice in the darkness.

"Annora."

It was a man's voice, deep and soft, no one I recognized. I sat bolt upright on my pallet, clutching the furs to me, although I slept fully clothed. At first I thought that perhaps it was the guard, but I had heard him speak, and he had a pleasant tenor with a slight country burr to it.

"Who's there?" I whispered.

"Someone who wishes to help you."

My eyes strained against the darkness, attempting to see who had spoken. It was not absolutely black, as a torch flickered halfway up the stairwell. And as I stared, I was able to see the outlines of a tall dark figure, shrouded in a hooded cloak, standing in the far corner of my cell.

I let out a shocked gasp and pushed the furs away from me, then scrambled out of bed. My thought was to go to the front of my cell and call for the guard, but the hooded figure was too fast for me. Even as I began to move, he was there next to me, a gloved hand covering my mouth as I parted my lips to scream.

"There, now," the stranger said, his voice pitched low. "Did I not tell you that I wished to help you?"

His cloak concealed his form, but I was now pressed up against him, and I could tell he was strong and tall, certainly no one I could possibly overcome in a physical confrontation. My tone a furious whisper against his leather-clad fingers, I asked, "Help me how? By invading my cell in the middle of the night?"

"That seemed wisest. I would not wish to be seen by your guard—although I admit he is not much of an adversary at the moment, as he is leaning up against the wall and snoring to wake the dead."

There was an undercurrent of amusement in the stranger's voice, and, despite myself, I relaxed slightly. If he had come here to assault me, surely he would not have announced his presence by calling out my name.

The strange man seemed to note the shift in my posture, for in the next instant he let go of me and stepped away. Not very far, just a foot or so, but enough that it seemed to indicate he trusted me not to cry out for help. Then again, if the guard was really snoring as badly as all that, there was a good chance he might not hear me, even if I called out for him.

"Who are you?" I asked the stranger.

"My name is not important."

"And you don't think it rude that you have my name, and yet you are unwilling to give me yours? How do you expect me to trust you if you will not give me that smallest of courtesies?"

He chuckled then. It was a warm, rich sound, and something about it made a little shiver go down my back. Or perhaps it was simply that I had just realized I stood on the cold stone floor in only my stocking feet.

"If it is so important to you, then you may call me Rumple."

"'Rumple'?" I repeated, certain he was teasing me. "That is not a proper name."

"Perhaps not, but it is the one I am giving you now. It will have to be enough."

I decided it was best to let the matter go. "Very well. I suppose I should not be arguing with someone who says he wishes to help me. But how can you? Do you have some way of getting me out of this cell?" For I reflected that he had obviously gotten in, and so possessed some knowledge that I most certainly did not.

"Not precisely. For there is no need of escape, if you can do as the king has asked of you."

So he was helpful...and mad. "That is impossible."

"Not with the right assistance. Please, Annora, take your seat at the spinning wheel."

More protests bubbled to my lips, but I had already told myself that I should not argue with him anymore, at least not until I had determined what he expected of me. At least he had made no assault on my person, save that hand over my mouth to keep me from alerting the guards to his presence.

So I made my way across the icy floor and sat down on the chair. "What now?"

"Pick up a piece of straw."

Sighing, I bent down and grasped the longest piece I could find, even though I knew its length mattered not at all. It could be long enough to stretch from here all the way back to my house, and it still would not make any difference. Straw was straw, and even if I could somehow manage to feed it through onto the bobbin, it would stubbornly remain straw, and nothing else.

The stranger's gaze was almost like a physical weight on my shoulders, even though I could not see his face. "Go on."

This time I did not bother to sigh. I only grasped the lead yarn with my left hand, and took the piece of straw in my right. A few presses of the treadle with my foot to get the wheel moving, and then I laid the straw on top of the yarn. It would hit the orifice and crumple, I knew, but I decided to humor the stranger.

Only...it did not. The straw seemed to meld with the piece of lead yarn, stretching and softening in my hand, and the faint bit of torchlight which made its way to my cell suddenly found an answering gleam in the golden thread that began to wrap its way around the bobbin.

My foot faltered on the treadle. "What in the world...."

"Don't stop," the stranger said, satisfaction clear in his voice.

What could I do but continue to pick up the bits of straw from where they lay, and watch as they somehow fused with the golden thread I had already spun? I worked and I worked, my shoulders beginning to grow tired as the night wore on and the pure metal filament grew thicker and thicker on the bobbin.

At last there was no straw left on the floor, and instead a spool of heavy gold where yarn should have been. For the longest moment I could only sit there and stare at it, and wonder how such a thing could have ever come to pass.

"Good," said the stranger. For the briefest instant I felt the weight of his hand on my shoulder, and then he moved away. "I think you have earned your life this night."

I rose from the chair, feeling my muscles protest as I did so. It had been several years since I had last spun, and I had never spent so many hours at it as I had tonight. But all that seemed to melt away as I stared in awe at the man in the hooded cloak.

"Who are you?"

"As I said. Someone who wishes to help you." He paused then, head tilting upward, as if at some sound only he could hear. "It is not quite dawn. Sleep, Annora, and know that the king will pardon you when the true morning comes."

And then he was gone, passing like a shadow in the night, even as I opened my mouth to thank him for his unlikely help. I blinked, certain my eyes must have deceived me, that he had merely slipped into a dark corner, but no—strain as I might, I could not see him anywhere. He had simply...disappeared.

Magic, my mind whispered at me, and I shivered and shakily made my way over to the pallet. How I would ever be able to sleep after a night such as this, I did not know, but the stranger's words did make some sense. I should try to get what rest I could, for most assuredly all would be clamor and commotion once it was discovered that I truly had managed to spin that straw into gold.

But although I lay down and shut my eyes, I could not get my mind to grow quiet enough for slumber. I kept recalling the soft, heavy weight of that golden thread against my fingertips, the way it quietly gleamed on its prosaic wooden bobbin. Such a thing was impossible, and yet...there it was.

Magic had once ruled this land, or at least that was what the storybooks said. Great mages wielded power to rival that of the gods, and had raised themselves to be above the common folk.

But those sorcerers' pride was their undoing, and the people rose against them and their tyranny. Now there was no trace of the mages, or the magic they had wielded. Every once in a great while, someone was accused of practicing the forbidden art. If they were found guilty, there was only one punishment the rulers here in Purth would mete out.

Those unnatural beings were burned at the stake.

And yet...magic.

There could be no other explanation, either for the gold itself, or the way the stranger had disappeared from my prison cell. I had read that the great mages could perform those sorts of feats, disappearing from one place and appearing somewhere else with as much ease as someone walking from one room to another.

There were not, of course, supposed to be any mages left. But I very much thought I had just encountered one. Why he had deigned to help me, at such great personal risk, I could not begin to guess. Surely the fate of one merchant's daughter should not matter much to someone who had such powers at his command.

But the ways of such men were said to have been inscrutable, and I doubted I would ever get any answers as to why this one man had used his skills to save my life. All I knew was that he had done so, and there, only a few feet away, was the answer to my unspoken prayers.

Somehow, unlikely as it might seem, I did doze a bit, for some time later I heard the most unseemly clatter and sat bolt upright in my pallet, looking around in some confusion. As I blinked, I saw the guard who came on duty in the early morning standing outside my cell, the tray which had held my breakfast lying at his feet. Scattered around it were a tin cup that had contained some water, along with a few pieces of bread and cheese.

"By the gods!" he exclaimed, staring at the thick bundle of gold thread that now rested on the bobbin. "Is that—"

"Yes," I replied, then pushed back the furs and my one thin blanket, and got to my feet. "I am sorry that it took me this long, but—"

"N-no, I am sure it will be fine," the guard said, his dark eyes round and astonished. "I must go—that is, I will send word of what you have done. Wait here."

What else would I do? I thought, amused by his discomfiture. But I supposed I should not be surprised that he should be so flabbergasted. To tell the truth, I still did not quite believe it myself, even though the evidence of the night's work sat only a few feet away, looking like strands of morning sunlight as they wound around the bobbin.

He left, and I did my best to straighten my gown and smooth my hair. Because I had not slept much, I was not overly rumpled.

Rumple. What an odd name. But then, I thought it was probably not the stranger's name at all, but a strange little nickname he had given me to avoid revealing who he truly was. Judging by the powers he wielded, I thought that bit of discretion only wise. Not that I would ever willingly give up his name—not after what he had done for me—but it was always better to be cautious.

It seemed as if I waited for some time. Eventually, though, I heard the clamor of booted feet on the stone steps that led down into my dungeon, and in the next moment I saw why my wait had been so lengthy. For it was not merely the guard returning, but Lord Edmar as well, and the king himself. I wondered how disheveled I actually looked, and then realized it mattered not at all. For the king and the duke were staring, transfixed, at the gleaming golden thread I had spun, and seemed not to see me at all.

The king stepped forward first, moving right up to the bars of my cell. "So it is true."

Perhaps I should have said nothing, but lack of sleep did have a tendency to hamper my discretion. "Of course it is. That is what you asked for, Your Majesty. Gold from straw." *And make of it what you will.* It came to me then that the king might see this as magic, and my life would still be forfeit. Had I escaped one terrible death, only to suffer one even worse? In that moment, I could not think which fate might be the more horrible...to have one's head struck off, or to be burned at the stake.

But the king did not appear to be contemplating my execution. He smiled, and blinked, then looked over at me, even as Lord Edmar came up behind his left shoulder. "So it is, my dear. That is...most excellent." The king flickered a glance at the duke, who did not appear particularly pleased. But then, of course he would not be pleased. I had succeeded, and so there was no reason for any "arrangement" to be made. Still smiling, the king went on, "It seems the merchant's claims were true."

The duke nodded. "That is...most astonishing, my lady."

"Thank you, Your Grace," I said crisply. "And now, since I have paid my father's debt, I believe I should be released?"

Again the two men exchanged a glance. Then the king nodded, almost imperceptibly, and Lord Edmar said in his smooth voice,

"Of course you will be released from this cell, my lady, but we would ask that you stay on with us at the palace for a little while longer. As an honored guest, of course."

I lifted an eyebrow, not liking the sound of that at all. "I don't understand. Why can I not be allowed to go home?"

The king stepped in, saying, "Ah, well, I must have my treasurer take up the gold and assay it, and determine its worth. Then that worth must be measured against your father's debt, and after that...we will see." He smiled then, most unpleasantly, and my stomach began an uneasy churning.

They clearly thought me only a simple girl, but I could guess their intentions. First one excuse, and then another, but it seemed obvious enough that they wished to keep me under their eye, where I could continue to spin more gold for them.

The duke had called me an honored guest, but I knew then that they would keep me their prisoner.

CHAPTER FIVE

At least my new cell was more luxurious than the last. I was given a suite that occupied almost an entire floor of one tower. The apartment was so large, I was not sure what they intended me to do with all of it.

Save one room, of course.

What appeared to have been a small study had been cleared of its furnishings, except a low couch placed up against one window, and the spinning wheel and a high-backed chair were placed in the center of the room. Next to it was set a large burlap bag of straw. Clearly, the king intended my gold-spinning activities to continue apace. And what would he do when he discovered my little trick could not be repeated?

Difficult to say. For all the king's talk of treasurers and assay, I was confident that what I had spun the night before should be more than sufficient to discharge my father's debt. No, I feared His Majesty's only motivation was greed, pure and simple.

At least I had bought myself a little time. The king, of course, could not lower himself to show me my new quarters, but the duke had accompanied me as I was removed from my prison cell and taken to the tower apartment that was to be mine.

"I hope you will find it sufficient, my lady?"

I didn't bother to tell Lord Edmar that the suite was larger than the entire top floor of my father's house, and far more grandly furnished...except for the spinning wheel, which looked as out of place there as I felt. Indeed, in my mind, it had begun to take on a rather ominous aspect, as it seemed to serve as a mute reminder of the king's expectations. I saw no reason to mention that, however, for I did not think His Grace would appreciate the comment. "The apartments are quite sufficient, Your Grace."

He nodded, but then moved closer to me. I couldn't help stiffening, although I hoped he hadn't noticed. "You have pleased the king, and so have pleased me as well." One hand touched a loose curl that lay upon my shoulder, and I tried not to flinch. "Although I must confess I had rather hoped you would be pleasing me in other ways as well."

"So I heard," I said tartly, and he moved back a fraction of an inch, brows drawing together. "I am sorry that you couldn't carry out your arrangement with my father, but I am sure the king would prefer he had his gold, rather than you having me in your bed."

The grey eyes widened, and then the duke forced a smile. "You have a very blunt tongue, my lady."

"I see no reason to dance around the issue." Indeed, I didn't. Perhaps it was the lack of sleep—and the relief of knowing I had been granted a reprieve, if only a temporary one—but caution did seem to have deserted me for the moment.

"Perhaps not." He gestured toward the spinning wheel. "Then I think it best that I leave you to your work."

"In due time," I replied. "I can only spin the straw into gold after the sun has gone down, and that is still some hours off." Which of course was a complete prevarication. There would be no gold spun from straw at all this day, either before or after the sun had set. I could not expect the stranger to lend his assistance a second time. But at least by saying I could not do my spinning by daylight, I might earn a little breathing space.

"I see. Well, I will leave you alone to refresh yourself." A pause, and then he was taking my hand and raising it to his lips. They lingered against my skin far longer than the gesture usually required, but I made myself stand quietly and not shudder. For some reason, I thought he might enjoy that, but a lack of reaction could only serve to put him off.

Which apparently it did, for he released my hand after that, his lips compressing slightly. "We will look in on you in the morning," he said, then bowed and left.

One did not have to be a genius to decipher the threat in those words. He would return with the king the next day, and if there was no more gold, only that pile of straw, then my life could still be forfeit.

Or at least my virtue.

I drew in a breath and told myself that I had already witnessed one miracle, and perhaps I would be able to witness yet more. In the meantime, I might as well do what Lord Edmar had said and "refresh" myself.

Which I did. The palace servants did not seem to realize that I was not an "honored guest" and instead the king's prisoner in everything but name, and so I was brought trays of delicious food, and warm water for a bath, and several more gowns, these ones even finer than the dresses I had been provided previously. I napped, too, still exhausted from my mostly sleepless night.

The one thing I wished for but knew I dare not attempt was to have some way to write my sister and let her know I was well, that I had not suffered any calamity. But a hurried search of my chambers showed there was no paper or ink. Besides, any missive I sent was sure to be intercepted and read...and most likely destroyed, if it contained information the king did not want to get out...and so I did not much see the point. I could only hope that my father had been informed of the "miracle" I had wrought the night before, and then had given Iselda some sort of comforting lie as to my whereabouts, since he at least would know I yet lived. My sister might not entirely believe anything he told her, but it would still be better than having no information at all.

Night fell. Dinner was brought, and the tray taken away again after I had cleaned my plate of the ragout of beef and vegetables, and the small loaf of bread and fresh-made butter. There had even been a small flagon of wine, which I drank as well. Perhaps it was not wise, wearied as I was, but if this was to truly be my last night on earth, then I should enjoy it as best I could.

I washed my face and braided my hair for the evening, then slipped into the luxurious bed of carved oak, with hangings of sky blue. The chemise I had been given to sleep in was of linen so fine it felt almost like silk against my skin, and the feather bed I lay upon was deep and soft, and yet sleep eluded me. Perhaps it was the lengthy nap I had taken this afternoon, although I guessed that my sleepless state had far more to do with what awaited me on the morrow. I could not forget that lascivious gleam in Lord Edmar's eyes. He must have seen some hesitation in my manner, something that told him the miraculous spinning of straw into gold would not happen two nights in a row.

Then a footfall, so soft I probably would not have heard it if I had not been lying there awake and watchful. I sat up in bed, willing myself to stay calm. Surely the duke would not lower himself to slip into my bedchamber like this, not when all he had to do was wait for my failure the next day....

A voice issued forth from the darkness, warm and ironic. "He is a greedy little man, our king, is he not?"

I let out a relieved breath. "Rumple."

He appeared then, looming over my bed, still in the hooded cloak he had worn the night before. Even though I knew he meant me no harm, I couldn't help recoiling slightly. After all, it was quite disconcerting to be confronted by a large black-shrouded man when lying in one's bed.

"Good evening, Annora," he replied, sounding casual enough. He reached behind him and grasped the chair that sat on the other side of my bedside table, then set it down next to the bed frame. After seating himself, he added, "It appears that my trick of last night was not sufficient to satisfy His Majesty."

"No," I replied. A faint drift of moonlight came in through the partially open curtains, but it was not strong enough for me to actually see him. I began to reach for the candlestick on the table next to the bed, but his gloved hand descended on my wrist.

"That will not be necessary."

"Why don't you want me to see you?" I asked.

Silence then, as his hood tilted to one side. He must have been watching me carefully, although I could discern nothing of his face or his expression. "There is no need for that."

"Because you are a mage, and if I can identify you—"

"What makes you say that?" he inquired, interrupting me. He did not sound angry, though, but rather amused. "I am no mage. Magic doesn't exist anymore."

"Then perhaps you would like to explain how you were able to turn straw into gold?"

"The alchemical sciences are not magic," he said calmly.

"That was alchemy?" I asked, not bothering to hide the skepticism in my tone. "I had always heard that alchemy required a great laboratory, and glass bottles and beakers and goodness knows what else. I did not see any of that last night."

"That may be how some practice that art, but my methods are...different."

"Ah. All right, then, it was alchemy. But, leaving that aside for now, you cannot say it was alchemy that allowed you to disappear into thin air the way you did. I saw."

"You saw nothing," he replied, voice still unruffled. "Or rather, you saw a black form disappear into a shadow. How do you know that there was not simply a hidden passageway, one I took to make my way from your cell?"

"I noted no such passageway."

"Of course you didn't, because it was hidden."

From the note of satisfaction in his tone, it seemed he thought he had outwitted me. But I would not be put off quite so easily.

"Very well, let us also leave aside how you could have come and gone from a dungeon that no one has ever escaped from. How do you explain your presence here tonight? The passages of this palace are well lit and well guarded."

The hood tilted again. "Do you always ask so many questions, Annora Kelsden?"

"I do, if their answers don't immediately present themselves. Are you also going to claim that there is a secret passageway here? I highly doubt that the king would house me someplace where anyone might come and go without being seen. Besides, I was awake this whole time. I only heard you when you were a few feet away. If you had come in through the door, or even the window, I would have noticed."

This time he actually laughed, although low in his throat, so the sound could not possibly be overheard. "Ah, well, I suppose you have me there. All right, we shall be honest with one another."

"We shall?" I asked, interest piqued. Was he now going to confess that he truly was a mage? For of course I did not believe his story about alchemy, not for one moment.

"Yes," he replied. "There is actually a trap door in the ceiling not too far from the foot of your bed. I lowered myself down through that."

Oh, of all the impertinence! I pushed the bedclothes aside and stood, reaching for the dressing gown that had been draped on top of the silk coverlet. Perhaps I should have been more concerned about my dishabille, but I did not get the same impression from this "Rumple" that I did from Lord Edmar. Mage or no, Rumple did not appear to have any particular designs on my person.

After knotting the sash around my waist, I turned back toward him. He had not moved, still stood there like one of the room's shadows come to life. "Why are you here?" I asked simply.

"Because it seems you are still in need of some assistance."

I could not deny that. "So you intend to help me again?"

"Yes."

How I wished I could see his face, could detect something of his expression! His voice was rich and deep, musical almost, but I could only glean so much of his mood by his inflections, especially since I could not claim to know him well.

Or at all, really.

"Why?" I asked.

He did move then, going from the bedchamber to the study next door, where the spinning wheel stood. The two rooms were connected by a door, so there was no need to enter the suite's central hallway. I could but follow him, wondering what his purpose was.

After stopping next to the spinning wheel, he reached out with one hand and touched it gently, so that the wheel began to move in lazy circles. "Does it matter?" he returned.

"It matters to me." Perhaps it was foolish of me to be so blunt, but I would rather the evil I knew than the one hidden from me. "I would like to know what you expect of me in return."

"Expect?" Rumple replied, sounding almost surprised. Then he went on, "Ah, I see. No, I am not like Lord Edmar, seeking to use my power to take that which a woman should always willingly give. I expect nothing, Annora, save that you sit here and spin this straw into gold."

Relief coursed through me at his words, although at the same time I was puzzled. If he did not expect...that...of me, then what was his purpose here?

"I don't understand," I said slowly.

"It is not necessary that you should."

I bristled at that comment, and he left the spinning wheel and came toward me. Again I was struck by the oddness of my situation, that I should be standing here and speaking so calmly with a man whose face I had never seen, who apparently had the skill to slip into a woman's chambers at night without being detected.

He extended a gloved hand to me, and I took it, not certain of what he intended. Then he covered the back of my hand with his free one in the ancient gesture of agreement, the one used to indicate a deal sealed in good faith. His hands were much bigger than mine, which quite disappeared between both of his. The fine leather of his gloves was warm against my skin, soft. I found myself wondering what his fingers looked like beneath that leather casing. Were they callused, the hands of a working man, or smooth, like those of Lord Edmar, someone who had never had to lift a finger in his life, except to ride on the hunt or train his falcons?

"Annora," Rumple said, "let me set your mind at ease. My only design is to make sure your life is not in danger. If that means I must return here every night to see that you spin enough straw into gold to make certain you suffer no threat, then I will. I expect nothing of you. Nothing at all."

"Nothing?" I replied, then managed a shaky laugh. "It does not seem like that fair a bargain."

He released my fingers, and his hand dropped back somewhere within the folds of his cloak. "Well, except perhaps a little company. If you do not mind."

"Of course I don't mind." But even as the words left my lips, I had to wonder again at his true purpose. He would come here, and use his powers—whether alchemical or magical—to create enough gold for a king's ransom, and want nothing of me except to be in my presence, perhaps to share some conversation?

"Very good. But I suppose now you should get started. You were awake until almost morning last evening, and it would not do to deprive you of your sleep every night."

I saw the wisdom in that. At the same time, my heart sank a little at the prospect of having to sit at the spinning wheel night after night, producing more and more gold to feed the king's greed.

But no. I would not allow myself to think that. I would sit here and produce another gleaming skein of golden thread, and perhaps that would be enough to convince King Elsdon that he had enough. After all, he already had storehouses full of treasure. How much more could one man—even a king—possibly need?

"You are very kind," I murmured, but Rumple only gave a noncommittal lift of his shoulders, as if he did not believe my words.

Deciding to let the matter go for now, I took my seat in the chair and gathered up some straw. Once again I laid it on top of the starter yarn—only this time it was not yarn at all, but the remnants of last night's gold threads—and watched as it somehow shimmered and twisted and transformed while I worked. This time around, I knew better what to expect, and so did not pause to gawk at that impossible skein of purest metal. It wound around the bobbin, growing thicker and thicker.

Since Rumple had said he desired conversation from me, I asked, "And is it—is it truly real? For I have read that long ago the mages could cast illusions that looked as real as anything, only they would melt away after a day, or a week." If that were the case, I would be in a great deal of trouble, should the king have his treasurer check on those threads of gold, only to find they had turned back into straw.

"It is real," Rumple said quietly. I noted that he did not bother to protest yet again that he was no mage. "It will not change back."

"Then that truly is a wondrous thing." I was silent for a moment, pondering what such a gift could do to change a person's life. For it meant that limitless wealth was his to command...or at least to command from another. Following up on that thought, I inquired, "Could you do this yourself? Or do you need someone else for your power to work through?"

Even as I asked the question, I did not think I liked the sound of it very much. To be used as a conduit for such power... it was frightening.

He seemed to note my unease, for he said at once, "I can do it on my own. That is, I could change a regular brick into a brick of gold, merely by holding it in my hands. But the lie your father told involved spinning straw into gold, and I know nothing of the weaver's arts. So you must do the spinning, and then I can let the enchantment flow through your fingers."

"So you are a mage."

"Of course I am." He paused then, seeming to regard me closely. "Does that frighten you?"

"I don't know," I told him. That was only the truth. Everything I had read about those long-ago wielders of magic had made them seem very fearsome indeed, but Rumple had done nothing to me that could be perceived as threatening. Indeed, the ones who had threatened me were the king and the duke, and not this strange man who controlled the sort of power the world thought long gone.

"That is an honest answer," he said with a chuckle. "I suppose it must be odd, to know that magic is not quite as dead as everyone thinks."

"Yes," I agreed. "Perhaps in some way I am not sure I entirely believe you, and yet there is this." I raised my right hand, which was unoccupied at the moment, and gestured toward the gleaming thread that wound itself around the bobbin as I worked the treadle. "With this power, you must be very rich."

"You think so?" Once again that note of amusement was back in his voice.

"So you are not?"

"Conspicuous wealth brings attention, Annora. I live comfortably, but not in any sort of fashion that would attract comment."

I considered that statement for a moment as I continued to spin, the pile of straw at my feet already almost gone. At first it did puzzle me that he should be able to produce as much gold as he wanted, and yet somehow did not. Surely one would want to have all the comforts that such wealth would bring. But then my father entered my thoughts, and I realized that if he had this power, it would not matter. He would find more and more ways to foolishly spend the wealth he created, and yet would still never be satisfied. Much better to know one's limits, to choose to only have as much as was needed to live well but not grandly.

"That makes a good deal of sense," I said.

"I am glad you think so." Rumple had been sitting on the small divan under the window while I worked, but he stood then and came closer to me. "You have almost finished."

"It did go more quickly tonight." As I spoke, I bent and gathered up the last bits of straw and set them in my lap. One by one they slipped from my fingers, turning to gold and winding around the bobbin. At last I was done. I reached out and touched the heavy thread, feeling the cool smoothness of it beneath my fingertips. I rose from my chair as well, adding,

"And if the king still deems that not enough to cover my father's debt, then I shall know for sure he is lying, and only keeping me here to provide more gold for his coffers."

The mage did not respond to that, but touched the golden thread as well, his fingers resting only an inch or so away from mine. My first instinct was to pull away, but I thought that would be rude, and so I remained where I stood. He was very close, so close that a fold of his cloak touched the dressing gown I wore. Although he had said he had no expectations of me, I could feel my pulse begin to race. It would be easy enough for him to reach toward me, to pull me against him....

But he did not. He moved away from me, saying, "It is only a little after midnight. Rest now, Annora. I daresay you have earned it."

And then he was stepping toward the window, and his cloak billowed around him. For a few seconds, the moonlight silhouetted his form, showing that underneath the cloak he had on the close-fitting breeches and doublet all the men of my land wore, along with high shining black boots. I still had no idea what his face looked like, but in form he seemed well-made, with broad shoulders and long legs.

After that I had no more opportunity to gape, for he was simply gone. In some of the books I had read, it had sounded as if the mages made a great fuss when coming and going, appearing in a shower of sparks or whatnot, but there were no such fireworks here. In one second he was there, striding purposefully toward the window, and in the next....

He simply wasn't.

I put my hand to my breast, felt my heart thumping there. Yes, he had decided to be truthful with me about himself...up to a point...and yet the way he had disappeared struck me with far more force than those magical golden threads I had helped him to conjure. Whoever he truly was, and wherever he had come from, he was like no one else I had ever known.

With a tinge of sadness, I thought, *Perhaps he is the only one of his kind....*

CHAPTER SIX

As shocked and startled as I might have been by Rumple's revelations, my unsettled state did not prevent me from falling into a deep, deep slumber, one which surrounded me in such oblivion that it took someone shaking me awake the next morning and an unfamiliar woman's voice saying, "My lady, you must get up. The king will be here at any moment," to make me startle out of sleep and sit bolt upright.

Standing above me was a woman I had never seen before, perhaps some ten years or so older than I. Her dark blonde hair was twisted into a series of intricate plaits and wrapped around her head, and she wore a neat but simple gown of dark blue piped with gold.

That uniform told me she must be one of the palace servants. "The—the king?" I repeated, panic clear in my voice. I looked down at the chemise I wore, the messy braid looped over one shoulder.

"Yes, my lady." She reached toward the foot of the bed and gathered up the dressing gown lying there. I had a vague recollection of pulling it off and draping it over the bed, right before oblivion claimed me. "There is no time for you to dress, but put this on."

I pushed back the covers and stood. My neck and shoulders ached somewhat, most likely from that intense session of spinning the night before. The serving woman held the dressing gown so I could shrug into it. Then I tied the sash tightly.

"Here," the woman said, turning toward the bedside table. I noted that a bowl of water scented with lavender sat there. She picked up the cloth lying next to it and dabbed my face. The lavender did refresh me somewhat, although it was certainly no substitute for a proper bath. "And let me see to your hair." With deft fingers, she undid my untidy plait and then pulled a comb out of her pocket.

No sooner had she begun to run the comb through my hair, however, than a knock came at the door. She handed the comb to me and hurried off to answer the knock, while I tugged through the worst of the tangles as best I could. I heard her say, "Your Majesty," and then I could do nothing except set the comb down and move forward to greet him, all too aware of my current unkempt state and wishing that I had not slept quite so late.

To my dismay, King Elsdon was not alone. No, the duke again accompanied him, a glint entering his eyes as he took in my dressing gown and loose hair. There was nothing I could do, save curtsey, and so I essayed one as best I could, praying that they would not notice the bare toes peeking out from underneath the silken folds of my dressing gown.

The king seemed singularly unconcerned about my appearance. "And what do you have for us this morning, Annora?"

"What you asked for, Your Majesty," I replied with as much dignity as I could muster. "You may see for yourself." In that moment, I did not care whether the serving woman overheard me.

But the duke did seem determined to keep my spinning a secret for he tilted his head at the woman and said, "Wait out in the salon."

She hurried out, even as I pointed toward the door that joined my bedchamber with the study next to it. Both men swept past me and into that room, although I couldn't help noting the way the duke glanced back at me, a smile touching his lips. No doubt he was thinking of how he would like to see me as I was, only after emerging from his bed rather than my own.

To let him see how he had discomfited me would only be a sign of weakness, and so I entered the study with my head held high, and did not meet the duke's gaze. The king was standing next to the spinning wheel, running his fingers over the thick mass of gold thread that rested on the bobbin.

"By the gods, Edmar, this is even more than she spun the night before last!"

"Does it please you, Your Majesty?" I asked.

"Very much, Annora," he replied, smiling. Somehow, though, that smile didn't quite reach his eyes, and I felt the beginnings of a chill somewhere in my midsection.

Even so, I thought I had no choice but to press on. "Certainly between what I spun last night and the night before that, it should be enough to discharge my father's debt. I thank you for your hospitality, but I think it is time for me to go home."

The king's eyes narrowed. "That is my decision to make, not yours, young woman."

Oh, gods. My feelings of foreboding apparently had not been exaggerated. I could not help but glance at the duke, although I doubted I would get any help from that quarter. He, too, wore a smile, but I could tell it was at my expense.

I was well and truly trapped here.

Desperate, I said, "Your Majesty, I have my own spinning wheel at home, one that suits me better than this one, grand though it might be. If—if you would like me to spin more for you, I am happy to oblige. But I could do so even more efficiently at home, with my own wheel."

"We will have it brought to you," he said, still watching me from between his eyelashes.

I knew then that it mattered not what I said or did. The king had happened upon a miraculous means of filling his coffers, and he had no intention of letting it go.

Not looking at him—for I knew he would see the hatred burning in my eyes—I replied, "That would be excellent, Your Majesty. Thank you." How I wished for the courage to ask for one small favor, only to see my sister for a few moments, but I held my tongue. Something told me that it was better for the king not to know how much I missed her. Why show evidence of a weakness he might attempt to exploit?

He nodded, then gestured toward the thread. "If you will take that, Edmar—"

The duke stepped forward and removed the skein of gold from the bobbin. I wondered then why he was tasked with such things, rather than one of the servants, and then realized that my king wanted as few people as possible to know of the miracles I wrought—or rather, that Rumple and I wrought—each night with the spinning wheel. The guard in the dungeon had seen something of the thread I had spun, and that could not be helped, but I guessed he had probably been handsomely paid to keep his mouth closed on the subject...if he was lucky.

And the study door was kept locked, the key in my possession. No doubt the serving woman who had awoken me had been admonished to keep away from that door.

Seemingly satisfied with his latest haul, the king gave me a dismissive nod. "Then we will leave you to prepare for your day, Annora. We will come back tomorrow."

"Not quite so early, I hope," I said tartly. After all, what did I care if I offended him? I had something he desperately desired.

As the king began to bridle at my tone, Lord Edmar stepped in, saying coolly, "My apologies for that, my lady. I fear my anticipation exceeded the propriety of visiting at such an early hour."

Which of course was a lie. I knew it was the king who had brought him here, rather than the reverse. But he was interceding to shield me from King Elsdon's wrath, and I had to be grateful to him for that.

But not overly so, for I knew he did so only to make himself look better in my eyes. *It will take a great deal more than that,*

Lord Edmar, I thought, *to coax me into your bed.* I said nothing, though, instead only inclining my head. That seemed to mollify the king slightly, or perhaps he had merely decided that he had wasted enough time on me, and wished to get to his breakfast. At any rate, they were soon gone, the serving woman shutting the door behind them.

"I am Rashelle," she told me, once we were safely alone together. "The steward has assigned me to you, my lady."

Even more evidence that the king intended to keep me here for a very long time. I wanted to sigh. That, however, would only tell the woman who stood before me that I was not pleased with my current situation. She had a kind enough face, and was quite pretty, but I could not allow myself to trust her. For all I knew, she had been placed here to spy on me, as well as to do my hair and fetch my bath.

A bath. That would be a good starting place. After that, well...I supposed all I could do was wait for darkness to come, and Rumple to return.

Two servants appeared late in the morning, carrying my scratched old spinning wheel with them. They set it down in the study, then picked up the one of gleaming walnut that I had used for the past two nights and spirited it away.

This time I did sigh, mainly because Rashelle was off in another part of my suite, dusting. I knew she did so only to have something to occupy herself, for the apartment the king had given me was spotless and beautiful, and did not appear to have been lived in for some time. At least, there was certainly no trace of its former occupant.

I mentioned as much to Rashelle, thinking it a harmless enough topic of conversation. To my surprise, she shot me a wicked smile, then said, "Ah, that is because it once belonged to the king's mistress. But she pressed her suit too hard, wishing to be queen, and he sent her away. No one has lived here for more than a year."

That would explain its current empty state, and also the luxury of the furnishings. The king had been widowed for some years, and so I supposed one could not begrudge him some form of female companionship, although it surprised me somewhat that he had been quite so open about it. Then again, I did not pretend to understand the workings of the court. They were as far above me as the stars in the heavens, and their movements were equally inscrutable.

I worried that Rashelle would stay in the suite, and I would have no opportunity for any privacy with Rumple. However, after she had dressed my hair for the night, and put away the gown of silver-stitched silk I had worn, she told me, "I will leave you now, my lady. But if there is anything you find you need, please ring the bell. It is in the main salon, in the corner by the hearth, in case you had not noticed it before this."

Although I had noted the bell pull earlier, I had had no reason to use it, as my meals had been brought up promptly, and Rashelle had scarcely left the suite. And I had no intention of using it now, unless something calamitous occurred. Right then, I was only itching to be alone, so that Rumple might return to me.

I thanked her, though, and after that she mercifully departed and shut the door behind her. The thought crossed my mind to wedge a chair under the door handle so no one could enter without my permission, but I soon abandoned that idea. After all, my strange mage friend had the ability to disappear in the blink of an eye, so even if someone did intrude without my leave, he would most likely be gone before anyone could discover that I'd had a visitor in my luxurious prison.

After taking up the lit candelabra that sat on one of the tables in my bedchamber and making sure I had the key to the door, I went on into the study. My poor battered spinning wheel looked very much out of place in that room of carved furniture and silk curtains, but there was nothing I could do about that. All I could do was hope that my plan to escape home hadn't backfired on me too badly. I had not used the wheel in several years, and, for all I knew, it might not still function properly.

When I sat in front of it, however, and began to work the treadle, the wheel moved easily enough, with a soft whispery sound that brought to mind winter evenings by the hearth back home, when I would spin soft yarn to be knitted into stockings and Iselda would lie on her stomach on the rug, reading one of her books. It was not, perhaps, the most ladylike of postures, but she had no mother to guide her in such things, and of course Father was rarely home. Even if he had been, I doubted he would have noticed.

Thoughts of Iselda awoke an ache in my heart. I had to tell myself that she was well, that as long as I kept making this golden thread for the king, she and my father would be left unmolested. Not that I cared overmuch what happened to my father at that point, but on the other hand, neither did I wish for my sister to be left with no parent at all. And of course I had no idea if I would ever be allowed to leave this place.

Rumple's arrival was hardly louder than the soft whispered hum of the spinning wheel. A shiver of dark movement caught my eye, a swish of his cloak, and then he was standing there in the corner, watching me as I set the wheel through its paces.

He stepped forward, then paused and cocked his head as he regarded me. "Was there something wrong with the other wheel, Annora? For this one appears to have seen better days."

I sighed. "No, there was nothing wrong with the other wheel, save that I attempted a stratagem which backfired on me. I had hoped that by telling the king I would spin better on my own wheel, I might be allowed to go home, but of course he would never hear of that, and instead had my spinning wheel brought here."

"That is unfortunate." This time, it seemed as if he took care to keep some distance from me, for he had stopped several paces away, the spinning wheel's bulk between us. "So what you spun last night was not enough to satisfy His Majesty, I take it?"

Something seemed to tighten within my chest. I swallowed, then said, "No, I fear it was not. Rumple, I do not think I can ever spin enough for him. He intends to keep me here to do his bidding and fill his coffers, night after night. How can I expect you to continue to come to my aid? Sooner or later, we must stop, and then the king will have me executed, or give me over to Lord Edmar to be his plaything."

Rumple seemed to stiffen at that pronouncement. Then he shook his head. "I will not allow that to come to pass."

Hope flared in me, and I rose from my chair and went toward him. From somewhere within I found the courage to place a hand on his arm, shrouded in the heavy folds of his cloak. It felt solid and strong beneath my fingers, as if he had reason to use his muscles. An odd tremor seemed to go through him, and then he stilled.

I was not sure what that meant, but I forged ahead, asking, "You can easily come and go from this place. Could you not spirit me away, take me with you the next time you disappear?"

"I cannot," he replied, his tone calm but sad. "My power is only strong enough to bring me hence, not to take you away with me. And even if I could, where would I take you? If I brought you home, the king's guards would only discover where you had gone and would bring you straight back here. And I fear that His Majesty would have lost patience, and would return you to the dungeon. At least now you are housed in some comfort."

That was true enough, although I hated to admit it. Despair began to edge its way up within me, and once again that unwelcome tightness seized my throat. I blinked, feeling the hot sting of tears within my eyes.

"And so there truly is no escape," I murmured, not able to speak any louder than that because of the increasing constriction in my throat. "I will be kept here forever, and the only release I can hope for is that the king will die someday, and perhaps Prince Harlin will find it in his heart to let me go."

I could say no more, because in that moment the tears which had been choking me suddenly overflowed, blurring the candlelit room, the shadowy figure who stood a few feet away.

Oh, the ignominy of it, to weep like a distraught child in front of one who commanded such amazing powers! But by then I truly was at my wit's end, the fear I had attempted to hold back the past few days now engulfing me as the dire nature of my predicament finally began to sink in.

Then I could feel arms going around me, heavy draperies of wool falling over my arms, warming my chilled and shaky limbs. Perhaps I should have startled away, but I sensed nothing predatory in Rumple's embrace, only a desire to lend me what comfort he could.

"Shh," he said, voice a soft rumble in my ears. "I know you are frightened, but you must not give up yet. I will think of something."

His words should have reassured me, but they did not. I continued to weep, my face burrowed into his chest, which felt quite broad and strong. Indeed, I understood then why a woman would go to a man for solace, because despite my worry, I could not help but notice how good it was then to have his arms around me. A strange little thrill moved through my body. I could not quite understand what it was, for I had never experienced anything like it before. All I knew was that I did not want it to stop.

It did, of course. After a few moments, once my sobbing had begun to quiet down, Rumple took me gently by the arms and held me away from him. And I realized what I had just done, letting a man I hardly knew hold me while we were alone together and unattended.

"I am sorry," I said, as soon as I had control of my voice again. "That was—that was unforgivable. I beg your pardon."

"It was quite forgivable, and understandable as well. You are a young woman who has never known anything but the safety of her home. And now you have been plucked from your family and brought here to serve the king's whims." He paused then, as if deciding how best to put what he had to say next. "I would think it far stranger if you did not break down at some point. But now that is over, and you must be strong. Can you do that?"

I nodded, lifting a fold of my dressing gown to blot my watering eyes, since I had no handkerchief with me. "I will try."

"Very good." Another hesitation, something in his manner seeming to suggest that he wanted to reach out and offer a reassuring hand on my arm or shoulder. But he did not, and instead turned toward the spinning wheel. "I will think on this, Annora, and do my best to find some way to free you from this place. In the meantime, though, I believe you have some gold to spin."

Managing a watery smile, I went to my chair and sat down, then gathered up some straw and set it in my lap. How odd that after only two evenings of such activity, it should already feel almost normal to me. I knew that Rumple was right—I must keep on spinning, so the king would have no reason to punish me.

And after all, my mysterious benefactor had kept me safe so far. I had to trust him now, and hope he truly could discover the means to save me forever from King Elsdon's clutches.

If he could, then he truly must be a very great mage.

The next morning, Lord Edmar arrived alone to retrieve the golden thread. It was on my tongue to snap that I was surprised the king should already think my activities so commonplace that he would not come to fetch his treasure, but I somehow managed to remain silent. Rashelle was puttering about the suite, continuing with her eternal dusting, but her presence now heartened rather than annoyed me. At least it meant the duke would not attempt anything too untoward. And I had taken the thread from its bobbin the night before and concealed it under my mattress, so there was no chance of her discovering it, unless she intended to remove the entire thing so she could turn it over. That she might find the gold was something the king seemed to have forgotten when he had set the maid to be my watchdog, but I did not want to take the risk either way. King Elsdon had already shown himself to be an intemperate man, and no doubt he would blame me if Rashelle managed to locate the thread.

"You are looking rather pale, my lady," Lord Edmar remarked as I handed the heavy wad of golden thread to him. "I think you need a good walk in the sunshine."

"Perhaps I do," I replied. "But since His Majesty has seen fit to keep me imprisoned in these chambers, there is very little I can do about that."

"But perhaps there is something I can do." His eyes shifted toward the window and then back to me. "Would you like that?"

I wished I could tell him that what I would truly like was to be sent home, so I could enjoy the fresh air in my own courtyard, but I knew that reply would only annoy him. "A taste of the wind would not be unwelcome."

"Excellent."

Rashelle appeared then, holding her feather duster, and so anything else he'd intended to say, he abandoned for the moment. He did not even try to kiss my hand—for which I was profoundly grateful—but excused himself, saying he would return when he could.

Which he did, later that afternoon after I had had a reviving noontime meal of fresh cheese and leek soup, and a lovely dish of spiced apples. By then the hours had begun to feel so dull that even the presence of the duke was not something to be despised. He was smiling as Rashelle opened the door to allow him into the suite.

"Good news, my lady," he said, bowing extravagantly over my hand. In the background, I could see my serving woman raise an ironic eyebrow, and my estimation of her went up slightly. At least she was not the type to be sent all a-flutter by the gallant gestures of a nobleman.

"Indeed?" I replied.

"Yes," he went on, apparently nonplussed by my cool reaction. "The king has agreed that it would be better for you if you were to walk in the gardens, and so I will take you there."

"How kind of him." My tone indicated that he was anything but kind, although I did feel a slight stir of anticipation within me. It would feel good to be out in the sun and the wind, even if I must do it while accompanied by Lord Edmar. I added, "It is very kind of you to take the time out of what must be a very busy schedule to do these things for me."

I watched as his lashes dropped over his eyes, as if he were attempting to measure precisely what I had meant by that statement. Then he lifted his shoulders. "It is the least I can do for a lady who has done so much for her kingdom."

There was little I could say in reply to that, not with Rashelle listening in. I summoned a smile. "Well, I thank you for it. And from what I have seen out the window, it does look to be a fine day."

"A very fine day, my lady. Let me show you."

He offered me his arm, and there was nothing I could do except take it. I must confess that it felt strange to step out of the rooms that had been my prison for the past few days, to walk through the corridors of the palace as if I truly belonged there. Curious glances came my way, especially from the ladies of the court, as if they were attempting to discover who this strange young woman with the duke might be.

In that moment I was glad that Rashelle had taken a good deal of care while dressing my hair that morning, and that I wore a gown in a warm dark teal color, flattering to my mahogany hair and hazel eyes. I did not think any of these fine lords and ladies would have been able to guess that I was only a simple merchant's daughter.

Well, not so simple, perhaps. I was, after all, hiding a very great secret.

For some reason, I recalled the way Rumple's arms had felt around me the night before, the strength of him. He had made me feel safe and protected in a way that my father most certainly never had. Actually, the mage's touch had made me feel things I had never experienced before…sensations I wasn't sure I should be feeling.

And certainly not thinking of while in Lord Edmar's presence.

To my relief, he did not seem to notice my preoccupation. We went down a corridor narrower than the one we had been traversing previously, and from there out a set of double doors that opened on a wide, shallow set of steps. Before us stretched the palace gardens, what seemed like acres of green lawns and carefully clipped hedges. The stately poplars were columns of fluttering gold in the brisk breeze that danced across all that manicured loveliness, touching my face like the caress of a lover.

"It's beautiful," I said.

"The king is very proud of his gardens," the duke said. "And this is only the beginning. Come with me."

He had held my arm this entire time, and I had dared not pull it from his while we were surrounded by others. Now, though, after we descended the steps, I gently slipped away, pretending eagerness to walk ahead. He did not protest, although I noted how he lengthened his strides so he could catch up to me.

"If you go down this central path, and then take the spoke that leads off to the left, you will be able to see something very fine."

I did as he directed, mostly because I did not know the gardens, and he did. They were not completely unoccupied, either; I saw members of the court walking here and there, getting their own fill of the mellow autumn air. In less than a month, it would be too cold to walk thus, but for now everyone was enjoying the season while they could.

Where we were headed, however, seemed to be empty enough. The hedges gave way to what were probably spectacular beds of iris in the spring, but now were only clusters of tall sword-like leaves. Past the soft rustle of the wind in the foliage, I heard a low murmur, as of water over stones.

The path ended at a small pond, where a stream fed into it on the far side. Swans glided across the water, pale and proud. I had only been in the country a handful of times, and yet here it seemed was a small piece of it captured within the palace walls, a place to go when the crush of city life became too much to bear. I wondered that all those who walked in the garden had not come here directly, because I could not imagine anything more beautiful.

"It's lovely," I breathed, going as close to the edge of the pond without muddying the hem of my gown as I could.

"I'm glad you think so." The duke wore high, fine boots, but I noticed he stood some ways off, as if he did not want to risk dirtying his footwear. "An antidote, I hope, to all those hours you spent in your apartments."

"Yes, and a welcome one." I paused then and watched as one of the swans took flight, beating against the air with its great strong wings. In fact, it launched itself so fiercely that it splashed water in my direction, and I hastily backed away.

"I fear I don't have much experience with swans," I added.

Lord Edmar smiled. "I find them to be quite a nuisance, but the king enjoys them."

His manner was so easy, so relaxed and friendly, that I almost wanted to let down my guard. I knew better, though. He was only pretending to be kind. What he desired from me was perhaps different from what the king wanted, but to both of them I was only someone to be used.

Whether something in my aspect shifted then, I could not know, but I saw the smile fade from the duke's face, and the familiar crafty glint entered his eyes. "I am curious, my lady. How precisely do you do it?"

The breeze was fresh, but not cold. Despite that, I felt a distinct chill along the back of my neck. "Do what, Your Grace?"

"You know what I am asking, Annora. Do not bother to play games."

I gave what I hoped was a negligent lift of my shoulders. "Nothing in particular. I suppose I merely think of how the straw is golden, and how it is so close to true gold, and as I spin...it just becomes the real thing."

One eyebrow went up at a sardonic angle. "You expect me to believe that."

No, I really didn't. Even to me, the explanation had sounded quite foolish. I couldn't tell him the truth, however, and so I was left with whatever makeshifts I could concoct. "Truthfully, Your Grace, I do not know how it works. It happened to me one day, and ever since then I've been able to spin gold. Not a lot, not so much that it would attract attention, but...." I stopped there, thinking of how my words were an echo of what Rumple had told me the previous night. In that moment I thought I understood the importance of not attracting attention.

Too late for that, however. My father had brought that unwanted attention down upon my head, and now I had to do my best to survive its consequences.

The duke regarded me for a moment, expression blank. In the bright afternoon light, I could see glimmers of silver in his dark hair, the laugh lines in the tanned flesh around his eyes. No one would deny that he was handsome, even though he was twice my age.

As I gazed back at him, wearing my best guileless expression, I watched his mouth purse slightly, as if something had just occurred to him. He moved closer, and laid a hand on my arm. Startled, I began to jerk it away, but his fingers tightened on the limb, and I could not move.

"Tell me, Annora," he said. That he had addressed me by my first name was not lost on me.

"Can you do these things because you are a mage?"

CHAPTER SEVEN

The world seemed to go very quiet. The wind in the trees, the low murmurs of the courtiers taking their afternoon constitutional on the garden's pathways...those all seemed very far away. All I could hear was the painful thudding of my heart within my breast.

Then I took in a quick, sharp breath, and let out what I hoped was a convincing chuckle. "A mage, Your Grace? I am only a simple merchant's daughter."

"Who can spin straw into gold."

"And that is all," I replied. His grip on my arm was almost painful, but I dared not show him my discomfort. "A peculiar gift, I am sure, but that is all it is. If I were a mage, could I not have escaped from my suite? Could I not have avoided capture in the first place? I know little of these matters, but I have always read that mages were great, fearsome creatures with all sorts of diabolical powers at their command. I am most certainly not anything like that."

For a long moment, he said nothing, only watched me with those sharp, hawklike eyes of his. Then at last he let go of me. I resisted the urge to rub my arm where he had grasped it. "You may say that, my lady, but you must admit there is something very peculiar about this 'gift' of yours."

"I will not deny that it is strange. Perhaps it is something given to me by the gods. As I am only a humble young woman, I dare not venture a guess."

That seemed to set him thinking. Whether he would believe the gods had blessed me with the gift of spinning straw into gold, I could not say. In these worldly times, the gods were given lip service more than anything else—an offering laid on an altar at harvest, a deity's name invoked when good fortune in a business dealing was desired. But whether most people truly believed the gods existed...that I could not say for sure. I must confess that most of the time I myself was skeptical at best. Now, though, having seen what Rumple could do, I did not know what I believed. His powers had to have come from somewhere. The gods? Possibly.

But it seemed as if my remark had thrown Lord Edmar off somewhat, or at least had given him something new to consider. He gave the faintest of nods, then said, "Perhaps. It is said that the gods once walked among us, and bestowed miracles upon those they found worthy. You, my lady, may be the recipient of such a gift."

"One that I am glad to put to the service of the realm," I responded. "Only...."

"Only?"

"Only I cannot help wondering how much gold the king truly needs," I said. "Our land has been at peace these many years. Of late the harvests have been good. So what is he going to do with all of it?"

The duke shook his head, then gave me an indulgent smile. "I cannot expect a sheltered young woman such as you to understand matters of state. But you must have heard that the Hierarch of Keshiaar lately married the sister of the Emperor of Sirlende. When two such great powers ally, the rest of us must be on our guard. Purth especially, as we share a southern border with Keshiaar."

On the surface, that explanation sounded logical enough. However, I knew that Keshiaar was a far, far greater power than my own homeland of Purth could ever hope to be. Because of that discrepancy, I did not think it would matter how much gold King Elsdon stockpiled. If the Hierarch truly wished to wage war upon my land, then he would fall upon us with the force of one of the great sandstorms that swept the deserts in his empire's southern reaches. Not that I thought such an attack was terribly likely. I could not profess to be an expert in politics, but from what I had heard, the Hierarch seemed to be a peaceable sort, not given to unwarranted acts of aggression.

"I see," I told the duke, since it seemed obvious that he was waiting for me to make some sort of answer. And I did think I understood, although not in the manner that Lord Edmar most likely guessed. With some, it mattered little how much wealth they accumulated. They must always have more, no matter what.

I did not say such a thing to the duke, of course. He would only see that sort of remark as a criticism of the king, something a woman of my standing should not dare to do. What his lordship sought to gain from all this, I did not quite know. Perhaps King Elsdon had promised him a small share of the golden thread I had spun in exchange for riding herd on me, or perhaps the promise of my person was enough for him, since it seemed to me his covetousness lay in different areas than in merely accumulating wealth.

A shiver passed over me then, thinking of what the duke might have planned for me. Apparently seeing the tremor, he said, his tone all solicitude, "Are you chilled, my lady? Should we go back inside?"

In truth, the mild afternoon air was comfortable enough. But I was glad of the excuse to have him take me back inside, for by then I had had quite enough of his company. "Yes, Your Grace, if you please," I replied. "The wind seems to have picked up a bit."

"Of course."

He offered me his arm, and I could not refuse it. I had to let him guide me back into the palace, and on up to my chambers. Once again I was glad to see Rashelle waiting for me inside, for it meant that the duke would most likely not press his suit. No, he preferred to take advantage of me when I was alone.

He did linger, however, pausing by the door and saying, "If you feel the fresh air has done you some good, I can come again tomorrow afternoon. Would you like that, my lady?"

Actually, I wouldn't like that, not at all. Right then I'd felt as if I'd had enough fresh air—and enough of Lord Edmar's company—to last me for days. Refusing him, however, did not seem to be a particularly wise thing to do. "That sounds lovely," I replied, hoping I sounded more enthusiastic than I felt.

Apparently I did, for he offered me a smile before bowing over my fingers once more. Then he slipped out the door. I had to thank the gods that he hadn't tried to kiss my hand. Perhaps he hadn't wished to, not with Rashelle hovering in the background, wiping down the marble surround on the hearth in the main salon.

Whatever the reason, he was gone without further incident. I shut the door and fought back the urge to sigh with relief. Instead, I came farther into the apartment, then went over to the side table, where a pitcher of water and a pair of silver goblets sat. As I poured some of the water for myself, Rashelle came closer, pausing a few feet away.

"He is a very fine man, is he not?" she said.

I lifted my shoulders. "I suppose many would say so."

"But you would not?"

"I did not say that. He has certainly been very…thoughtful." I paused then, as I did not know how much of my circumstances she had even been told. Certainly not the whole truth, but did she know that I was only the daughter of a merchant, and not someone who, under normal circumstances, would have had cause to spend any time in the company of one so exalted as Lord Edmar?

Her expression was mildly inquisitive, but I could see nothing more in it than simple curiosity. However, that meant very little. I did not know her, and it was entirely possible that the king—or his steward, more likely—had placed her here as a sort of spy, to see what kind of information she could glean from me when my guard was down.

What none of them understood was that my guard was almost always up. It was a practice that became necessary when raised by such a one as my father.

"The fresh air has wearied me somewhat," I told Rashelle then. "I think I will lie down for a while."

At once she became concerned, asking if I needed a cool cloth for my head, or perhaps some tea rather than the water I had been drinking. I turned down both of these offers, then went into my bedchamber and shut the door. Of course it would take more than a half-hour of fresh air to tire me, but the excuse seemed the best way of getting myself some much-needed privacy. I would lie down for a while, and then she would bring me my supper.

And then eventually night would arrive, and she would go. And Rumple would come to me once more.

I did not quite want to admit to myself how much I looked forward to seeing him again.

He appeared as I had expected him to, some time after Rashelle had excused herself for the night, and I felt the palace dreaming and quiet around me. Perhaps somewhere far below, people still drank and danced and flirted, but I heard nothing of that if they were. And I knew little of such things as well; in my mind, palace life had always seemed to be a whirlwind of social activities, but I knew it was quite likely that I had formed the wrong impression. The king was not a young man anymore, and his son, Prince Harlin, was by all accounts a fairly sober type, much better suited to sit on the throne than his father. I did not want to wish anyone ill, but neither could I quite banish from my mind the notion that I—and the kingdom itself—might be much better off if it was Harlin who ruled over the kingdom of Purth, rather than King Elsdon.

I was already waiting in the study when Rumple appeared. By now, I was not so concerned about meeting him in my dressing gown and with my hair down in a plait. The gown covered my chemise completely, and it did not seem that the mage cared one way or another what my hair looked like, or indeed seemed to even notice that I was female. Yes, he had held me the night before, but he had done so to offer me comfort, nothing more.

"You have survived another day, I see," he said as he stepped into the center of the room, once more seeming to materialize from the shadows.

"Yes, no thanks to Lord Edmar. I fear his latest theory is that I must be a mage myself, for how else could I turn straw into gold?"

At that remark, Rumple paused. I could not see his face, but it seemed as if he frowned within the folds of his hood. "What did you say to him?"

"The truth, of course. That I was no mage, and that perhaps this strange ability of mine is rather a gift from the gods."

"What was his reply to that?"

I shrugged. "He seemed to take my words at face value, or at least he did not press the matter."

"That is something, I suppose. Typical, though, for him to start questioning you about the very thing he and his king desire most."

"I suppose now he has gone past his initial surprise that I was able to do it at all, and is beginning to wonder how. But for the time being, he seemed willing to set his questions aside."

"Of course he was," Rumple said, an edge entering his tone. "It would not do, after all, for the woman he desires to be revealed as a mage."

My cheeks heated at that remark, but I did not bother to deny it. The duke had made his intentions obvious enough. I had acknowledged it to myself, but it was quite something else to have Rumple state the matter so baldly.

"At any rate," I said hurriedly, "the best thing is to conjure more gold for the king, so they have nothing to take exception at."

"Is that the path you truly wish to take?"

I had begun to move toward my chair and the wheel next to it when Rumple's words stopped me. "'Path'?" I echoed in some confusion. "What path can I take, save to keep spinning this gold? Or rather, have you help me spin it."

He crossed his arms. "Yesterday evening, I told you that I would do what I could to discover a way to release you from this makeshift prison the king has put you in."

"And have you discovered such a way?" My tone was light, but underneath, my heart had begun to race. I felt I would not even care so much to keep spinning for the king, as long as I could do it from my own home, where I could be with my sister and in familiar surroundings. The only difficulty there would be to keep my activities with Rumple from her, but I felt I could devise some way to do so. I certainly did not fear any discovery by my father, as I could not even recall the last time he had set foot in my chamber.

"I believe I have," Rumple replied. "After careful study, I have decided that the best thing to do would be to sue for your release."

The suggestion was so completely unexpected that for a moment I could only stare at him, mouth slightly agape. Then I managed to recover myself, and I said, "Sue...the king? Are you mad?"

"Not at all," he said calmly.

True, the people of Purth were known for being litigious sorts. More than once my father had been compelled to hire a lawyer to settle some suit or another brought against him. I supposed it was better than crossed swords at dawn, which long ago had been the usual means of settling all manner of disputes, including business ventures gone wrong. But to sue the king....

"On what grounds would I even bring such a suit?" I asked, glad that I had been able to conceal most of the alarm I was currently experiencing. "After all, this is not quite the same as suing a neighbor because the roots of his tree are undermining the wall around your property." That example was the first thing to spring to my mind, a nonsense lawsuit my father had spent a good deal of money he couldn't afford getting dismissed.

"No, it is somewhat more involved than that," Rumple said. "But you have excellent grounds. You are an innocent woman, and have not even been accused of a crime. The law states that anyone held by the king or his proxies must be charged within the first two days of imprisonment, or that person must be set free. Have any formal charges been brought against you, Annora?"

Of course they had not. I had been kept here under a sort of ominous hospitality. If I cooperated, and provided the gold the king desired, then I could stay in these luxurious apartments. If not, then I would be returned to the dungeon. That was bad enough, even setting aside my continuing worry that my family would also be punished if I failed to produce a sufficient amount of golden thread.

"No," I replied. "I was not—that is, I did not think the king needed to follow the same rules as anyone else."

"Ah, but he does," Rumple said. He went to the spinning wheel and gave it an idle turn with one finger, watching as the wooden spokes began to move lazily around and around. "He may be the king, but that does not mean he can do whatever he pleases. His limits are broader than most, but they still exist."

"And I as a woman can file such a suit?" I had never heard of such a thing being done before. True, occasionally women were involved in legal matters, but in most cases as an adjunct to their husbands, and nothing more.

"Yes, you can." A gloved hand clamped down on the wheel, preventing it from spinning any longer. "In fact, that is one area where your father has actually done you a service, for as a woman who has reached her majority and is neither married nor betrothed, you are entitled to enlist legal aid on your own behalf."

"I can?" I asked, startled. Once again, this was new information, but welcome information for all that.

Rumple turned back toward me. "Tell me, Annora—have you heard of Queen Jenelda?"

"Of course. She was...." I paused to recall my studies in Purthian history, now several years behind me. Not that they had ever been all that extensive; my father had believed in giving his daughters only enough education so they wouldn't embarrass themselves. Bookishness was not counted of much worth to most prospective husbands in our class. "She was the wife of King Bannic, was she not? He died only a few years after they married, and she acted as steward for their son, who was an infant at the time."

"Exactly right," Rumple said. He sounded pleased. Perhaps he had thought I wouldn't remember. "But what is often not taught—and I can see why, for I misdoubt that many fathers would want their daughters to know these things—is that Queen Jenelda passed many laws during her time as steward that were intended to better the lot of the women within her realm. One of them is the statute which declares that young women who have reached the age of twenty and have no husband or betrothed to speak for them can seek legal aid on their own. It has been almost a hundred years since her death, and her work on the behalf of the women of Purth has been mostly forgotten...or concealed...but no one has repealed those laws. So you can use them to your benefit now."

I nodded. In that moment, I felt both excited and afraid. Did I have the courage to do such a thing? And if I declined, told Rumple I did not think I could go through with it, would he still help me in spinning the golden thread, or would he wash his hands of me, thinking me a weak-willed fool without the strength to take the true assistance he offered?

Put that way....

Voice low, I asked, "If we do this, who will represent me? You?"

At that question, he chuckled and immediately shook his head. "No, Annora, I have a few skills, but I have made only a casual study of the law. I cannot make this case for you."

"Not that casual, it seems, to have recalled a law most would prefer remained hidden."

A shrug. "The law has always fascinated me, although I am in no position to actually practice it."

"Because you are a mage?"

That question was followed by a long silence—so long, in fact, that I began to wonder if he intended to answer me at all. "Among other things," he said at last.

His tone was so carefully neutral that I thought he must be hiding something. But for all the help and advice he had given me so far, I did not feel I knew him well enough to probe further. Besides, a lawyer was someone who must be out in the world a good bit, and for someone like Rumple, who had to hide the truth of what he was from everyone he met, the law would not be the most practical of vocations.

"Do you have someone in mind?" I inquired. It seemed best in that moment to move on to the practicalities of the matter at hand.

My question appeared to come as a relief to him, for he squared his shoulders and then nodded. "Yes, I do. His name is Ryon Jamsden, and he has offices not far from my residence."

"So you live in town?" As soon as the words left my lips, I regretted them, for it seemed to be quite an impertinent question to ask, considering that Rumple had so far volunteered almost no information about his own background. And for some reason, the notion of him living in Bodenskell, in some unassuming townhouse surrounded by people who could have no idea of what he truly was, struck me as not very likely.

But he shrugged again, replying, "Yes, I do. How else do you think I can come and go here so easily? Magic is mine to command, but only up to a point. It is one thing to send myself here to the palace, a journey of less than a mile. It is quite another to have the strength to do so when traveling a large distance."

Yet again I wished I could ask more questions about his powers, about what he could and could not do. But he had certainly not given me permission to make such inquiries, and so I put them aside for now. "And you think this Master Jamsden will take my case? After all, it cannot be without risk for him."

"I know he will. He is not the sort to back away from a challenge. In fact, he delights in taking on the suits that no one else will."

That did sound rather heartening, although I had to wonder how Master Jamsden managed to make a living at his profession if he continually accepted cases that were unwinnable. That thought brought me to another concern. "I—I have no way to pay him—"

"Nonsense," Rumple said crisply. "I shall pay him. And before you protest, remember that it is nothing to me to conjure the gold Master Jamsden will require."

That was true enough, and yet it seemed I was becoming more and more indebted to this man who had appeared from nowhere to lend me his aid. Surely he must expect something from me in return, no matter what he might have said about wanting only to share my company.

In my heart, I thought it might not be such a bad thing if his expectations were somewhat different from what he had told me. True, I had never seen his face, but I knew he was tall and well-built, and his voice was not that of an older man. At least he was kind, which was more than I could say for many of the men of my acquaintance.

"I will be forever in your debt, Rumple," I said slowly. "And please—I do not wish to offend you, but does all this aid only stem from a desire to help me? For I must confess that I am having a difficult time understanding why you would do so much for someone you have only known for a few short days."

"Length of acquaintance should not dictate one's desire to help," he replied. He did not sound angry. Actually, he did not sound like much of anything at all, as if he were keeping his tone as neutral as he could so I would be unable to divine anything from it.

"I understand that, but—"

A sigh escaped his lips, not of weariness, I thought, but of exasperation. He made an impatient gesture with one hand. "I do wish to help you, Annora, but yes, I must confess that desire does not stem from a motive of pure altruism. Aiding you means making things difficult for the king, and that is an outcome which is worth a great deal to me. Do you understand?"

I still didn't, not completely. But I was rather perversely relieved that this was not all to do with me. Rumple had some grudge against the king, and I was merely a tool he had decided to use to help him carry out that grudge. Perhaps one day he would tell me why, but in the meantime, I would have to content myself with knowing even this much.

"I do understand," I said clearly. "Thank you for telling me. And now I suppose we must get on with this spinning."

CHAPTER EIGHT

The door to my suite banged open with little ceremony early the next afternoon, and the king came raging in, followed by a man I did not recognize. The stranger was slight and vaguely rabbity-looking, with a pink nose and eyes set too close together, and he held a sheaf of papers in one hand.

"What is this?" the king shouted, tearing the papers from the rabbity man's hand and hurling them to the floor, where they scattered all over a rug of priceless Keshiaari weave.

I had been sitting on the divan in the main salon, working on some embroidery, for Rashelle had been kind enough to bring me a hoop and floss earlier that day. At the king's explosive arrival, however, I got to my feet and curtseyed, all the while attempting to hide the embroidery hoop behind my back. "What is what, Your Majesty?"

"That!" he growled, pointing at the papers, which were even then being gathered up by the other man. "You dare to file suit against *me?*"

Oh, dear. My gaze flicked to the rabbity man, who finished picking up the papers and straightened, although he did not appear much more impressive at his full height than when he had been bent over. Could this be Master Jamsden? Somehow I doubted it; his appearance did not seem to match what Rumple had told me about the lawyer he planned to hire.

I raised my chin. "I am sorry, Your Majesty, but I had no other choice, since it was quite clear to me that you intend to keep me here indefinitely, even though no charges have been brought against me."

"Charges?" he repeated in outraged tones. "*Charges?!* Why, look at this apartment! That gown you are wearing! The jewels in your ears and on your fingers! Who has given all that to you?"

"You have, Your Majesty," I said calmly. "And I would say it was all very generous of you, save that I asked for none of it. All I wished was to be sent home to my family once I had"—I hesitated then, for I did not know how much the rabbity man knew of the services I had rendered for the king—"once I had performed that one task for you. But you would not send me home, and would instead keep me prisoner here. In a very fine prison, true, but still a place I do not have the freedom to leave."

During this entire speech, the king's pale blue eyes had opened wider and wider, his cheeks flushing with apoplectic color. "You dare to speak in such a way to me? I am the king!"

My heart began to race, but I told myself that to reveal any weakness now would be to give the king an opening he would most surely exploit. "Yes, Your Majesty, but the king of this land must abide by its laws as well. Because I was not charged with any crime within the allotted timeframe, I should have been allowed to go home."

He rounded on the rabbity man, demanding, "Is this true, Holtson?"

"I, well, yes. That is—" He faltered, then shot me a look of mingled terror and annoyance, as if asking how I could possibly have put him in this sort of untenable position. "It is the law, Your Majesty. She has the right to sue for her freedom. And the right to speak with her counsel alone," he added in a rush, as if steeling himself to do so before he lost his nerve.

"Ridiculous," the king growled, but I noticed the sidelong glance he gave me. I could have been misreading him completely, but it almost seemed that a grudging respect had entered his expression. Most likely he was wondering how a sheltered young woman like myself had even come up with the notion of contacting an attorney.

Of course the idea had not been mine, but I would never admit such a thing. All I could do was hope that he wouldn't inquire how in the world I'd managed to do so in the first place, because of course there was no way I could have gotten word to a lawyer without outside help.

But then he did ask the question I had feared the most. "And how is it that you were able to seek this help, Mistress Kelsden?"

"I—" The words seemed to catch in my throat, and I swallowed, hard. The last thing I wanted was to cause any trouble for Rashelle, but she was the only person I had any contact with. I had to hope that because she was a servant and therefore must do as she was told, she would not be held to account for the lie I was about to tell. "I gave a note to Rashelle, and bade her have it sent to my father's house. Oh, she did not know what the note contained," I added quickly as the furious color began to rise in the king's cheeks. "She thought I had written to my sister. But the note was a plea for help to Master Jamsden, who had provided legal counsel to my father once upon a time. That is how he came to my defense."

King Elsdon's eyes narrowed, and I could tell he fought to contain his anger. "Very well, Mistress Kelsden, but do not expect anything much to come of it. You will have one hour to speak to your lawyer, and no more."

Because I did not want to annoy him further, I only assumed as meek an expression as I could muster, and then nodded.

"Come, Holtson," the king commanded, then began to stride toward the door. Just as his lackey moved to open it for him, he rumbled ominously, "Do not think that this removes your current obligations from you. Lord Edmar will be stopping by tomorrow morning. Do you understand?"

I nodded once more.

"Troublesome wench," he muttered, and then was gone, slamming the door behind him.

I did not even have the opportunity to let out a sigh of relief, for Rashelle emerged then, eyes enormous.

"The king seemed very angry," she whispered.

"I know," I said cheerfully. "I'm suing him for my freedom. And I believe I will be speaking with my lawyer soon, so if you could see if there is some tea...?"

She swallowed, then hurried out of the suite.

And I, suddenly realizing that I had just experienced an open confrontation with the king and somehow lived to tell the tale, sank down onto one of the divans to await the arrival of my lawyer.

Master Jamsden was younger than I had expected, probably no more than thirty, and tall and well-favored. Indeed, if it were not that I had far more important things on my mind, I would have thought he was the kind of man I might have been happy to have as my betrothed, if my father had had the good sense to seek out someone like that for me.

My new lawyer introduced himself with the slightest of bows, and then immediately sat down on the divan facing mine. On the table between us was the tea Rashelle had brought up, but he did not appear to even notice it.

"Now, then," he said, his tone brisk, "Master Slade was not precisely forthcoming about the particulars of your case, so I will need you to tell me exactly everything that has transpired over the past three days."

"Master Slade?" I had never heard the name before.

"Tobyn Slade, the man who hired me. He lives in my district."

So that was Rumple's true name. I wondered why he had bothered to conceal it from me. I hoped that he would not be angry with Master Jamsden for revealing it now.

"You know him well?" I asked. Yes, I had been given one precious hour with my lawyer, but even so, I wasn't about to pass up the chance to glean from him whatever information about Rumple—*Tobyn Slade*—that I could.

"Not terribly well. Our paths have crossed a few times."

"And have you ever...have you ever seen him?" I inquired. Gods, that sounded so desperate, even to my own ears. In that moment, though, I was almost beyond caring. I needed to know more about this mysterious man who had insinuated himself into my life.

"No, I fear I have not. He told me once that he had the pox when he was a very young man. I suppose that is why he thinks there is a need to cover himself so. But that is no concern of mine."

"Oh," I said, feeling myself quite let down. Perhaps it had been foolish of me to imagine he was handsome under that hood, and yet I doubted any other young woman in my situation would not have done the same.

What does it matter, really? I scolded myself. *His actions are what is important here. Besides, your experiences with Lord Edmar should have been enough to teach you that a handsome face counts for very little.*

That all sounded very practical. Now if I could only convince myself of the truth of those words....

Then I had to return myself to the present, for Master Jamsden was speaking again.

"...I believe there was originally the matter of a gambling debt?"

I blinked. "Gambling...oh, yes. My father, I fear, has something of an excess of zeal when it comes to the dice table."

"And he made some outrageous claims, claims which you were brought to the palace to prove."

"Yes," I said, my tone uncertain. Master Jamsden had said that he would need all the particulars of what had happened to me over the past three days, but if I told him everything, then I would be revealing secrets about Rumple...*Master Slade,* I reminded myself...that I had promised to keep concealed.

The lawyer appeared to note my hesitation. After giving a quick look around and determining that we were quite alone—for I had told Rashelle that I needed to speak to Master Jamsden in private—he said quietly, "You need not fear revealing Master Slade's secrets to me. I know of his, ah, particular gifts."

"You do?" I responded, startled. Surely Tobyn must trust Master Jamsden deeply, to have told him of something that could cost him his life, should it get out.

"Yes," Master Jamsden said. "He hired me for a legal matter several years ago, and told me the truth about his talents so I would have all the facts of the case."

"And it did not bother you?"

The lawyer's dark eyes glinted with amusement. "Has it bothered you, Mistress Kelsden?"

"Well, no. That is—" I floundered for a moment, then went on, "I mean to say, it is because of Master Slade's 'particular gifts,' as you put it, that I am still alive now. I surely would have forfeited my life if I had not been able to give the king the gold he desired. But I must confess I am surprised that you have accepted this information with such equanimity."

"I am a man who deals in facts, Mistress Kelsden. I do not think we have nearly as much to fear from users of magic as we have all been taught. For is not Master Slade ample proof that people with such gifts can live among us and yet do no harm? The laws of this land are barbaric in regard to their treatment of those who possess the ability to do magic, and it is shameful that we have not revised them. This is not the world of a thousand years ago, when all was beaten down by the wars between the mages. Enforcing laws based on the events of a dim history long past do no one any good."

I stared at him, somewhat surprised by the impassioned nature of his speech. "It seems as if this is a cause dear to your heart."

He shrugged. Master Jamsden wore a simple black wool doublet with no ornamentation, but somehow the severity of its lines only served to emphasize the width of his shoulders.

But they are not so broad as Master Slade's, I thought, then wanted to shake my head at myself.

"It is not so much that this particular cause is dear to my heart," the lawyer said. "It is more that I wish to fight injustice wherever I see it. It is especially painful to see such barbaric laws still in effect here in Purth, where in so many other places on the continent, the old practices are slowly giving way. Why, did you know that the consort of the Mark of Eredor is a gifted mage herself, and quite openly uses her magic?"

Of course I did not. The land of North Eredor was thousands of leagues away, far off beyond Seldd and on the western slopes of the Opal Mountains. I heard very little of what might be happening in lands such as that. It was not deemed necessary for a young woman such as I to possess such knowledge. But to be told that magic was not universally reviled...well, that gave me a little hope.

Hope for what, precisely, I didn't want to admit to myself. That I would finally be free from the king's clutches, and that Master Slade and I might run off someplace where he could be allowed to practice his magic without threat of reprisal? Foolish notion. Ridiculous, really, when he had never given any indication that he cared anything about me, except to ensure my safety at the king's expense.

"That is very interesting," I told Master Jamsden, since he had been watching me, obviously expecting a reply.

"So it is," he said. I could tell from his inflection he had thought he would get more of an answer from me than that. But then he seemed to square his shoulders. "So, then, Mistress Kelsden, now that you know it is safe to reveal all to me, please give me your account of what led you to being held here by the king."

Which I did. I tried my best not to embellish, or to reveal anything more than I absolutely needed to of what had passed between Master Slade and myself. Certainly I did not tell the lawyer of how I had broken down that second night, and how my benefactor had held me while I wept. I debated whether I should mention anything of Lord Edmar and his suspected intentions—mainly because I knew it would be embarrassing to the extreme—but then I decided it would be better if I did. For all I knew, that particular collusion between the duke and the king had contributed to my being kept here against my will.

Throughout my recitation, Master Jamsden wrote swiftly in a leather-bound book he had brought with him, his pen scratching against the paper, the tiny inkwell he had produced from an inner pocket sitting on the low table before us. When

I was done, he kept the book open so the ink would dry, but his gaze was fixed on me.

"This is quite a grave matter, Mistress Kelsden," he said. "For it was put down hundreds of years ago that no man—or no woman—could be held without the proper charges being filed. The king's greed has blinded him, or at least has made him believe that he can be above the law in this. I will write up my arguments and submit them to the High Court. Because the king is a peer, that is the body which must listen to this case. Going to a simple magistrate is out of the question."

I nodded, although I must confess that half of what Master Jamsden had said went quite over my head. Yes, of course I knew that a High Court existed, but its activities certainly had nothing to do with me. "How long do you think this will all take?" I asked him. For I had heard of some cases being dragged out for months or even years, if the parties involved had the funds to keep paying their legal counsel.

He seemed to understand my worry. "Not too long, I should think. This is not a simple property dispute or quarrel over a contract. It involves someone being held against their will, and so I think the court will give your case the priority it deserves." A quick glance down at the book where he had made his notes, followed by a nod, as if he was satisfied that the ink was now dry. He closed it and tied it shut with a ribbon attached to the binding, then tucked it away in a pocket. After that, he rose to his feet, while I did the same.

"Thank you, Master Jamsden."

"Thank me when this is all done, Mistress Kelsden," he replied. Up until that moment, his manner had been matter-of-fact, but a look of concern passed over his features then. "Just remember to stay strong, for you are in the right in this."

He bowed at the waist, while I nodded and attempted to assume an expression of what I hoped was something resembling fortitude. And then he was gone, letting himself quietly out the door to my chambers.

I sank back onto the divan then, my knees suddenly quite shaky. For better or worse, it seemed my case would go to court very soon.

Unfortunately, I was not left to my own devices for very long. Rashelle had not even returned before I heard a knock at my door. Since she was not there to answer it, I got up from where I had been sitting and opened the door myself.

Lord Edmar stood outside. Inwardly I cursed, wishing I could have ignored that knock, even though I knew there was really no way for me to have done so.

His expression was bland, pleasant, even, and yet I detected a tension in his manner that did not bode well for me. However, I was determined not to let that put me off.

"Your Grace," I said coolly. "This is a surprise."

He did not react, but only asked, "May we speak?"

Of course I would have liked to say no, but that was not an option allowed me, I feared. Instead, I inclined my head. "Certainly. Do come in."

He moved past me and stopped in the main salon, surveying the room. Perhaps he was looking to see if Rashelle was anywhere about with her ubiquitous feather duster. If only

I had not told her that she could take her time in returning! When I had sent her off, I had thought Master Jamsden would require a full hour to speak to me, but he had been here for rather half that amount of time.

But I would not let the absence of a chaperone, even one as inadequate as Rashelle, discommode me. For some reason, I felt better now, knowing the lawyer would speak for me, and hurry things along as best he could.

I came into the salon and stood a few paces away from the duke, then said, "I fear I have no refreshment to offer you, Your Grace, save some lemon water. But I will pour you a glass if you would like."

"That won't be necessary." His eyes narrowed then. "You have gotten quite good at playing the grand lady, Annora. So grand that you do not even fear to go up against the king himself."

Ah, so that was why he was here. I supposed I should have guessed that the king would send his lapdog to speak with me, rather than confronting me himself. Once a day appeared to be his limit when it came to dealing with commoners.

Lifting my shoulders, I replied, "I regret that I was forced to this extremity. But His Majesty would not relent, and so I had no choice but to use legal means to seek my freedom."

My words did not appear to mollify the duke in the slightest. "From the way you speak, Annora, one would think you were still locked up in the dungeon. Have you not been given every comfort? Do you not reside in a beautiful suite? Has the king not given you gowns and jewels and a woman to wait on you?"

"Yes, he has given me all these things," I retorted, "save the one boon I actually asked for. I am not one to care for jewels, or gowns, or a woman to come at my beck and call. I want only to be returned to my family, and the life I was living before all this began."

"Oh, and a pretty life that was," the duke sneered, "with not even a maid to wait on you, and a father who squandered his wealth and yet still waited to see if he could sell you off to the highest bidder."

It was no more than I already knew, and yet hearing Lord Edmar say such a thing merely served to make me that much more furious. Lashing out at him would only make matters worse, however, and so I pushed my anger aside. Tone cold and controlled, I said, "Do you think you are telling me anything I do not already know? I am not responsible for my father's actions, only my own. And whatever you may think, I am blameless in all this. Am I not supposed to assert even the few rights I do have?"

His expression softened then, and yet I somehow knew he had altered his aspect on purpose, seeking to throw me off guard. "No one is saying you do not have rights, Annora, but to do such a thing is quite beyond the pale. Do you not under-stand the precedent you will set, if you somehow succeed? The king will lose face, and worse, be shown as someone whose commands can be subverted. Do you truly wish to weaken the kingdom in such a way, simply to prove a point?"

"Not to prove a point," I said, speaking slowly, for until the duke had pointed them out, I had not really thought of the ramifications of my actions. I had only thought that if I won, I would be able to go home. Certainly I had no wish to make the king look powerless, an easy target. But really, it was his own stubbornness and greed that had forced matters to such a pass. All he had to do was let me go, and all of Lord Edmar's gloomy predictions could still be avoided. "But to get my family and my life back. They may not seem much to you, Your Grace, but they are the world to me. *My* world, small and mean as it might appear to you."

To my surprise, he smiled at those words. Not even a mocking smile, which I might have expected, but rather one of sympathy and respect. But perhaps I was flattering myself, seeing something I wished to see. "I think, Annora, that there are not many who would choose the simpler things instead of the grand and mighty, especially in exchange for so little."

So little? I thought then. *What Rumple...Tobyn...helps me spin in one night would feed every household on my street for at least a six-month.*

I did not bother to say such a thing aloud. For someone like the duke, born to wealth and power and knowing nothing else, my simple existence probably did not seem all that appealing. And parts of it were not—namely, my father's weakness for the gaming table—but there was a quiet comfort in that life. Some had remarked that my beauty should have been shown off at court, where I might have attracted suitors, despite my lack of a dowry. That had never mattered to me, however. It was true that I hoped some day to have a husband and a family, but I had not been one of those girls who dreamed of attracting the attention of a peer.

"Perhaps there are more people like that than you might think," I said simply. "At any rate, I would be more than happy to drop my suit, if the king would only allow me to go home. You may pass that intelligence on to him, although I doubt it will do much good."

"No, I do not think it will," he agreed. A silence fell while he studied me for a moment. I tried not to fidget under that keen grey gaze. Surely he must take his leave, now that I had shown myself to be intractable.

What he said next, however, surprised me so much that I couldn't help starting.

"But what if you were not held here against your will, but as a member of the court, on equal standing with them? What if you were here as my wife?"

I could only stare at him. Then I mustered a shaky laugh and said, "Your Grace, you certainly cannot think to lower yourself in such a way. The daughter of a merchant, when any of the kingdom's high-born young women would be so much better suited?"

"If I cared for that, I would have married one of them already," he replied. "Besides, none of them are nearly as beautiful as you."

The compliment probably did not have its intended effect, for it only dismayed me more. "Your Grace, I—"

"Edmar," he cut in. "Surely we do not need titles when we are speaking of such matters?"

That was even worse. My fingers knotted in the heavy silk damask of my skirts. The duke was still watching me with that sharp, hawkish stare. It was certainly not the gaze of a lover—not that I would have wished for him to regard me as such. As I searched for the proper words to make my reply, I knew he stared at me in such a way because he did not have any tender feelings for me. He wanted me...and the king wanted me...and if I agreed to be Lord Edmar's duchess, then I would be neatly trapped, and each of them would have gotten what he desired.

"Edmar," I said, hoping the use of his given name might placate him somewhat, "this is a very great honor you are doing me, but...."

"But?" he repeated, eyes narrowing.

"It is also very sudden. May I have some time to think on it?"

He did not like that, I could tell; a muscle in his cheek twitched, and I saw how his jaw tensed. But then he gave a reluctant nod, and said, "You may think on it, Annora. Only do not take too long."

To my relief, he did not reach for my hand to kiss it...or worse. No, he merely gave me a courtly bow, if one that appeared a little too brusque, and then made his way back to the door of my suite. Without any further farewell, he was gone.

I drew in a shaky breath. Yes, I had given myself some time...but how much?

CHAPTER NINE

For once I was glad that I could not see my benefactor's face. He stood in the study, anger radiating from every inch of his black-swathed body.

"He asked you to *marry* him?"

"Yes," I said wearily. The tumultuous day had taken its toll on me, and waiting up for Rumple—*Tobyn,* I reminded myself for the hundredth time—had not been easy. As much as I wanted to speak to him, I'd wanted to take to my bed that much more, and not rise from it again until all this had been resolved. Unfortunately, life was seldom that accommodating.

"So they counter our gambit with one of their own," Tobyn said, his tone musing. "I take it that he did not much care for your answer."

"No, I think not, but I also think he knew he could not press his suit too strongly, or else appear churlish. However, I doubt that I can hold him off for more than a few days."

"It may not take that long. Master Jamsden came to speak with me after he had filed his paperwork with the court this afternoon, and he said it sounded as if they may be willing to hear your case as soon as the day after tomorrow."

My eyebrows lifted. Yes, I had been told that the court would treat this matter with some urgency, but I had not expected events to move that quickly.

Tobyn must have noted my surprise, for he went on, "It appears that the justices of the High Court do not have any great opinion of our king. If there is a way to make life more difficult for him while remaining within the bounds of the law, then they will seek it out."

I couldn't help chuckling a little at that revelation. "No wonder he was so incensed. Poor man, he must believe he has no hope of winning."

"I would hesitate to call him 'poor man,' but yes, he is most likely facing an uphill battle here."

Some of the tension seemed to leave Tobyn as he spoke. No doubt it was better for him to be thinking of how we were provoking the king, rather than the unwelcome news that Lord Edmar had asked me to be his wife. Although I dreaded to think what the outcome of my refusal would be, I also felt slightly cheered. Surely Tobyn wouldn't have seemed quite so incensed if he didn't have at least the barest beginnings of some sort of feelings for me.

He had been standing a few paces away from me, while I sat in my chair next to the spinning wheel, but he came closer then. Not for the first time, I breathed in the soft scent of sweet woodruff that seemed to permeate the folds of his cloak. It

was a comforting aroma, one that reminded me of my child-
hood, when my mother had taught me how to use the herb to
make sachets for our wardrobes and clothes presses. After she
was gone, however, my father did not see the use in wasting
valuable space in our kitchen garden for herbs when we could
be growing vegetables instead, and so we had not had those
sachets for many years.

"But you, Annora," Tobyn said. "How are you faring in all
this?"

I lifted my shoulders. "As well as I can. The king blusters,
but he has not made any direct threats against me. Probably
now he dares not do anything, since Master Jamsden has filed
the papers with the court, and they know something of what
His Majesty has been up to." Pausing, I slanted a glance up at
Tobyn. As always, I could see nothing of his face. I had begun
to wonder whether he wrapped some sort of cloth around his
cheeks and jaw in addition to pulling the hood of his cloak so
low. Otherwise, shouldn't I have been able to see *something*? I
went on, "What I cannot understand is why the duke should
be willing to sacrifice himself, just to satisfy the king's greed."

"I doubt many men would consider marriage to you to be
any sort of a sacrifice," Tobyn said dryly.

A rush of warmth went over me at his praise. But I tried
to appear unaffected by his words, replying, "I am not so sure
about that. However, the duke has always seemed to be a confirmed bachelor. He must be counting on a good deal of the
king's favor by marrying me to keep me from getting away."

"Perhaps. Actually, Lord Edmar was married not so long
ago, to the daughter of an earl. But her attempts to give him an

heir only led to her death, and he did not seem inclined afterward to seek a replacement for her."

"So he loved her," I murmured, experiencing an odd pang of pity. It appeared that even the duke had met with his own share of tragedy.

"I doubt it was anything quite so romantic," Tobyn said, his tone laced with sarcasm. "More that he was now free from the marriage which had been arranged for him, and he saw no reason to go rushing back into its bonds. True, he would at some point require an heir for his estates, but that could wait. After all, a man does not have the same restrictions of age in such things as a woman does."

Which had never seemed quite fair to me, but then again, so many things about the way the world worked were not fair. So Lord Edmar had enjoyed his time as a bachelor, and only now had decided it was time to give that life up, because he wished to curry favor with the king.

And he desires to bed you anyway, I thought with some distaste. *Why not kill two birds with the same stone?*

"Then I fear he will not be as easy to put off as I had hoped," I said. My heart sank a little, for somewhere deep inside I had thought that if my suit was successful, and the king thwarted, I would have heard the last of the duke. But I feared that now he might still try to pursue me, and get a mother for his heirs and an easy source of gold in one fell swoop.

"Perhaps not," said Tobyn, "but it does no good to concoct misfortunes that may never come to pass. There is always the chance that he will decide you are more trouble than you are worth."

At those words, I glanced up at him through my lashes. "Do you think I am so very troublesome?" I inquired.

It was possible that he smiled, but of course I could not see it. "Not at all, but then, I might have a slightly different perspective on the situation than the duke." He gestured toward the spinning wheel. "We might as well get on with that."

True. Although each evening the process seemed to go a little more quickly, it still took more than an hour for the two of us working together to create the thick knot of gold threads that Lord Edmar came to collect every morning.

I pulled my chair closer to the wheel, then gathered up some straw. My foot worked at the treadle, and once again the bits of straw were drawn from my fingers and transmuted somewhere along the way to something fine and precious.

"When did you first learn this?" I asked Tobyn, for he seemed content to watch quietly as I worked. Perhaps he was still brooding over the duke's unexpected offer of marriage to me. At any rate, it seemed best to speak of something else, something that might shift his thoughts elsewhere.

"Some ten years ago, when I was not so much older than you are now."

Ah, that confirmed one of my suspicions. So he was my senior by a decade. Not that I really cared one way or another. It was still far better than the gap of twenty-odd years that separated Lord Edmar and myself.

"Did you have someone teach you?"

A long silence then, so long that I wondered if he did not intend to answer me at all. But, to my surprise, he took one of the side chairs from where it had been placed up against the wall and set it down next to me. This was the first time he had ever done such a thing, and I hoped it was an indication that he intended to share confidences.

"I did," he said at last. "My powers began to manifest when I was young, probably around ten. As you can imagine, it was rather terrifying to think of going to retrieve a ball I had dropped, and to suddenly have it spring into my hand, or to begin fumbling for a tinderbox, only to have the candle I'd intended to light illuminate itself, all on its own. To be sure, at first I thought I was going mad, or had been cursed in some way. That seemed to be the only explanation. But then my father hired a new tutor for me, and soon afterward Master Osford began instructing me in much more than merely geography and mathematics."

A tutor. So Tobyn's family must have been of some means. Merchant, like my own? Possibly, but I didn't want to interrupt his narrative to ask. So I only nodded, and he went on,

"You see, those few of us who can still practice magic can sense one another. It is difficult to explain how, only that it's something we can feel, like distant thunder. So when my powers began to awaken, Master Osford knew of this, and came to me as someone my family would never suspect."

"Didn't they notice when you did not make much progress in the more...traditional...subjects?"

He shifted on his chair, and again I got the impression that he might have smiled beneath the hood. "Oh, Master Osford was quite learned on a variety of topics, and so my studies did not suffer overmuch. What he did see was that I had a particular mastery for manipulating physical objects, and so we focused on making that skill stronger. I am not very good at altering the weather, or conjuring illusions, but I can change straw into gold, or send myself from one place to another by mere force of will, or"—and here he fished for something in his pocket—"change a pebble into a flawless ruby."

His fingers were curled around what he held, and he opened them, revealing a stone dark as blood sitting on his palm. It caught the light from the candelabras placed around the room like a sanguine blinking eye.

"For you," he said simply, then placed it in my free hand, the one that sat idle while my left held the straw that was being fed to the bobbin.

For such a small thing—perhaps only a little more than an inch across—it felt very heavy in my palm. "I can't—" I began, but he shook his head.

"And why not? It is nothing I took from anyone else, nothing that anyone will miss. It is something I made for you."

How could I refuse it, after he had made such a speech? "Thank you," I said quietly. "It is very beautiful."

"You should have beautiful things. Ones that truly belong to you, and which aren't simply given on loan as a sort of bribe."

A bribe. That was precisely what the king had given me—this apartment, the clothes I wore, the earrings I placed in my ears or the necklaces I wore around my throat. They had not been provided out of thanks for the riches I had already given him, but as an inducement for me to keep on spinning the gold.

"I will treasure it," I told Tobyn, and he nodded.

"And you will not have to worry about having a setting to house it in." He got up from his chair and went to the spinning wheel, then pulled away some of the golden thread I had just spun. His gloved fingers moved in an intricate pattern, and before I could even see what was happening, the fine threads of gold had been fashioned into a setting of cunning detail, with flowers and vines surrounding an opening just the exact size of the ruby he had given me. At the same time, I thought I heard the whisper of a few strange syllables, as if he had murmured the words of a spell while he was creating the setting for the ruby.

Then he spoke in a more normal tone. "If I may borrow that for a moment?"

I handed him the ruby, and he took it and slipped it into the setting he had created. A few more golden threads became a shining chain. As I stared up at him, my eyes wide, he came to me and settled the piece around my neck. There was something very intimate about that touch, even though gloves hid his fingers and he did not have to brush my hair aside, as the braid Rashelle had put it in for the night was looped over one shoulder.

The silence felt very thick in that moment. I knew I should speak, but words seemed to fail me. There was so much I wanted to say to him, but I worried he would think me foolish. After all, we had only known one another for such a very short time, and even then, ours was an acquaintance of a few stolen hours here and there. It was only that I had never before met anyone like him. In truth, I was not sure whether there could *be* anyone else like him.

At last I murmured, "It's exquisite. I will treasure it always."

"I am glad it pleases you." Another of those pauses, and then he said, his tone somewhat lighter, "I fear I have given away my secret. For I am known to some members of the gentry as Slade the jeweler, and that is how they think I support myself. I am sure if they were ever to discover that the jewels they wear had a magical origin, they would not show them off quite so proudly."

"Well, I will certainly not tell anyone," I replied. "Indeed, I now feel doubly grateful, for I am sure your work is *very* exclusive."

I had said this with a teasing note in my voice, but I wondered after I had spoken those words whether he would take them as they were intended. Certainly I did not mean to make light of the beautiful gift he had given me. Yes, the king had provided jewels for me to wear, but none of them were half as lovely as the pendant Tobyn had created.

"Oh, very exclusive," he agreed with a slight chuckle. "Why, the ladies of the court must wait at least six months to receive their custom orders from me."

"And do you do that merely to torment them, since I just watched you make my pendant in only a minute or so?"

"I have found that it is better to delay gratification sometimes." He fell silent then, as if he had said more than he first intended.

In my life, I had not had much experience of gratification, delayed or otherwise. But since it seemed that we had wandered onto an unintentionally awkward subject, I thought it best to move on and return to the original thread of our conversation. "And this Master Osford? How long was he your tutor?"

"Until I turned eighteen," Tobyn replied, relief obvious in his voice. "At that point, he said he had taught me as much as he could, and that the rest of it was up to me, to my own study and practice. His strengths lay more in enchantments of the air and the wind, smoke and fire, and so my own talents diverged from his quite a bit. So he went off, in search of his next pupil, I suppose."

"Are there so very many of you?" I asked. "Those born with mage blood, that is."

"He seemed to imply that there were more than one might think, but it is very hard to say, since those of us who have these gifts must hide them, or mask them in commonplaces as I do. There are none here in Bodenskell, other than myself, or else I would have sensed their presence. But that does not mean there might not be some up in Daleskeld Province, or down in Willensur by the seacoast. From time to time I have thought that perhaps I should go searching for others with magical blood, but I have always been loath to leave the city. I have ordered my life well enough here, and to go forth from that life is to risk exposure."

"I am sorry," I said then, and he tilted his hooded head at me.

"Whatever for?"

"Have I not interrupted that orderly life? You come here to the palace each night and risk being discovered, only to help a girl you did not even know before a few days ago." I stopped then, and it was my turn to give him a speculative look. "Indeed, how is it you even discovered my predicament? For it was certainly not the sort of thing the king wished to advertise."

Tobyn did not reply at once, but went back to his chair and sat down. "No, it was not, but I am always on the alert for anything which might sound as if magic was involved. I have a few...well, informants or spies, for lack of a better word. I ask them to tell me if they hear of anything unusual, and then I investigate further. The story of your father's boasting at Baron Levender's birthday gala, and then the appearance of the king's guard at your house, did not precisely pass unnoticed. So I looked into the matter a little further, and realized that you had been caught in the middle of a terrible lie, and an even more terrible predicament, through no fault of your own."

A small pause then, as he seemed to stop and weigh what he should say next. In that moment, I was very conscious of how close he sat to me, how, if either of us shifted just the least amount, our knees might brush against one another. I wished I had the courage to do so, but something seemed to stop me, and I remained still, except for the slight movements of my foot on the treadle to keep the wheel spinning.

And of course Tobyn did nothing to move closer to me. I thought then of what Master Jamsden had said, of how Tobyn had told him that he had had the pox as a young man, and had been forever scarred by that terrible disease. Did he now think he was unworthy of another's regard, simply because of a misfortune that was none of his own doing?

I knew I could not speak of it. For one thing, Master Jamsden had told me the story in confidence. And for another, I'd certainly not had enough encouragement from Tobyn to dare broach such a subject. He certainly had not said or done anything to indicate he had any interest of that sort in me.

Save when he held you in his arms, I thought, then wanted to shake my head at myself. He had done so to comfort me, and for no other reason.

It was so quiet that the sound of the spinning wheel whirring away seemed unnaturally loud. When Tobyn spoke again, I almost jumped.

"Master Jamsden would say that I had something of his crusading streak. But I am not one to idly sit by and watch another be treated so unjustly, especially when I possess the skills to do something about it. And so that, Annora, is why I interrupted my so-called 'orderly life.' I could have done nothing else, when presented with someone so in need."

His words awoke a strange ache in my breast. I could not say precisely what that ache even was, for I had never experienced such a sensation before. I wished I could turn to him and have him put his arms around me again. I wished I had the courage to push back his hood and tell him that whatever he had suffered in the past, it mattered not at all to me, except that I thought it grossly unfair for a man of his courage and strength to be so buffeted by fate.

Most of all, I wished I could be as noble and as brave as he. Perhaps then I would have the strength to lay my lips on his, and let him know that, while I was not sure I was deserving of his regard, I would do my very best to earn it.

But because I was a coward, I knew I would do none of those things. My foot continued to pump away at the treadle, and I continued to feed the straw into the shining strands that wrapped themselves around the bobbin. Voice low, I said, "And I thank you for it, Master Slade. Every day, I thank you for what you have done for me. I hope there is some way I can repay you."

I allowed the slightest hint of a question to enter my words. Perhaps he would hear that inflection and understand that I wished very much to thank him and repay him. With myself, for I had nothing else to give.

However, he seemed not to understand, or to ignore what I was attempting to offer. "No repayment is necessary, Annora, except the knowledge that I was able to get you the justice you deserve."

"Oh," I said, my tone flat. Was that truly all he wanted? It seemed I was surrounded by men who wanted something from me—the king, Lord Edmar, my father—and yet the only man I actually desired to give something to apparently would have nothing of it.

An awkward silence fell. Perhaps Tobyn finally had begun to comprehend that my gratitude was of a slightly different nature than he had first believed, and did not know quite what to do about it.

I took in a breath, then asked, "Why 'Rumple'? Why did you not give me your true name when first we met?"

He chuckled. I fancied I heard something of relief in that low laugh, but I did not look over at him, but rather continued to feed straw onto the guide thread in my left hand as if it was the most important thing in the world.

"That was an old nickname of mine," he said. "I fear I was not the tidiest of little boys, and would sometimes wad up my shirts and stick them under my pillow when I went to sleep, rather than put them in the hamper as I was taught. On several occasions I pulled them out from under the pillow the next morning and wore them down to breakfast, whereupon my mother laughed and called me 'Rumple.'"

"Where is she now?" I asked, for there was a note of sadness in his voice as he spoke of his mother.

"The same place yours is," he replied. "With the gods, in the next world. As is the rest of my family."

The words slipped out. "Because of the pox?"

Tobyn had been sitting quietly enough in his chair, but at that question he seemed to startle, the black-gloved hands clenching on his knees. "Did Master Jamsden tell you that?"

"He mentioned something in passing. That is all." As I made that reply, I hoped I would not be getting that worthy gentleman in any kind of trouble with his employer. But neither did I wish to lie. Perhaps I hoped that if I let Tobyn understand I already knew of what he was attempting to keep hidden, it would not be such a barrier between us.

With a sudden, abrupt movement, he got to his feet and once more crossed to the window. His back to me, he said, "Yes. Because of that. I was an only child, but that particular... misfortune...came to visit both my parents as well."

"When?" I asked quietly.

"I was eighteen."

Eighteen. Only a few years younger than myself, and yet an event that had happened far enough back in his past that he'd had more than a decade to come to terms with it.

"I'm sorry."

He shrugged, but even I could see the studied nonchalance of that gesture. "That was a long time ago. It could have been worse, I suppose—I did recover, after all. And although I had been left alone in the world, I could use my magic to give me the semblance of a trade, which meant I was able to support myself. There are many who did not fare nearly as well."

Even so, I had the impression that he would have given a good deal of that stability to have escaped the pox unscathed. I thought it best not to say such a thing, though. Instead, I lifted my foot from the treadle and stood, then went to pluck the shining mass of thread from the spinning wheel's bobbin. "Another good night's work," I told him, hefting the golden strands on my palm.

"Well enough," he replied. But I saw that he did not even turn to look at the fruits of our labor.

True, the amount had not varied much from night to night. However, this was the first time he had not bothered to inspect the gleaming gold thread.

I fought back a sigh and slipped the mass of thread into the pocket of my dressing gown, which sagged dangerously but did not, thankfully, show any signs of tearing. Wishing to change the subject, I asked, "What should I say to the duke when he comes to retrieve the thread tomorrow morning?"

At last Tobyn did shift away from the window. His change in position did not provide me with any particular relief, though, for I could tell by the rigid set of his shoulders that he did not deem my new topic of conversation any more welcome than the last.

"That, I suppose, is up to you," he replied. "Do you wish to be a duchess?"

"Of course not!" I snapped. "I thought I had made my opinion on the matter sufficiently obvious. But if you need me to spell it out for you, then no, I do not wish to be Lord Edmar's wife, nor the wife of any other peer."

Another of those pauses. I thought he studied me closely, but I could not tell for certain. "And what do you wish?" he inquired, his voice dropping lower. It had softened slightly, and something about those smooth, warm tones made a shiver go down my spine.

I swallowed. I could not tell him what I truly wished. It would be so very forward of me. Worse, I knew he would never believe me, even if it was the truth of my heart. For of course, how could a woman like me desire him, scarred as he was?

It seemed better to choose the most obvious answer. "I wish to—to return to my life," I told him. "That is all."

"That is a very simple wish."

"Not so simple as it sounds, I fear." He did not move, and I pressed my lips together, willing myself to find the courage somehow. To do just one simple thing. Not a kiss; no, nothing so forward as that. But....

I reached out and laid a hand on his arm, finding it beneath its concealing layers of wool. Despite the thick fabric, I could feel the strength of him, the solid muscle under my fingers. One would have thought he spent his days at a forge, rather than willing those beautiful pieces he created into being from the very air itself.

My heart beat once, twice, thrice. He stood still, not stirring, and I hardly dared to breathe. Then at last he reached up with his free hand and laid it on top of mine. No, I could not feel his flesh, for the leather glove which covered his skin prevented that. But I could at least sense the heat of him, the power in those fingers as they rested against mine.

We stood that way for a long moment, neither of us speaking. In a way, that was enough. I had never been kissed, but even so, this—merely resting my hand on Tobyn's arm, and feeling his hand on top of mine—somehow felt far more intimate.

Finally, he spoke, although his voice was barely above a whisper. "Annora, what is it you are doing?"

"I don't know," I said honestly. "All I know is that I *very* much do not wish to marry the duke."

Tobyn laughed at that, although the sound seemed almost shaky to my ears. "Then we will have to make sure that does not happen."

He moved then, so I was compelled to remove my hand from his arm. I could not be angry with him for that, however, because immediately afterward he took both my hands in his, and held them tightly. We stood there for a long moment, my hands encased in his, while I breathed in the sweet woodruff of his cloak and reveled in the warmth of his body, so close to mine. And then, at last, he let go. The silence was very loud, and I did not know how to break it. So I stood there, until at last he said, "Good night, Annora," and was gone.

Perhaps I had wished for more than that. But it was a beginning at least, and so I was content.

CHAPTER TEN

The next morning, I prepared myself as best I could for my meeting with Lord Edmar. I arose early, and chose the most becoming of the gowns the king had bestowed upon me, the rich crimson one with the golden embroidery. If it perfectly showcased the pendant Tobyn had created for me the night before, well, perhaps that was my way of sending a subtle message.

Not that the duke would recognize the pendant for what it was, of course. He would only think it yet another of the pieces the king had given me on loan. But I knew that Tobyn had given it to me, and I would wear it as my sigil of what had passed between us the previous evening. Perhaps some might think it no very great thing, to have simply held hands as we did, but I knew better. It had changed something between us. Before, he had made sure to keep his distance. Now, though, I had taken a step or two toward him. Not all the way, of course.

That would take some doing on my part, for it was clear that he thought himself irretrievably damaged.

I would not lie to myself. Of course it would have been better if he was whole and unblemished. I had seen the scars the pox left behind, and they could be quite terrible. But my feelings for Tobyn had awakened without my ever seeing his face. I loved the sound of his voice, the subtle ironic edge to his laughter. And I loved even more the impulse that had driven him to give me succor. He had not known who I was. He only knew I was someone facing an unjust punishment, and so had come forward to bring his most unusual skills to my aid.

Indeed, it seemed that I loved *him,* strange as it felt when I admitted that truth to myself. Or rather, I thought I loved him. Having no experience of the emotion before—at least in terms of loving a man, rather than a member of my family—I could not say for certain if the way my heart beat a little faster when I thought of him, or how a delicious kind of heat passed through my body whenever I remembered how it felt to have his hands clasped around mine, meant that I was in love with him. But from everything I had heard and read, it did seem that somewhere over the past few days, I had given my heart to Tobyn Slade.

Which meant that of course I could not marry Lord Edmar. It would have been impossible before, and now, with this new realization dawning in me, I realized that it would be even more wrong.

I had arrayed myself this morning rather the way a knight might don his armor before he went into battle. The finery was not intended to make me more attractive to the duke, but rather to gird me with the outward appearance of an equal, even though I knew we were anything but alike when it came to our relative ranks in the world.

The ball of shining thread sat inside a small carved box on top of a side table. Rashelle had already tidied up the main salon, and so I knew there was little chance of her discovering it. Besides, I had told her that I would be meeting with the duke this morning, and that I must do so alone.

At that confidence, her eyes had lit up, and I guessed she thought I intended to accept his suit. For of course there could be no secrets at court; I had not said anything to her directly, but she appeared to know that the duke wished to make me his wife. In her manner, there was something of an air of anticipation. Perhaps she thought I would keep her in my service once I was the Duchess of Lerneshall, and that would be quite the elevation for her, to be lady's maid to a great duchess.

I could not disabuse her of these notions. Even if I had tried, I was not sure she would have believed me. After all, who would be foolish enough to refuse a duke's offer of marriage?

A knock came at the door, and I took a breath, then went to answer it. With Rashelle gone, I must be my own servant.

Lord Edmar waited outside, looking quite resplendent himself in a black velvet doublet trimmed in gold, and with a heavy chain of gold around his neck. I offered a curtsey, then said, "Do come in, Your Grace."

He moved past me to head into the main salon, which was where we always held our conversations. The door to the study with its spinning wheel was shut and locked, and I found myself glad of that. Every time I looked at that spinning wheel,

I could only think of Tobyn...where he was, what he might be doing at that same moment. No doubt he was safely home, creating another of those beautiful pieces of his. Did he take off his gloves to work, so he could feel the gold and silver under his fingertips as that wondrous gift of his molded the metal?

I wondered what his hands looked like.

But there I was, distracting myself when I should be focused fully on the duke. He had stopped in front of one of the divans, and was sending me a rather quizzical look.

"Here is the gold," I said hastily, then went to the box where I had concealed the thread. After I pulled it out, I went to him, the gleaming mass resting on one outstretched hand.

He did not take it from me, though. For a long moment, he stared down at it, and then his grey eyes flicked back up to my face. "That is not why I came here, Annora."

"I know," I said. "But the king will expect you to bring it to him."

A nod, and he reached out and took the thread from me. He hefted it in his hand, as if weighing the amount, before slipping it into a pocket of his breeches. "You are very conscientious."

"I am only doing as the king bade me."

"True." His gaze had never wavered during that exchange, and it was more difficult than I imagined to keep from glancing away. I did not much enjoy being on the receiving end of such a gaze...at least not when it was Lord Edmar concentrating on me so closely. Perhaps if it had been Tobyn, I would have felt much different.

"Some spiced cider?" I inquired then, remembering that I had asked Rashelle to leave some refreshments for us before she went. Offering the drink gave me the excuse I needed to break the contact, to make it seem perfectly natural that I should turn away from him.

"I think not." He crossed his arms. "I have given you the night to think on what I asked of you. I would like to have your answer."

Although the room was comfortable enough, with a cheery fire in the marble hearth to dispel the chill of an autumn morning, my hands felt like ice in that moment. To buy myself some time, I picked up one of the pewter mugs filled with hot cider and took a sip. That was a little better. At least the heat from the warm metal helped to penetrate my cold fingers.

Then I turned back toward the duke, who watched me, arms crossed, one eyebrow at a slight angle, as if he already knew what I intended to say but wanted to hear how I would say it.

"Your Grace." My voice shook somewhat, and I drew in another breath, hoping that would steady me. "Please believe that I understand the honor you have done me by asking me to be your wife. But at the same time, I feel it is impossible for me to accept your offer."

Quiet then, for a long, long moment while the fire crackled away into the silence, one log breaking apart and settling against the grate with a soft *thump*.

He spoke. "That is your answer to me?"

"Yes, Your Grace. Truly, there are many more women here at court better suited to be the wife of a duke. I know nothing of how to be a grand lady, after all."

Then I held myself still, for he was watching me with narrowed eyes, eyes the color of a frozen lake, and I was chilled all over again. Perhaps it had been foolish of me to send Rashelle away. But what could a simple maid do against the wrath of a man like Lord Edmar?

He took a step toward me, and another. We stood very close, so close that I knew I could not get away, should he decide to reach out and seize me. So I remained where I was, hoping that he could not hear the frightened beating of my heart.

"A bold stratagem, my lady," he said, and gave me a mocking little bow, barely more than a brief nod of his head. "It is not every woman who thinks she can fare better on her own, rather than shelter herself with a title and a husband who seeks to protect her."

"So you would protect me?" I inquired. Skepticism laced my tone; I saw no reason to conceal my doubt from him. "From what, pray? Your king?"

"He is your king as well, Annora."

Much to my misfortune, I thought, although that was one sentiment I did not dare utter aloud. "True. But it is because of him that I am here at all, and so I am not sure why you would think it strange that I desire protection from him."

Lord Edmar shifted his stance slightly and I stiffened, worried that he would reach out to me, do something to force an intimacy I most certainly did not desire. But he did not, instead saying, "You think it is the king's fault that you are here night after night, spinning gold for him? Rather, the blame should be laid at your father's feet, for if he had not spoken so rashly at

Baron Levender's birthday gathering, none of this would have come to pass."

Well, I could not deny that. I lifted my chin and replied, "Perhaps the two of them can share the blame equally. Not that I care much for assigning blame, as what's done is done. And as for protection, I believe I will wait to see how my counsel fares when he goes before the High Court tomorrow. All of this will be moot if he wins me my freedom."

That comment angered him, I could tell, for his jaw set, and his eyes glittered. "You may be placing your faith in a spurious hope of rescue, Annora."

I began to think that I should have been more careful about provoking him. But then, what else could I have done? I feared my only utterance that would have pleased him would have been for me to accept his proposal, and of course that was something I would never do.

"If I am, then I will face the consequences when the time comes."

"Will you? Are you prepared to spend the rest of your life locked in these chambers? For I assure you that His Majesty has no intention of letting you return to the life you once knew. I am offering you some form of escape. And I believe," he added, gaze lingering on my lips, "you may not find it quite as distasteful as you now think."

Somehow I kept myself from shuddering. Oh, this duke was very sure of himself. But then, why should he not be? For his entire life, he had had his wealth and his title and his looks on his side. To be refused by a commoner such as myself must have been quite a blow to his pride.

"That is a word you have chosen, not I," I replied. "I do not believe I have ever said such a thing. True, you are a good deal older than I"—his face darkened when I uttered that remark, although he did not interrupt—"but that would not be a hindrance in many cases. No, it is simply that you do not love me, Lord Edmar, and I do not love you, and so becoming man and wife is quite out of the question."

Almost as soon as those words had left my lips, he threw back his head and laughed. "Love?" he said with some derision, once he had recovered himself. "When has love had anything to do with marriage? It is a contract involving wealth and property, and the getting of heirs. Nothing more."

My own jaw clenched. "Perhaps that is how you view the matter, Your Grace, but I see these things very differently. And that is why I know we would not suit."

His eyebrow was cocked at an ironic angle, and I knew he was no longer angry with me. No, I had just given him a reason to think me a fool. A naïve child, with no knowledge of how the world really worked. It could be that I was, but I would rather be a foolish child than a world-weary adult.

"Would it change your mind if I were to woo you, to write you poetry and bring you flowers and say that no other woman exists on this earth besides you?"

The mental image of him doing any of those things was so ridiculous that I had to smile. "No, it would not, Lord Edmar, for I know the truth in your heart. I have no doubt that you will find your duchess soon enough, but she will not be me."

He smiled in return, but I saw that the expression did not reach his eyes. Perhaps he was not angry any longer. That did not mean he was still not dangerous.

"The king will not be happy to hear of this," the duke said, the warning clear behind his words.

"I doubt he will, but as it seems to me that he has not been happy about much of anything for a good span of time, this particular piece of news should not materially change his disposition."

Lord Edmar shook his head, as if deciding that he was quite done with me. Indeed, he bowed and said, "Then I will take my leave of you, Annora. I cannot say I precisely wish you luck, for I will not be at cross-purposes with His Majesty. But I do hope that this decision of yours will not cause you any unforeseen trouble."

"I thank you for that, Your Grace," I replied. "As always, I must hope for the best."

For a second or two, he said nothing. Then his shoulders lifted. "I fear that if I were you, I would prepare for the worst."

No immediate doom seemed to befall me, however. The duke made his farewells and left, and some time after that Rashelle returned, bearing a tray with my lunch. If the king had decided to punish me for my intransigence, at least he did not intend to do so by starving me.

Despite that, I spent a long, weary afternoon, worrying the whole time whether I would be summoned to His Majesty's presence to explain myself. Or perhaps he would come rushing in as he had before so that he might upbraid me in person.

Neither of those things happened, however. I embroidered, read a little, went to the window and watched people moving about in the gardens below. Now they wore cloaks against the brisk wind, for the sunny conditions of a few days earlier had been replaced by banks of lowering clouds. Rain seemed to be imminent, although I would have no chance to feel it or smell it on the grass and the fallen leaves, not here in the shelter of my tower prison.

Although I could have sworn there had been none when I first came to my suite, I also found paper, pen, and ink in one of the drawers of the desk in the study. Had Tobyn left it there for me, knowing that I fretted about my sister? It seemed the sort of thoughtful gesture he might make.

Thus gifted with the means of doing so, I sat down to write a letter to Iselda. True, I had asked Master Jamsden to pass word along to her that I was well and unharmed, but I thought it might be better if I wrote her directly. I could hide the note until night fell and Tobyn came to help me spin the king's unending skeins of golden thread. Then I would give the letter to my benefactor, and he could make sure that it came safely to my sister.

At first I was not sure how much I should tell her, but the two of us had always been honest with one another. It was one way of fighting back against our father's continual misrepresentations as to his activities, or the actual state of the household budgets. We could not control what he did, but we could make very sure that we did not do the same thing to one another.

So I explained how Father's boasting had brought the king's attention upon me, and how I must stay here to do his bidding. I told her of how Lord Edmar wished to marry me, so that I might remain safely under their control, but that I had a counselor who would be fighting for me before the High

Court, and that I hoped he would prevail so I might be sent home very soon.

The one thing I did not mention was the assistance Tobyn had given me. Nor did I say anything about his powers. The letter should be safe enough, since I would be handing it directly to him, and he would get it to my sister somehow from there, but I did not wish to take even the slightest chance of revealing the powers he had worked so hard to hide. If his mage blood should be discovered because of anything I had said or done, I knew I would never forgive myself.

Supper came and went, and eventually Rashelle retired to the servants' hall after braiding my hair for the night and banking the fire down low. I went to the study and sat at the spinning wheel, impatient and wishing for Tobyn to appear. It was not that he was particularly late, but the day had felt overlong already, and I wanted nothing then except the comfort of his presence.

Eventually, he did come, seeming to step forth from the shadows in the room. I had been half-dozing, eyelids heavy with weariness, but as soon as he moved toward me, I startled awake and rose to my feet.

He was the first to speak. "It seems you have done somewhat to annoy His Grace."

I could hear the slight lilt in his voice, and so I knew Tobyn was pleased, no matter how Lord Edmar himself might be feeling about my refusal. "Did you think I would do anything else?"

"No," he replied. "That is, I had no reason not to believe you when you said you did not wish to be a duchess. But I doubt there are many who would have faulted you for changing your mind, when confronted by the reality of such an offer."

"Once my mind is made up, I rarely change it," I said. "At any rate, even if I had not already been set on my decision, Lord Edmar's remark about marriage having nothing to do with love most certainly would have prevented me from ever contemplating such a union."

Tobyn had paused on the other side of the spinning wheel, as he often did. My revelation made him tilt his head toward me, as if in surprise. "And you believe it does?"

"Of course," I said stoutly, even though my own parents' example left something wanting when it came to the notion of marriage as a union of true souls. Perhaps I had read too many of my sister Iselda's chapter-books. Then, as Tobyn seemed disinclined to reply, I added, "Did your parents not love one another?"

"No, I believe they loved each other very much. But some would say they were the exception rather than the rule."

His voice was carefully neutral, and I thought perhaps I had carried the conversation into regions that were uncomfortable for him. It was too late to turn back, however. Besides, I would be lying to myself if I did not admit some curiosity as to Master Slade's own views on the subject of love. Did he think it a foolish construct, the way Lord Edmar seemed to, or had he merely cut himself off from affection and desire because he had decided he was now too scarred, too unworthy, to ever have it offered to him?

"I am not so sure of that," I said slowly. "True, I did not have much of a good example in my own household, but I blame my father's faults for that. On the other hand, I have had the opportunity to observe the other families on my street, and they seem to be quite affectionate households. Why, Master and Mistress Marisdon have eight children."

"I suppose that would be evidence of a good deal of affection," Tobyn replied dryly, and hot blood rushed to my cheeks. No, I did not have any great knowledge of the particulars of becoming with child, but I knew the act required a good deal more intimacy than merely a kiss.

"At any rate," I went on, attempting to keep my tone steady, "I would certainly not marry someone whose only reason for doing so was to keep me safely at hand for the king's pleasure."

"No, I suppose you would not." He put his hand on the spinning wheel and gave it a gentle turn so that it began to revolve slowly. "You seem to be a woman of rare and passionate spirit, Annora Kelsden."

His praise only made me flush that much more. At the same time, I felt a stirring of hope. Surely he would not say such things to me if he did not wish to continue what we had begun the night before. Only the most tentative of steps, true, but all journeys must begin somewhere.

And so I came around the spinning wheel to stand next to him. Not too close, but enough that once again I could smell the sweet herbal scent which arose from his garments. I hoped that perhaps he would also note the rosewater lotion Rashelle had given me to put on my face and hands, and might find it pleasing.

Before I lost my nerve, I reached out and took his hand. He startled, but then he seemed to relax, and even to wrap his fingers around mine. Once again I was surprised by his warmth...and by the way that warmth seemed to find its echo deep within me, awaking a longing I did not completely understand.

"Last night," I began, but he shook his head.

"Annora, that was...." The words trailed off, as if he wasn't sure what to say next.

I could guess, however. "Was what? A mistake? A moment of weakness?"

"Yes, both those things."

"All we did was touch our hands together. As we are doing now. What is wrong with that?"

A sigh came from deep within the hood. "You say that because, whatever you might be thinking, this is nothing more than misplaced gratitude."

"Indeed?" I returned. "Do you truly think me such a fool that I would immediately bestow my affections on whoever came to my aid? If Master Jamsden succeeds with the High Court tomorrow, does that mean I will fling my arms around his neck and kiss him, and proclaim my undying love for him?"

"No, of course not." The words sounded strangled, as if Tobyn had had to force them out. "You know I do not think you any kind of fool. But—"

"But what? If I do not know my own heart, then who else can know it? Yes, our acquaintance has been short, but I have never met anyone like you, Master Slade. I know what I feel. And perhaps"—I hesitated, but as I had already unburdened so much of myself, I did not see the point in holding back now—"perhaps you feel something the same, or else you would not be praising my 'rare spirit.'"

"Even if I did, this would be impossible. All I can do is see you safely returned to your father's household."

"'Impossible'?" I flung back at him, then stopped myself. My tone had begun to rise, and although the study was safely ensconced between other chambers in my suite and did not share any walls with the apartments to either side, I did not think it wise to be quite so strident. Lowering my voice, I continued, "I would like to know why you think 'this' is impossible. Are you already wed, or promised to someone else?"

"Of course not," he said. The words came out as barely more than a harshly rasped whisper. "I have no one."

"Well, then," I returned, as if that should take care of everything.

He crossed his arms. "You say that very blithely, Annora. But, even setting aside the matter of only knowing one another for a few days, you must understand that a man such as I does not have the...liberty...to bestow his heart wherever he chooses."

"A man such as you? Do you mean because you are mage-born, or because you believe the pox has rendered you unfit for female companionship?"

"Both," he replied, in that same strangled tone.

"And if both those obstacles were removed?" I asked. I held on to him tightly, so that he would have to tear his hands from my grasp to get away. "What would your heart tell you then?"

"That is immaterial, because my mage blood and—and my disfigurement—are part of who I am. I cannot change them."

"I am not asking you to change them!" I cried, forgetting my vow of a few moments earlier to keep my voice down. "I am only asking you to tell me whether you care anything at all for me."

Of course he did not respond. His hands lay still in my grasp. He would not try to get away, but neither would he show me any encouragement by twining his fingers around mine. Oh, I wished I had the courage to push him away, to show him what I thought of his intransigence, but somehow I knew that I must not. I must continue to cling to him, to show him that I could be quite as stubborn as he.

"Tell me, Tobyn," I whispered. "For if you do not, then I will not press you further. I can only beg you not to lie to me."

At last his hands did move, clutching mine, pulling me closer to him. "Of course I care. What man with a beating heart would not? You are brave and strong and beautiful, and you should be a duchess, or something much grander than a woman shackled to a man who dares not even show his face in public."

Those words made my heart sing. Or perhaps it was simply his delicious nearness, the way only an inch or so separated our bodies. And there I was, clad only in a chemise and dressing gown, no heavy court dress and boned undergarments acting as armor between us. Again one of those delicious warm thrills moved over me. I could not say exactly what it was, only that I wanted him to pull me even closer, to feel his arms around me, his hands on me....

I let out a little gasp, knowing I must not allow my mind to continue down those paths. Not here. Not yet. "But I do not wish to be a duchess, Tobyn. I've already told you that. As for the rest...." I paused, thoughts racing furiously. It seemed clear enough to me that he did care, but only held back because of his own perceived defects. Since I cared little for those, why not remove any other impediments to our being together? "Purth is harsh to those who have magical blood, but it is not that way in all lands. Master Jamsden told me of how magic is allowed in North Eredor, of how the consort of the Mark herself is mage-born. Why could we not go there?"

"You would do that? Leave your family, the only land you have ever known?"

Put that way, the prospect did sound rather daunting. But was that not always the woman's lot, to go where her man took her? If I had accepted Cordell's proposal, I would have remained in Purth, but I might have been living several days' ride from Bodenskell, or even farther off. Chances were that I would not have seen my family that often. "For you, I would," I said stoutly.

"You don't know what you are saying, Annora—"

"Perhaps I do not. Or perhaps I know it here,"— and I let go of one of his hands so I could touch my finger to my chest— "even if my mind would agree that I am not being at all logical."

"No, you are not being logical. But then, neither am I. Else I would never have allowed you to take my hand last night, or indeed this evening, either."

Something in his tone sounded almost sad, as if he were troubled by what he perceived as his own weakness. I almost reached for his hand again, but then decided I had something better in mind.

Moving quickly so I could not stop myself, I wrapped my arms around him and laid my head against his chest. For one startled second, he went completely still, as if attempting to decide what he should do next. But then his arms closed on my waist, pulling me more tightly against him. The wool of his cloak settled around us both, enclosing us in a cocoon of sweet-smelling warmth. Never before had I felt so safe, so sheltered.

So loved.

For he must love me as well, or else he would not have held me thus, would have found a way to maintain some distance between us. I lifted my face toward his, but within the shadow of his hood, I could see nothing at all.

That did not matter, it seemed, for he bent to me as well, and somewhere in the space between us, our mouths met, coming together so perfectly that their joining must have been inevitable. True, I could feel something in the shape of his lips that told me the scarring had touched them as well, but in that moment I did not care. This was what a kiss should be, an awakening of the fire within one's soul, bringing to life desire that had only slept until that moment.

My mouth parted, and I could taste him then, a lingering sweetness, possibly from some wine he had drunk with dinner before coming to see me. It did not matter, for I had not known a kiss could progress into this, a touch so intimate that it seemed as if we must learn everything of one another in that moment.

I clung to him, for how long, I could not say. Eventually, he pulled away from me, shaking his head.

"I should not have done that."

"Why not?" I retorted. "It seemed as if you very much wanted to. And I wanted you to as well."

"You have placed your trust in me—you are vulnerable—"

Such talk needed to stop. It seemed the easiest way to accomplish that was to go up on my tiptoes and kiss him again, the pressure of my mouth ending such foolish arguments.

"I am not vulnerable," I told him, once I thought he had been sufficiently quelled so I might speak without argument. "I believe I know very much what I want. And that happens to be you."

A muffled sound arose in his throat, half-groan, half-sigh. "Ah, Annora, you think that, but how can you know for sure? You have never even seen me."

True, I had not. However, I had touched his lips, felt the scarring there, and, for whatever reason, it had not bothered me at all. "No," I replied. "But I have heard your voice, and felt your arms around me, and tasted your kiss. All of these seem far more important to me than what you look like."

"You say that, and yet I fear you do not understand what the pox did to me. I am not...like other men."

"Then let me see," I said boldly. "That way I may prove to you that I care little for what that wretched disease might have done to scar your face."

He went still and silent then, and finally shook his head. "Not yet. Not because of how I think you will react," he added quickly, as I opened my mouth to protest, "but because I would like to live this pleasant lie for now, the one where you do not believe it can possibly be as bad as I have intimated."

"My knowing will not change anything," I told him.

"Perhaps it will not. In the meantime, though, it is getting late, and the king must still have his wretched gold."

That was true. If Master Jamsden succeeded on the morrow with his plea before the High Court, this might be the last time I ever had to sit at this wheel and spin gold for a greedy king. But in the meantime, I must play my role.

"One more kiss, to see me through it?" I asked, and Tobyn rewarded me with a reluctant chuckle.

"If that is the price I must pay...." He bent and kissed me, but softly and swiftly.

I wanted more, but I knew that would have to suffice for now. After he had straightened, I took my seat at the spinning wheel, gathered up a measure of straw, and got to work. This time, neither of us spoke as the skein of gold on the bobbin grew thicker and thicker. What more could we say? We had come to some kind of an accord, and until I knew of my fate the next day, it did not seem the right time to make plans.

Not until I was done, at least. As I got up from my seat and lifted the golden thread from the spool that held it in place, I slanted a look up at Tobyn. "Are you so very sure you cannot take me away?" I asked. "That is, you can come and go like the mist. Why should it be that much more difficult to make another person disappear as you do?"

He shook his head. "I have told you, Annora—my magic only allows me to transport myself. Believe me, if it were that simple, I would have spirited you away days ago. To someplace safe, like your aunt's home."

"You know of my Aunt Lyselle?" I asked, surprised.

"I have learned a good deal about you and your family, yes. And I believe she would have shielded you while Master Jamsden prepared your defense. But all that is moot, because doing such a thing is far beyond my abilities."

I heard a disappointed note in his voice, as if he berated himself for his shortcomings. Which was foolish, because he certainly possessed more extraordinary skills than any other man I had ever met. "It does not matter," I said quickly. "For Master Jamsden will prevail tomorrow, and I will be free, and then we can plan together what to do next."

"You sound very confident."

"Master Jamsden was confident, and so I will be as well."

That reply made him chuckle, and he kissed me again, this time lingering so we could taste one another again. My body was all shivering heat, and I thought then of how my bedchamber was so very close....

No, that was quite out of the question. Well-brought-up young ladies did not entertain such thoughts. Or if they did, they certainly did not speak of them aloud. As if to save me from my own indiscretions, my mind went to the letter to Iselda, which I had hidden in the desk drawer. I went to it and pulled it out.

"Would you see that this gets to my sister?" I asked as I handed the folded piece of paper to Tobyn. There had been no sealing wax that I could find, but I was certain he would not look at the letter's contents. "I fear my father has not told her much of what has happened to me, and she should know that I am well, and safe."

"Of course," he replied, before he took the letter from me and slipped it somewhere within the folds of his cloak. "I cannot go to your house myself, but I will see if Master Jamsden or one of his assistants will take it in my stead."

"That will be fine. I should have realized that running such an errand yourself would be impossible."

"Do not worry about that," he told me, then bent and kissed me again. Softly, only a brush of his lips against mine, but even that was enough to send those delicious shivers all over my body once more. "Good night, Annora."

"Good night, Tobyn," I said softly, as he stepped away from me. "Tomorrow, everything can begin anew."

He did not reply, but reached out to touch my cheek. And then he was gone, disappearing into the shadows of the night.

I knew this would be that last time we would be forced to part in such a way.

Chapter Eleven

As a woman, I was not allowed to attend my own hearing. The law gave me the right to have a lawyer present my case, but women were not allowed in the courtroom. All I could do was wait in the suite that had become my prison, and hope that good news would reach me soon.

Under other circumstances, such anxious waiting might have been quite nerve-wracking. But even as I sat there, the neglected embroidery hoop in my lap, I recalled the touch of Tobyn's lips on mine, the strength of his arms around me. So much still remained to be said between us, and yet I thought we had come to an understanding. The attraction that had flared between us could no longer be denied. What that meant for our future together, when we had not yet spoken any words of love, I could not be sure, but somehow I knew there would no longer be any question of remaining apart.

Midday came and went, as did the tray with my lunch, and still I heard nothing. By then I had abandoned my needlework altogether and stood at the window, watching as the rain promised by the cloudy day before finally began to fall. Those few who had braved the cold in the gardens fled for the shelter of the palace, some of the ladies running in a most unseemly fashion. But even that sight could not bring a smile to my lips, for the unease that had started to flare some time earlier had begun to grow into outright dread.

At last there came a knock at my door. Mouth dry, I turned away from the window, even as Rashelle went to answer that knock. I heard her speak, low, murmuring, followed by the deeper tones of a man's voice I did not recognize.

As I approached, I saw that he was one of the footmen, dressed in the now-familiar blue and gold of the royal house. He bowed, but not very low—perhaps an indication of my lack of rank. Still, he sounded polite enough as he said, "My lady, His Majesty requests your presence in his audience chamber."

Which could mean everything, or nothing. Did he intend to give me a formal farewell, or, if Master Jamsden had not succeeded, did the king wish to humiliate me in front of all his courtiers?

It did not matter, I supposed, for I certainly could not refuse this command couched as a request. "But of course," I said, as calmly as I could. Ignoring Rashelle's wide-eyed look, I went out the door and followed the footman as he led me down the corridor.

Several days had passed since my outing with the duke in the gardens, and I found myself trying not to stare as I passed by intricate tapestries and formal paintings and small carved tables that served as stands for priceless statues and vases. The hallways were not terribly crowded, but neither were they empty, which made me hope that not all those in court waited in the audience chamber, hoping to see the fate of the commoner who had had the nerve to refuse a duke.

Even so, that chamber seemed full enough as I entered. The footman stopped near the door, but inclined his head toward the throne. His intention seemed clear enough; I was to approach the king alone.

I lifted my chin and did my best to ignore the avid stares of the noble lords and ladies who stood to either side. In that moment, I was glad of my borrowed finery, for in my gown of rich blue damask, I did not look like the daughter of an impoverished merchant. Tobyn's ruby pendant rested in the hollow of my throat, warm and heavy, giving me courage.

As the throne drew near, I saw that King Elsdon sat upon that impressive chair of carved and gilded oak. Next to him was a young man I did not recognize, but who I guessed was the king's only son, Prince Harlin. He must have favored his late mother, for he was handsomer than his father, with a head of thick brown hair and forthright blue eyes, not the king's pale, unsettling hue, but the serene color of a mountain lake.

Standing on the dais, but not seated, was Lord Edmar. His gaze flicked toward me and rested there for a second or two before returning to the king. The dismissal was obvious, and I felt my heart sink. Then again, what had I expected? I had refused him, and therefore was of little worth in his eyes.

Otherwise, I could not tell from his expression what the High Court's judgment in my case might have been. My own eyes shifted to the king, but he appeared equally impassive.

Perhaps that was a good sign? Surely if my suit had been dismissed as frivolous, he would look far more cheerful than he did now.

I had no choice but to approach the dais, however, then pause a foot or so away and perform the best curtsey I could manage. Behind me, I heard a few tittering laughs, no doubt the good ladies of the court amusing themselves with my ineptitude. Anger flared, but I tried to keep my own expression as neutral as the king's. I did not want them to see how they had discomfited me.

"Your Majesty," I said.

"Annora Kelsden," he replied. His hands grasped the arms of his throne, fingers tightening over a pair of smooth-carved orbs of onyx. "The High Court has heard your case."

And? I wanted to ask, but I held my tongue. The king clearly had news he wished to deliver to me, but it was equally clear that he wished to do so in his own time.

"It was decided that you should be allowed to go free."

Joy leapt in my heart then. As I stared up at His Majesty, however, a cold trickle of fear stirred somewhere in my midsection. He did not look angry, which was what I had been expecting, given that the court had just thwarted his wishes and granted me my freedom. No, instead something in his eyes was considering, weighing. For just the briefest fraction of a second, his attention seemed to flicker to the young man sitting next to him.

What that meant, I had no idea. Prince Harlin was watching me, but only in an idly curious way, as if he was not certain why I should have been called here like this at all. That made two of us, I supposed. Since the king had not prevailed in keeping me as his prisoner, I had to wonder why he had not quietly let me go home, rather than make a spectacle of me in front of all his court.

"Thank you for sharing the court's decision with me, Your Majesty," I said, my tone all politeness. "Then may I assume that I will no longer be enjoying your hospitality, and may return to my father's house?"

"Not precisely," he replied. Once he again he glanced at his son, who appeared to note something odd in his manner as well, for the younger man sat up a little straighter in his own throne-like chair, his eyes beginning to narrow. "Your worth to this kingdom, Annora Kelsden, is far too great to be squandered in the household of a mere merchant. Indeed, you are a jewel not even worthy of Lord Edmar here."

My brows drew together in a frown, even as I fought desperately to appear as placid as possible. The icy fear that had started somewhere in my midsection now seemed to pass over my entire body. Was this some sort of horrible joke at my expense? Had the king brought me here merely to humiliate me?

Once again I allowed a quick glance over at the duke. At the king's mention of his name, Lord Edmar had stiffened slightly, but the same half-smile touched his lips as before. I would learn nothing from watching him. Perhaps it was foolish of me to think I could. After all, he was a veteran of the court, and knew what manner of games might be played here. As I was a hopeless novice, I could only watch and wait.

King Elsdon stood then, and so his son rose as well, his forehead now wearing a puckered little frown to match my own. "Because of your great worth, Annora, I have decided that you must remain here as a member of my household. It is my command that you marry my son, Prince Harlin."

At that insane statement, delivered with all calmness and authority, the watching members of the court let out a collective gasp, and the prince rounded on his father, eyes blazing.

"What madness is this, sir? Have you forgotten that I am already wed to a princess of Farendon?"

"Who has been your wife these three years, and has yet to provide you with an heir. Or," the king added, mouth curling with contempt, "even a daughter who might allow us to make an advantageous alliance. We shall have the marriage annulled, and send her back to her father."

"This is preposterous!" Prince Harlin spluttered, but the king held up a hand.

"Steward, if you will clear the hall."

Immediately following this command, a tall man with a forbidding brow stepped out from the far end of the dais. He held a silver-tipped rod of black wood in one hand and raised it as he spoke. "The king desires you all to go."

I heard murmuring, but the group of nobles who had been watching the display—several of them wearing expressions of glee at being witness to such a juicy bit of gossip—all obediently turned and made their way from the audience chamber. Even Lord Edmar, who shot me a sardonic glance, complete with raised eyebrow, as he passed me by. Within a moment or two, they were gone, and the footmen had shut the doors behind them. All that was left behind was a ghost of the perfumes they wore, and a glittering comb that must have fallen from a lady's hair.

Through all this activity, I had been rooted more or less frozen in place, uncertain as to what I should do. Surely this had to be some monstrous joke of the king's, although I had to admit to myself that I could not understand why he would choose to create such a scene in public.

As I stood there, Prince Harlin turned from his father and sent me an almost pitying glance. "I assume, my lady, that this pronouncement of His Majesty's comes as much as a surprise to you as it does to me?"

My voice seemed to fail me then, and I could but nod.

"So then, sir, it seems you must explain yourself to both the lady and me," the prince said. He sounded more calm now, as if he had gotten over the initial shock of his father's preposterous proposal and now wished to get to the heart of the matter.

King Elsdon lifted his shoulders. Around his neck, a chain of heavy square-cut garnets and gold glittered. "What is there to explain? The lady has a resource this kingdom needs far more than a tenuous agreement with a land far enough away that I doubt very much they would ever come to our aid."

"Strange that you did not have such a low opinion of Farendon's might when you betrothed me to one of its daughters." The prince folded his arms and gave his father a measuring stare. "Or is it merely that you thought it a good deal at the time, but now believe you have something better? Although I must confess some difficulty in attempting to discern what that might be. No insult meant to you, my lady," he added, with an apologetic glance in my direction.

How could I take any insult from his comment? I was only the daughter of a merchant. Many would have said I was reaching far too high in attempting to align with a duke, but the prince himself? King Elsdon's sole heir? It was quite unthinkable.

"I did not take any offense, Your Highness," I said quietly.

The king said, "Annora here has the means to give our kingdom riches without end. With her at your side, you could make Purth the greatest realm on the continent."

Prince Harlin shook his head. "Father, I understand that there is something strange here—else you would not have first attempted to have her marry Lord Edmar—but how on earth can one young woman possibly do as you say?"

A gleam came into the king's pale eyes. "I will show you. And you, Annora," he added, "you will come along as well."

That was an invitation I wished I did not have to accept, but I knew I had no choice. Just as I could not protest this insane match the king was proposing. It was one thing to turn down the duke, but for a commoner to decline the suit of the prince himself? That was bordering on treason. No, my only hope was that Prince Harlin truly loved his wife, and would have nothing of this annulment, no matter what his father's wishes might be.

So I followed meekly as the king stepped down from the dais and went out through a door halfway hidden by a set of heavy velvet draperies. The prince was only a few steps ahead of me, confusion and anger clear in the stiff set of his shoulders.

How I wished then that I had some way to call Tobyn to me! But he was most likely safe at home, and though he possessed great powers, none of them seemed to include the ability to speak across the miles. In this, it seemed, I would have to fend for myself.

We walked down a corridor far less grand than the ones I had traversed to reach the audience chamber. This hallway seemed to be in an older section of the palace, or perhaps one used mainly by the servants. The walls were plain white plaster, with dark beams overhead, and the floor beneath our feet age-darkened wood. And soon enough we came to a set of stairs that led downward. The king surged ahead, and I gathered my skirts in my hand so I might not trip, for the way was not well lit.

Prince Harlin turned back toward me. "Do you need any assistance, my lady?"

Blood heated my cheeks at his solicitude, and I shook my head. "No, Your Highness. I think I shall do well enough. But thank you for the offer."

He nodded and went on ahead, a few paces behind King Elsdon. I had not expected the prince to be quite so kind, not when his own father was apparently attempting to force him to marry me. But perhaps he had realized this was none of my doing, and that I was quite as reluctant as he.

The air seemed to grow colder and almost dank as we descended the steps. When we reached the bottom of the staircase, the floor beneath my feet was now stone. A few wan candles flickered from sconces on either side, but I still found it difficult to see clearly. I could not begin to guess where we might be going.

The prince seemed to have some idea, though. "Why on earth are you taking us to the treasury, Father?"

"You'll see."

The treasury. Of course. King Elsdon would show his son the evidence of my craft, and then the prince would have to decide whether angering the king of Farendon was a fair trade for apparently unending supplies of gold.

Of course he will not, I told myself. *It is clear enough that Prince Harlin is a man of honor, no matter what his father might say or do.*

I had to hope my estimation of the prince was correct. Unfortunately, as I had seen of late, greed could do strange things to a man's soul.

We stopped in front of a large iron-barred door of thick oak. Two guards stood watch there, but they bowed deeply to their king and prince, eyes flicking in some curiosity toward me.

"Your Majesty," one of the guards said.

"I wish to enter."

They bowed again, and the one who had not spoken retrieved a heavy key from the chain at his belt and then inserted it in the door's lock. He opened it, stepping aside so we might enter.

The chamber seemed vast to me, but that might have been because it was quite dark. More candles sat on sconces near the door. Their light, however, only served to illuminate the area nearest us. All the rest was in shadow, although I got the impression of large bulky shapes—casks or chests or other means of storage—lurking in the corners and along the walls.

"Take up one of those candles, Harlin," the king commanded his son. Prince Harlin lifted a pillar of beeswax from the sconce nearest him and held it in one hand. Even in the uncertain light, I could see the grim set of his mouth. Yes, he was humoring his father because he must, but it seemed clear enough that this entire undertaking was distasteful to him.

"Over here."

The prince followed his father into the darkness, moving from the chamber we had just entered to a smaller one with shelves all along the walls. I kept close to Prince Harlin, for I did not want to be too far away from that candle. It was so very dark down here, and I fancied I heard the squeaking of rats in the distance. I tried to tell myself that my imagination was playing tricks on me, that of course they would make sure these storerooms were free of vermin, and yet I couldn't help startling at every questionable sound.

Along all the shelves were ranks of boxes in various sizes. None of them seemed to be labeled, and I wondered how the king and his treasurers possibly kept track of everything contained within them. But he seemed to know where he was going, for he went to the far wall and lifted one of the wooden containers, then pulled off the lid. Even in the light of that one wan candle, fine threads of gold gleamed within the shadows of the box.

"Is that...?" Prince Harlin began, then hesitated.

"Gold," his father said. "Pure gold, spun for me by Annora here. Hers is a most miraculous gift, for all she must have is the commonest of materials—straw, which is grown in every pasture—and she can turn it into this most precious of metals."

He set down the box lid and lifted the skein of golden thread from the box so the prince could see its bulk.

Truly, as I had worked, I had not thought that what I produced was quite so significant. But seeing it held up like that, in the king's trembling hands, I realized that what I created each night truly was a fortune. No wonder he refused to let me go.

Prince Harlin's expression seemed to mix wonder and skepticism, and he glanced over at me, brows drawing together. "Is this truly your work, my lady?"

I hated to lie to him, but I knew I had no choice. Tobyn's identity, his gifts, must forever remain a secret. "Yes, Your Highness."

His frown deepened. "How is this possible?"

"I—" Once again, I found myself struggling to find a reply that would not incriminate the man I loved, nor make it sound as if I possessed forbidden powers myself. But the prince required some answer, so I said, "To be sure, Your Highness, I cannot precisely say. I only know that one day my sister was joking with me, saying that I spun thread so fine that I could probably do the same with the straw in the stable, rather than the wool I was using. It seemed such a silly notion that I had to try it. So I did...but what wound itself around the bobbin of my spinning wheel was not straw, but golden thread."

"There must be some kind of magic at work here," Prince Harlin said in musing tones.

My blood went cold, for I knew all too well the penalty for using such forbidden powers, and I had hoped the prince would not question me too closely, not with his father standing there and practically glowing with pride at this astonishing addition to his treasury.

The king, perhaps realizing that the last thing he wanted was to have the notion of foul magic attached to the miracle of my gold thread, broke in, saying sharply, "Of course it is not magic. Look at this lovely young woman—how can you accuse her of using something so dreadful to create something so wondrous? No, let us say rather it is a gift from the gods, who have chosen to smile down upon her—and indeed our kingdom, too, for Purth benefits from this miracle as well." His gaze sharpened as he stared at his son. "And this is why she must be forever joined to our house, so that there is no risk of anyone else being able to exploit this talent of hers."

In a terrible way, I supposed that what the king had just said did make some sense. The kingdom was prosperous enough, but its fields of sheep and cattle, and its few mines to the north, could not compete with the fabled riches of Keshiaar, which lay beyond our southern border. Yes, treaties had kept the peace between the kingdoms for generations, and there was no reason to think the current Hierarch of Keshiaar would do anything to break that peace. Still, the knowledge that one possessed the means to buy whatever armies and armaments necessary to secure one's borders was a powerful motivator when it came to making sure the source of that wealth could not get away.

And so it seemed I was fairly trapped, for I could not do anything to protest that I did not possess such a skill after all. The gold had appeared each night, which meant it had to have come from somewhere. Tobyn's gifts, if I revealed them now, would be enough to keep the kingdom's coffers overflowing with gold and gems, but I doubted the king would show him the same consideration he had shown me. Instead, Tobyn would be put to work night and day, for a user of magic such as he would not be afforded any courtesy. No, he would most likely be told he should be glad that he was not immediately put to death.

Prince Harlin fixed his father with a stern look. "Whatever Mistress Kelsden's skills, they do not warrant my putting aside Princess Lorelis. That would create very bad blood between Purth and Farendon, two lands who have always been allies. Besides—"

He stopped then, distress clear enough in his fine features, although he did not look at me. I thought I understood the cause of that distress—their match had of course been made for the sake of politics, but it seemed Prince Harlin cared for his wife, and had no desire to have the marriage dissolved. In that moment, I allowed myself a tiny bit of relief. Surely there was no way the king could force his son to do such a thing. He would have to abandon this mad plan.

But King Elsdon also seemed to know what his son was thinking. A sneer pulled at his thin lips, and he snapped, "What, do you fancy yourself in love with the girl? Love is for commoners, and for those who do not have to concern themselves with matters of state. At any rate, Lorelis is a pale, plain little thing, certainly no match for Mistress Kelsden here."

Was any compliment ever less welcome? I stared down at the stone floor beneath my feet, wishing myself miles away. Unfortunately, I did not possess any of Tobyn's gifts, and so could only remain where I was. At least it seemed as if I was meant to stand meekly by while these two great men discussed my fate. I did not think I could have trusted myself to respond with any great wit or intelligence, given my current circumstances.

Prince Harlin did not appear to suffer from the same constraints, however, for he retorted, "Whatever your feelings on the matter, Father, I would ask you to remember that Her Highness is both my wife and the daughter of the king of Farendon, and therefore is deserving of your respect at least, even if you cannot accord her any particular affection."

"Since she has not been able to perform the only function for which she is required, I am not so sure she is deserving of my respect." The king glanced from his son to me, and I kept my eyes downcast. I did not want to see what he might be thinking. "But we will leave that aside for now. I only wished for you to see what Mistress Kelsden has to offer our kingdom, so that you may make an informed decision. I will let you think on it."

"I could think for a year, and yet I would not change my mind."

No apology this time—not that I thought I required one. Rather, the apology should be given to Princess Lorelis, for putting her in the middle of a very ugly quarrel.

"Do not be so sure of that," the king said darkly. He placed the skein of golden thread, which he had been holding the entire time, back in the box, then set its lid on top and returned it to its place on the shelf behind him. "But we will leave this for now. I find I weary of trying to make you see reason."

With that, he turned and began to head back toward the door of the treasury. Lips set in anger, Prince Harlin followed, candle still in hand, and so I took up the rear. Neither of the men glanced back to see how I fared, and I realized they probably did not care overmuch. I was the cause of their argument, or at least the one they would admit to. The true cause was King Elsdon's greed, but neither of them were probably inclined to admit to such a thing.

In silence we returned to the main floor of the palace. The prince gave me a curt bow and then stalked off, no doubt to his own apartments. Finally, the king honored me with a glance, but I would rather he hadn't; something in it was cool and appraising, although he put on a smile as he looked down at me.

"He will see reason soon enough, Annora. In the meantime, you must be patient."

I nodded. In that moment, I did not trust myself to speak, for something that might have caused me grief later most likely would have left my lips.

We stood outside the door to the audience chamber. From the corner of my eye, I saw one of the footmen approach, and the king nodded at the man.

"See that Mistress Kelsden is returned safely to her apartments."

"Of course, Your Majesty," the footman replied with a bow. "My lady?"

I went to him, then followed him as he led me down the corridor, away from the king. With each step, my heart seemed to sink further. Yes, the High Court had given me my freedom, but it was clear enough that His Majesty cared nothing for its judgment. He would keep me here until Prince Harlin capitulated.

And if he does not? my mind taunted me.

I feared I had no answer for that.

CHAPTER TWELVE

I tried to compose myself. The king might be flouting the law at the moment, but, as Master Jamsden had pointed out, he was not above it. All I must do was wait for Tobyn to come to me this evening, and then I would tell him of the terrible events of this afternoon. He would enlist Master Jamsden's aid once more, and my counsel would file some sort of an appeal. That was the next step, was it not? I couldn't be sure, as my knowledge of the law was shaky at best. Besides, my thoughts kept darting here and there, agitated, unsettled, like a mouse in a field with a hawk hovering low. No matter what I did, I could not seem to stop shaking.

What if the king did prevail at last? Prince Harlin was a good man, but I did not know if he had the strength to continue to defy his father. He might eventually decide that it was better to give in to preserve the peace in his own home. Although annulments were very rare, they had occurred several times in my kingdom's history, mainly for the same reason King Elsdon had stated—failure to provide an heir. For of course barrenness was always the woman's fault.

I glanced at the hour candle on the mantel. Still some time before dinner, not that I would have the appetite to eat anything once my tray arrived, considering the way my thoughts were roiling. Perhaps if I had not met Tobyn, had never tasted his kiss, then I would not be so dismayed at the thought of becoming the prince's wife. After all, he was not so far off from me in age, and handsome and honorable. Many young women might have dreamed of such elevation in their station, combined with such a personable man, but I was not one of those women. I did not want to be a princess. I only wanted Tobyn, and a life far away from the king's machinations.

Rashelle had been keeping away from me, seeming to sense the thundercloud of my current mood. But a knock at the door came then, and she hastened to answer it, even as I sat and brooded into the flames dancing in the hearth. That knock did not improve my state of mind at all, for I guessed it was Lord Edmar coming to crow over me, or perhaps the king himself, full of plans as to how I might seduce the prince away from his wife's side.

Then I heard Rashelle exclaim, "Your Highness!" and I rose to my feet at once. Had Prince Harlin really come to see me in my chambers? What could such a visit possibly mean?

But as I made my way to the entry of my suite, I found myself stopping quite dead, for standing there was not the prince, but a young woman attired in a gown of soft blue silk, sapphires gleaming around her throat and in her ears.

I had never seen her, but I knew this must be Princess Lorelis. At once I swept into a curtsey, murmuring, "Your Highness."

She gave me a sort of abstracted frown, gaze flicking sideways toward Rashelle. "Mistress Kelsden, if I might speak to you in private?"

"Of course," I replied. "Rashelle, if you would—"

"Yes, my lady." She bobbed a curtsey of her own, then fled out the door. I thought I detected just the slightest hint of regret in her expression, as if she would have dearly liked to stay behind so she might hear what the princess had to say to me.

Well, she was not the only one. I also wished—but at the same time dreaded—to know the purpose of this interview.

No, actually, I thought I knew quite well what that might be.

"Some tea, Your Highness?" I inquired as I led her into the main salon. "I fear the water is not quite as hot as you might desire, since Rashelle brought it up almost half an hour ago now, but—"

"No, nothing at all," she replied, then added, "Thank you."

By then she had stopped with her back to the fireplace. It was not yet dusk, and so the candles had not been lit. However, enough light came in through the windows for me to see that King Elsdon's estimation of the princess had really been quite unkind. She had thick fawn-colored hair piled in elaborate braids and curls on the top of her head, and her eyes were large and brown, framed with heavy dark lashes. Yes, her skin did not possess much color, but the texture was fine, and her features were regular enough. Perhaps she was not what a man might consider to be a raging beauty, but she was certainly pretty enough.

"Oh," she said, faltering somewhat as I turned to face her. "It is true. You are so very beautiful."

I began to shake my head, but she forestalled me.

"No, it is true. I had hoped it was not, that the king was merely exaggerating, but—"

"The king came and spoke to you?" I asked, forgetting my manners in my indignation. It was one thing for him to browbeat and cajole his son, but to come to this poor young woman with his ridiculous demands?

"Yes," she said. One beringed hand twisted in the heavy silk of her skirt. Truly, she appeared so ill at ease that one might have thought she was the daughter of a merchant and I the princess, rather than the reverse. I began to see why Prince Harlin would fight so hard to protect her. She seemed to awaken that instinct in anyone who gazed upon her.

Except, of course, her father-in-law.

"He should not have done that, Your Highness," I told her. "Especially since nothing is going to come of this ridiculous notion of his."

"You may say that, Mistress Kelsden, but I have lived here as the king's daughter for the past three years. I have seen his tempers, his willfulness. He always gets his way. Always." Tears glittered in her eyes but did not fall. She blinked. "And he will get his way in this. I will be sent home in disgrace, and you will be the next queen of Purth."

I stared at her, searching for the right words to say. The princess seemed quite defeated already. My first instinct was to tell her she was being silly and jumping to conclusions, just as I might have admonished my own sister Iselda when she launched into a particularly elaborate flight of fancy. However, I knew that was not the best way to approach the situation.

"Please sit down, Your Highness," I begged her. "Let us discuss this calmly."

She took in a breath and nodded, then made her way to the nearest divan and sank down upon it as if her legs had given way beneath her. I wished she had not refused my offer of tea, for at least that would have given me something to do. But since she had, I could only settle myself awkwardly on the edge of the divan that faced hers. After I sat, I wondered whether I had made a serious blunder, for perhaps I should have waited for her to invite me to sit down.

If I had, Princess Lorelis showed no sign of noticing. Indeed, she was far too bound up in her own worry and misery to notice any gaffes on my part. She knotted her fingers in her lap and stared at me with imploring brown eyes.

"Has His Highness spoken with you?" I asked.

A nod, but she still looked stricken. "Yes, and he said that I should pay no mind to his father's blusterings, that nothing would come of all this."

"You see? His Highness is steadfast, and I certainly have no designs upon him."

"You don't?"

"Of course not," I said stoutly. "That is not to say that His Highness is not a very fine person, but I would never conspire to steal someone's husband from them. At any rate, I am in love with another, and would never even think of anyone else but him."

"Oh," the princess replied, eyes widening. "I had not heard that. Who is he?"

I hesitated. Perhaps it had been foolish of me to tell her that I cared for someone else, but I had only been seeking to reassure her that my heart was already given elsewhere. "I—I cannot say, Your Highness. It is better that no one knows who he is, for then he will not be in any kind of danger."

"Ah, of course." She nodded again, expression serious. No doubt she was thinking of her intemperate father-in-law, and how he definitely had the capacity to seek vengeance on anyone I might name as a suitor, and therefore be seen as a rival to the prince.

"So I think it is only a matter of standing firm, and eventually the king will see reason." I had to hope that would be the case. In that moment, I felt as if I was speaking as much to reassure myself as I was the princess. I realized, upon looking at her more closely, that she must not be much more than a year or two older than I, which meant she must have been very young when she was sent here to be Prince Harlin's bride. How lucky she was that at least her future husband had been young as well, and handsome and kind. Many princesses were not nearly so fortunate.

"His Majesty is not so very good at seeing reason, I fear," the princess said, and then paused, as if she had just thought that saying such things to a commoner like myself was perhaps not all that wise. Then she made an off-hand gesture, perhaps in an attempt to brush away any self-doubt. "I thought him quite fearsome when I first came here, but in the beginning he was all joviality. It was only as time wore on, and His Highness and I still had no son, that I could see his patience with me beginning to wear thin."

And no doubt he was not very kind about it. My own father's faults were numerous, but I had to hope he would not have behaved similarly in a similar situation. "It is not the king's regard that should concern you, but that of your husband," I told her. "And he will remain your husband, no matter what the king might say."

"Yes, that is what His Highness told me." Lorelis smoothed the heavy silk of her skirt over her knees, palms flat on the fabric. Sapphires sparkled on her fingers to match the ones in her ears. "He said that only he can sue for annulment, and he has no intention of doing so, and therefore his father can bluster all he likes."

I had not known that, and Her Highness's words relieved me somewhat. For what could the king do to coerce his unwilling son? Hold a knife to his throat? I rather doubted it.

"You see?" I said gently. "There is no reason to worry. But I am sorry if anything I have said or done might have caused you distress."

"No, not that," she replied at once. "Or rather, I was worried, when I heard how lovely you were supposed to be. That is not your fault, however." She seemed to catch herself, and gave a little shake of her head. "No, that is not what I meant. Only that your beauty is perhaps a gift of the gods, and certainly not a fault."

A curse, perhaps. For if I had been a plain girl, my father would have married me off as soon as he could, knowing that I might not get a better offer. Instead, he had held on to me, thinking of me only as a prize that might be used to bargain his way out of trouble. Surely the duke would not have had such an interest in me if I had been ill-favored.

But if I had been married off early, I would never have met Tobyn, and so I could not curse my present lot overmuch. All I wanted now was a way to extricate myself from this situation.

"Clearly, my looks matter very little to His Highness, which is as it should be," I told the princess. "He must care for you very much, or he would not defend you so vigorously to his father. And so I think we must all wait until the king wearies of this game, which will be uncomfortable for everyone involved. But in the end he must relent."

"I do hope you are right, Mistress Kelsden," Princess Lorelis said. She glanced up at the hour candle on the mantel, and a flicker of worry passed over her face. "It grows late, and I will be expected down at dinner. I see no point in giving His Majesty yet another reason to be displeased with me." Rising from the divan, she added, "I will tell my husband of your kindness to me. He...was not all that approving of you when last we spoke, thinking you must be colluding with the king somehow, but it now is clear to me that you have no interest in being queen one day."

A stab of annoyance went through me, but I found myself nodding. I had no wish for an argument at that point, especially when there was no need to defend myself to the princess. Prince Harlin could think what he liked. Perhaps if our situations had been reversed, I would have thought rather the same thing.

Still, my tone was probably sharper than I had intended as I replied, "No, Your Highness, I can assure you that I have absolutely *no* desire to be queen."

She didn't seem to hear the annoyance in my voice, or at least affected not to notice. "Thank you, Mistress Kelsden. I shall sleep better this night, and I hope you will as well."

An almost queenly incline of her head, and then she was off. Because Rashelle had made herself scarce, the princess was forced to let herself out. Perhaps I should have hurried ahead to open the door for her? Ah, well, too late now.

But once she was gone, I felt myself sag a bit. Although I would have said I had no appetite at all, right then I did wonder if the constant confrontations had begun to wear me down, and I required some food to restore me. Presumably Rashelle would be back soon with my dinner tray. Then, not so very long after that, I would see Tobyn again, and we could discuss what to do. There had to be some way he could use his magic to get me out of this place, no matter what he might have said in the past to the contrary.

When Rashelle appeared a few minutes later, she did have my tray...but she had also not come alone. A rather forbidding woman, seeming to be of an age with my father, had accompanied her. As Rashelle hurried into the main salon to set the dinner tray on one of the tables there, the strange woman paused where the entryway opened up into the salon and fixed me with a narrowed eye.

"I am Mistress Thranson, the chatelaine. It has been decided that you should no longer be left accompanied during the evening. There have been guards stationed outside your door each night, but that is not sufficient. Rashelle here will sleep in the small room off your study."

I stared at this apparition with a sinking heart. The one solace I had had throughout this entire ordeal was the chance to see Tobyn each night, to know that we could speak and plan... and then kiss...without fear of interruption. But now, to have a chaperone just on the other side of the room where I must work at the spinning wheel? It was not to be borne.

Although I knew I fought a losing battle, I still decided that I must register some sort of protest. "Mistress Thranson, Rashelle has been a very good attendant for me, but I fear I see no need for her to attend me night and day. I would not wish to deprive her of her own quarters in the servants' wing."

A tightening of her already thin lips, and Mistress Thranson replied, "Do not worry about whether you are depriving her of anything, my lady. She is here to serve you. And I know there is a comfortable bed in that chamber, so she will not suffer in any way."

True, that room did possess a bed. Not so large and elaborate as the one I slept in, but still, it was most likely a more comfortable situation than wherever Rashelle might sleep in the servants' wing. I had only been in and out of the chamber off the study two or three times at most, and so I did not recall much else of the furnishings. Most likely it had belonged to the lady's maid of the king's mistress, the one who had been sent packing some time ago.

During this exchange, Rashelle had been standing off to one side, listening to our debate. I turned to her and said, "And what are your thoughts on this matter, Rashelle? For if you would prefer to keep our current arrangement, I will do what I can to make sure nothing changes."

She shook her head, even as Mistress Thranson said, "It does not matter what she does or does not prefer. She is a servant in the king's household, and will go where she is told."

There was such a note of command in the older woman's tone that I knew I dared not continue to argue the subject. I might have been put in this suite under the guise of being an honored guest—and possible new bride to the prince—but I had no power here, no say in anything, except perhaps which gown I would wear that day.

Also, I worried if I protested too much, Mistress Thranson might become suspicious, and wonder why I was so concerned about sleeping without a chaperone in the suite. That would never do. All I could hope then was that Rashelle would turn out to be a heavy sleeper...or perhaps that Tobyn might know a bit of magic to make sure she slumbered soundly, even if that was not her usual habit.

"Of course, Mistress Thranson," I said then, and hoped my tone was sufficiently meek. "That room will do very well for Rashelle, and perhaps it will help her in the mornings, too, for she will not have so far to go to ensure that the fire is lit and the hot water for my tea already available when I rise in the morning."

This sop to her wishes did not appear to mollify Mistress Thranson overmuch, for her mouth remained compressed. Voice somewhat acid, she said, "It is her duty to awake early enough to make sure such things are managed, and you should not have to worry about her comfort. Of course, perhaps these matters were viewed differently in the household of your merchant father than they are here in the palace."

If I had been affecting the manners of a great lady and attempting to pass as a member of the court, perhaps such an utterance would have offended me. But since I knew my origins all too well and had done nothing to hide them, I only smothered a smile. No doubt the good mistress was imagining a house with some ten servants or so, and not our meager three. Well, two, now that Cordell had gone.

"Perhaps," I said mildly, hoping that she would let the topic go. I could see that she was intractable on the subject, and by that point I only wished to get to my dinner, rapidly growing cold under its silver-lidded tray.

Whether it was my tone or something else in my face or manner, I could not say, but Mistress Thranson seemed satisfied by my response. "Rashelle will get her things from the servants' wing and be back soon. Enjoy your supper, my lady."

It sounded more like a command than a pleasant request. She turned on her heel and headed back to the door, Rashelle tagging along a few paces behind. Then they were gone, and I was alone.

But not for long. Biting back a sigh, I took up my dinner tray and attempted to resign myself to an existence where Tobyn would no longer have free run of my suite.

I did tell Rashelle that I must do something for the king each night in the study, and that I must not be disturbed for any reason. Her blue eyes lit up with curiosity, but she knew better than to pry, especially in a matter involving the king. No doubt she had already been wondering why the study door was always kept locked. Unfortunately for her, she would get no further illumination from me. It would have been too difficult to explain away that spinning wheel, and why I only used it at night.

"Of course, my lady," she said, and left it at that.

Her response did not do much to reassure me. That night I stayed in my bed much longer than I normally would, waiting to make sure she slept before I ventured forth. True, she had been warned that I would move about the suite at night, but I thought it better that she be asleep before I tiptoed into the study.

As soon as I had shut the door and locked it behind me, I heard Tobyn's voice, pitched low. "So we are to have a chaperone, it seems."

"Yes," I murmured, hurrying across the room to him.

At least there was no nonsense this time about trying to stop me; he took me into his arms at once, warm, comforting, his lips brushing the top of my head before he drew me closer so he could kiss me properly on the mouth. Despite everything, warmth flowed through me. Somehow I could not be quite so worried when in his presence.

He said, "You have had quite the day, haven't you, Annora?"

"So you've heard?"

"I heard some rumor of further foolishness by the king. Does he truly think he can have the prince's marriage annulled?"

"He seems to believe it with all his heart," I replied, my words barely above a whisper. Yes, I had stopped to listen at Rashelle's door and thought I heard a faint snore from within, but even so I knew I must be careful. "Of course, Prince Harlin is fighting him, and it seems he must be the one to seek the annulment, but...."

My words died away. I thought again of what Princess Lorelis had said, how the king always got his way. Of course he did. He was the king. What could any of us possibly do to prevail against his power, his position?

Tobyn's voice was also no more than a murmur, but it still seemed to reverberate through me, soothing, calm. "My dear, it is surely not so bad as all that. As you said, the prince must be the one to initiate his separation from Princess Lorelis, and that does not seem very likely. What all this has done is show how very desperate the king is to keep his source of gold close by. He was never to be trusted, but now?" I felt rather than saw Tobyn shake his head. "I fear for you, Annora."

Well, that was not very reassuring! I pulled away and gazed up into the shadows that forever obscured his face. "Then take me from here," I whispered fiercely. "There must be some way, something you have not thought of."

He seemed to tense. "I have already told you that the magic I possess is not of that sort. I cannot turn you invisible, nor snap my fingers and have you safely back in your father's house. No, we must think of something else."

What that might be, I couldn't begin to guess. He stepped away from me and went to the spinning wheel, one gloved finger touching the sharp end of the spindle. "In the meantime," he went on quietly, "let us give the king the gold he desires above all else...but perhaps not quite so much of it."

I stared at Tobyn, mystified. "But will that not only anger him?"

"Perhaps. If he asks you why there is not as much tonight, you will tell him it is because you are tired and distracted, and now you are to have no privacy at all. If you make it seem as if your maidservant's presence here is affecting your ability to produce the gold, it is possible that he may decide it is not such a good thing for you to have a chaperone after all, and will send your lady's maid back to sleep in the servants' wing where she belongs."

His suggestion made some sense, and yet I worried about invoking the king's wrath. Then again, what on earth could he do to me? I was already the next thing to a prisoner, and he seemed to be bent on making me his son's wife, even though neither of us would have anything to do with such a mad enterprise. Perhaps it might be better to show King Elsdon that the prodigious amounts of gold I'd been providing him were by no means a surety.

"Very well," I said quietly. "Let us do just that."

I settled myself at the wheel and took up the straw, just as I had done many nights before. And once again the gold flowed out, although I noted that the thread did not seem to be quite as thick this time, and its weight upon the bobbin when I was done not nearly as heavy as it should be. I lifted the golden thread, then went to Tobyn, who had been watching in silence the whole time.

"It does seem quite meager," I told him, handing him the little golden ball of fibers.

"In contrast, yes, it does. But it is still enough to feed a family for a year." He went quiet as he weighed the product of that night's work in the palm of one gloved hand. "Ah, well. We will see where this stratagem takes us. In the meantime, I have Master Jamsden working on your appeal, although neither of us is terribly sanguine about its hopes of success."

Neither was I, but I saw no reason to state the obvious. "Thank him for his efforts," I said. "Even if it should prove that they are in vain."

Tobyn made no answer, instead slipping the ball of golden thread into the pocket of my dressing gown. For the briefest second, I could feel his fingers brush against my hip, and a thrill went through me at that touch. How I wished he would not pull away, would perhaps slide his hand up to my waist.

But of course he did not. He took a step backward, voice unruffled as he said in quiet tones, "We shall see. In the meantime, it is best if I go."

I wanted to beg him to stay. After everything I had suffered that day, I wanted only to feel his arms around me again, to experience the reassurance of his touch, even if I knew such comfort was misleading at best. With all that, I managed to nod meekly and murmur, "Yes, I suppose it is best."

A sort of low growl came from his throat, and in the next instant he was beside me, head lowering so he might taste my mouth again. I opened my lips to him, wanting nothing more than this, the two of us joined, if only for a few seconds.

He whispered, "Ah, Annora. Every day it becomes more difficult to leave you here. But take heart, my darling. You shall not be the king's prisoner forever."

Another kiss, one that left me gasping, and he was gone, my arms reaching for empty air. I let out a startled little sound, then closed my lips and hoped I had not been loud enough for Rashelle to overhear. Perhaps one day I would get used to how Tobyn came and went.

In the meantime, I patted the ball of thread in my pocket, then blew out the candles in the study and closed the door behind me, locking it as I left. Outside the door to the room where Rashelle slept, I paused, then listened for any sign that she might be wakeful. But I heard nothing, save the same soft snores from before. It seemed that she had slept through the entire time Tobyn was here.

I uttered a mental prayer to the gods for watching over me, then tiptoed back to my own bedchamber, where I pulled off my dressing gown and slipped under the heavy quilted counterpane. It seemed we had survived our first night with a chaperone. I could only hope there would not be many more such nights.

Chapter Thirteen

"What is this?" the king thundered, and I had to do everything in my power not to cower like a kicked dog.

"It—it is your gold, Your Majesty."

"And where is the rest of it?"

"I—" I quailed, then said, not quite meeting his eyes, "That is all there is."

"Lord Edmar?"

The duke had been standing off to one side, watching this exchange. When the king addressed him, he offered an elegant, if somewhat negligent, shrug. "I did look around her suite, Your Majesty. I saw no sign that she had hidden any of it. And the chatelaine questioned the maid, who swears she has never taken anything from Mistress Kelsden's suite."

We now stood in the king's private apartments, thank the gods, and not in the audience chamber. Prince Harlin was nowhere in evidence, an absence for which I was quite grateful. He and I might be allied against King Elsdon in one matter, but that did not mean we were anything close to comfortable around one another.

When Lord Edmar had come to collect the gold that morning, he'd frowned at the meager amount I offered, and did not quite believe my explanation that I was wearied and unable to produce anything more than that. No, he had poked into every drawer, every cupboard, had even gotten down on his knees and looked under the bed while Rashelle stood off to one side, a horrified expression on her face. No doubt she had never thought she'd see a great man like the duke crawling around on the floor of a bedroom. Or perhaps she was worried that she had left some dust mice under the bed.

If she had, Lord Edmar gave no sign of noticing her poor housekeeping. He got up, brushed off his knees, and said, "I believe His Majesty would like to speak to you about this."

And so I had come to the king's apartments, which were quite richer than anything I could have imagined, with their floors of inlaid wood, and gilding on the carved beams overhead, and hangings of velvet and silk. His Majesty had not looked all that happy to see us, and his expression had grown sourer still when he regarded my pitiful offering.

"If you have not hidden the rest of the gold," he snapped, squeezing the ball of golden thread Lord Edmar had given him in his hand, "then why is there so little of it?"

"Because that is all I was able to manage, Your Majesty," I replied. My voice shook somewhat, and I did what I could to school myself to calm. After all, I knew he could not hurt me, not if he wanted more gold. Even less gold than he had expected was still better than none at all.

"'Manage'?" he repeated in incredulous tones. "What else on earth do you have to *manage*, Mistress Kelsden, other than one meager skein of gold each night?"

I have to manage your ridiculous tyrannies, I thought angrily, *which are just as bad as anything my father made me suffer.*

I had reclaimed some of my courage, but not quite enough to allow me to say such a thing out loud. Instead, I met his gaze as best I could and said, "I would not say that any of the gold I have provided is precisely meager, Your Majesty. But after yesterday's tumult, and then not being given the peace and quiet I needed to work, I am actually quite surprised that I was able to produce as much as I did. If this goes on...."

My hope was that the words would trail off in a significant manner, forcing the king to follow the veiled threat to its logical conclusion. Unfortunately, he was far too full of bluster for that.

"Tumult? What tumult? And you are alone in your suite, Mistress Kelsden, so I cannot see what you mean by saying that you have no peace and quiet."

"I am not alone," I said calmly. "Not any longer. Now it has been decided that I must have my lady's maid with me at all times. Why, I am not sure, as guards have always been posted at my door, and the windows in my apartment look out on a sheer wall some fifty feet high. I doubt there is much chance of someone scaling that wall to find entry, and a lower chance still that I would attempt to escape that way. I cannot lie and say that I do not wish to go home, but on the other hand, I would prefer to do so with all my limbs intact."

The king's expression was a study in outrage, while I got the distinct impression that Lord Edmar wished nothing more than to burst into laughter. Perhaps it had been some time before anyone had confronted His Majesty in such a way. Perhaps they never had...and therein lay the problem.

"You impertinent—" He broke off there, as if unable to come up with a phrase that adequately described my cheek.

"I do apologize if you think I was being impertinent, Your Majesty. I was only telling you the truth of my situation."

He glanced over at the duke, as if imploring him to step in. With a slight shake of his head, Lord Edmar uncrossed his arms and came toward me. "Mistress Kelsden, forgive us, but I believe both His Majesty and I are having a difficult time understanding why the presence of your lady's maid should discomfit you so."

"Because it takes a great deal of concentration to spin straw into gold. Why do you think I perform that task in the quiet hours of the night? Because it is the only time when I know I can work undisturbed. And if I have to worry about my maid knocking on the door, or asking if I want a glass of milk...well, then, you see the difficulty."

Once again the two men exchanged a glance. The king spoke. "But you must see, Mistress Kelsden, that your status has changed immeasurably. As the affianced bride of my son—"

I couldn't help laughing outright at that description. "The what? I beg your pardon, Your Majesty, but I think His Highness might have a different view of the situation, given that he is already happily married and clearly has no interest in me at all. So I cannot see that there has been much change in my status, when all is said and done."

King Elsdon's jaw jutted in a way that I had begun to recognize did not bode well for me...or anyone else who might stand in his way. "He is adjusting to the idea. He will take you as his wife, for the good of the kingdom."

"Indeed?" I said dryly. "I must confess that I don't precisely enjoy the idea of being 'good' for someone. You make me sound like a spoonful of cod liver oil."

The duke grinned, saying, "Ah, Mistress Kelsden, I think most men at court would agree you are far sweeter than that."

This remark did not seem to please the king, for he shot a venomous look at Lord Edmar before returning his attention to me. "He will see reason. As you will as well." The entire time he'd been clutching my pitiful contribution to the treasury in his hand. Now he tossed it onto a side table, where it landed with an oddly musical sound. "Do not offer me such a meager showing again. Do you understand?"

I nodded, too cowed to say anything else. Yes, he might be full of bluster and the most wrong-headed man I had ever met...but he was also the king. I dared not defy him openly.

It seemed that Tobyn's and my plan had failed.

All was not lost, however, for later that day Rashelle informed me that she would be sleeping in the servants' wing that night. I expressed surprised at the abrupt about-face, assured her that the change had nothing to do with my opinion of her service... and exulted inwardly.

She had more news to impart, however. It seemed that not long after my audience with His Majesty, the ambassador from Farendon appeared at court, more or less demanding an audience. News had reached him of the king's plans for an annulment, and he wished to make certain that this was all merely rumors and gossip, and nothing of the truth.

Although the small doses I had had of the king were more than enough, I could not help wishing that I might have been present during that conversation, if only to see what his excuses to the ambassador might have been. Yes, such actions weren't entirely without precedent, but those previous annulments in my country's history had come about after a much longer period, when some ten years had passed without an heir being produced. Prince Harlin and Princess Lorelis had barely been married three years, and she was a young girl hardly out of the schoolroom when she came here. Asking for an annulment in such circumstances must have sounded wildly precipitate.

Gossip did spread at court like fire in a hay field—which I assumed was how Tobyn had somehow managed to hear of the king's plans as well—but no one seemed to be talking much about the outcome of that particular conversation between the king and the ambassador, or at least they had not done so in front of my maid. What that meant, I couldn't be sure. I could only be glad that I would be able to see Tobyn without having to worry about Rashelle overhearing our exchanges.

I was waiting for him that night, watching the one corner where he most particularly liked to appear. As soon as he stepped forth from the shadows, I ran to him and threw my arms around him.

"It worked!" I exclaimed. "That is, the king was very angry, but he must have decided that it was not worth the risk to get so much less gold than he had expected, and so Rashelle has been returned to the servants' wing."

"That is very good news," Tobyn said, but he did not sound particularly enthusiastic.

I stepped away from him and glanced up at the hood which shrouded his face, wishing for the hundredth time that I might be able to see something of his expression. How much longer did he intend to conceal himself thus? Surely by now he must know that I cared only for him, and not what the pox might have done to his face. "What is wrong?" I asked. "I would have thought you would be pleased."

"I am. It is good to not have to worry about being overheard. But...."

"But?"

"Just that I am concerned, after hearing something of the outcome of the king's meeting with the Farendonian ambassador."

That reply surprised me. "And how is it you know anything of that?"

"I could say it is because I have my spies, but really, it is more that my clients number some of the wealthier ladies of the court, and they do like to gossip when they come in to discuss a commission. Lady Aurelis came with her attendants to order a new diadem, and she was all abuzz."

"But how is it that she heard anything at all? It is not as if the king and the ambassador had a shouting match in front of all the court, is it?"

That question did elicit a chuckle. "No, of course not. You are sequestered up here in your tower, Annora, for otherwise you would know that very little happens at court that does not end up being the subject of that night's dinner conversation. Perhaps a door was not shut all the way, and a servant overheard something. Perhaps the ambassador was grumbling as he took his leave of His Majesty. One way or another, these things tend to get out."

"Then I am very glad I do not really live at court," I said with a slight shudder. "One could never call one's life one's own."

"Not really. Not in the way you are used to. At any rate, the interview did not go well. The ambassador seemed to make it clear that Farendon would never let such an insult to one of its royal daughters pass by lightly."

"They would go to war over such a thing?" Such a notion seemed incredible to me. Yes, an annulment would be quite the insult to Lorelis, but....

"Wars have been fought over less." Tobyn must have noted the worry in my face, for he reached out and took my hands, then gave them a reassuring squeeze. "I am not saying that is what will happen here, but I do think the ambassador's response has the king rethinking his strategy."

"Well, good," I replied. "For he is being quite mad about the whole thing. If what the ambassador said has made the king reconsider his actions, then he will have to abandon the notion altogether. Perhaps he will realize that this whole scheme of forcing me to stay and make gold for him is foolish, and he will let me go."

"That would be the best outcome," Tobyn agreed. But in the next instant he was pulling me against him, holding me tight, his arms wrapped around me as if attempting to shield me from some hostile outside force.

"What is it?" I whispered. "Why are you so worried?"

"Because I fear losing this one option will only make the king that much more desperate. And desperate men can do terrible things."

I could not deny that. Right then, I wished our kingdom was just a little richer, just a little larger. Peace had existed between Purth and its neighbors for many years, but these things could, as the ambassador's veiled threats seemed to prove, change in an instant. If we had Keshiaar's mines or Farendon's rich farmlands, perhaps we would have fared better. But a good deal of the kingdom was hilly and rocky, not suited for much more than grazing sheep. More fertile land lay to the south, where the estate Cordell had inherited most likely was located, since he had said it possessed a vineyard. Even so, Purth's wealth was not nearly enough to compete with any of the neighboring kingdoms. King Elsdon's desperate need for gold still seemed alien to me, and yet I thought I understood somewhat of where that desire had been born.

And because I knew all this, I would not contradict Tobyn. I could only let him hold me in his arms as I tried to tell myself that comfort was enough, and all would be well.

Unfortunately, my experiences of the past week told me I was being far too optimistic.

Despite my misgivings, nothing occurred during the next several days to make me think anything was terribly amiss. True, the king showed no sign of letting me go free, despite

Master Jamsden's appeals to the High Court. They could pass their judgment, but they did not have the power to force King Elsdon to do other than what he pleased.

Because we did not want to upset him, Tobyn and I made sure that the amounts of gold spun in the night were at least equal to what I had produced in the past. Each morning, Lord Edmar would come to take it away. I could tell nothing from his brisk and breezy manner what confidences—if any—the king had shared with him, and I dared not ask. The unsettled nature of my existence then did worry me, but I did not want to press for too much information. That would only tell the duke I was not yet reconciled to my situation. Better that he think me meek and cowed for now.

At least I saw Tobyn every night, and after the gold had been spun, we were able to steal a few kisses before he left. Being in his presence comforted me somewhat, although I still wished he could find a way to free me, one that did not involve the impotent wranglings of the High Court. Every time I asked, however, he would only shake his head sadly and say it was not possible.

"For you know you would be long gone from here, if I but possessed the talent to make such a thing happen," he told me. I could hear the regret and the impotent anger in his voice, and I knew he was uttering the truth, and nothing more.

One thing he did bring me that was of some comfort was a letter from my sister Iselda. How he had gotten it from her, I did not know for sure, although I guessed Master Jamsden had been involved somehow. I had read it so many times that

I practically knew it by heart, this one small connection with my family.

Dear Annora, she had written, *I am so glad to know that you are well. Father has been in quite a state this week, and I can see why, since you have told me that it is mostly his doing that you are locked up in the palace. I suppose there are worse places to be locked up, though. A dungeon, or a cave in a cliff, or an abandoned mine. What does it look like? Is everything made of solid gold? Are all the ladies very fine? I would love to see it for myself, although of course I should not like being locked up.*

I am trying to keep on with my studies, for I know you would be disappointed if I did not. It is hard to concentrate, though, knowing that you are off being held in a tower, like a princess in one of my stories. Do you think anyone will come to rescue you? I daresay I can't think of anyone who would even know how to scale a tower wall, but of course you are older and have a larger acquaintance than I do.

Maralys down the street has a cat who had kittens. Father has been in such a strange mood this week that he even said I could have one when I asked him, and you know how he feels about animals in the house. I am hoping he will not change his mind, for I have picked out the sweetest little gray and white kitty, and I would be quite sad if she ended up going to another home.

Well, Master Amardon is here to quiz me on my sums. I must say goodbye now, for he will be cross if I keep him waiting.

Your affectionate sister,
Iselda Kelsden

Each time I read this missive, it brought a smile to my face, for I could so clearly hear my little sister's voice in my head. She did not seem overly distraught by my situation, but then, she was always one to see romance and adventure in everything. Good thing I had said nothing to her of Tobyn; news of a hooded man with magical powers being my suitor would have sent her into transports.

But then, he did almost the same thing to me. Still he would not let me see his face, and I decided I would not let that matter. I had fallen in love with *him,* not what he looked like. Indeed, did not ordinary people change over the years anyway? Their faces became lined, or they grew plump. They were not, in appearance, at any rate, the same people their spouses had fallen in love with so many years earlier. Perhaps Tobyn was doing me a favor in forcing me to be in love with the man and not his face.

What mattered far more was how my heart thrilled at the sound of his voice, so filled with yearning when he said my name, or how his arms felt around me, or the sweetness of his kisses. Even with all that, I knew he held himself back. We were alone together, and it would have been easy enough for him to guide me to my bedchamber so we could let matters progress further. He cared too much about my honor, though, to ask such a thing of me. Not that I would have minded. I had begun to understand that our kisses, as dizzying as they might be, were only a prelude to much more satisfying pleasures, although such things must be forbidden to an unmarried woman.

And Tobyn had said nothing of marriage, spoke very little of a possible future together. At times, I almost felt that he held back because he believed we could not have such a future, although he had not said anything of that nature to me, possibly fearing an argument. I would not bring up the subject, either, for really, our acquaintance was still so new. I knew my feelings, examined them when I was alone, told myself sternly that I must be very sure of them, for Tobyn still seemed reluctant at times, as if fighting with himself over whether he should surrender to the connection between us.

More than a week had passed since I was brought here to the palace. Even though a span of ten days or so should not seem so very long, my life before becoming the king's prisoner had begun to feel indistinct and dim, like something I had read in a book. Sevendre passed into Octevre, and I wondered if King Elsdon would ever relent and allow me to return to my family. Because he had apparently given up on making me his new daughter-in-law, I did not even have visits from Prince Harlin or his wife to break up the monotony of my days. At night I had Tobyn, if only for an hour or so, but during my waking hours I only saw Rashelle, who seemed less inclined toward conversation than she once had, perhaps because of some admonishments from Mistress Thranson.

But then there came a knock at the door that afternoon, and there again was Lord Edmar.

I gazed at him in some confusion as I set down my needlework, for earlier that day he had already come and retrieved the previous night's gold from me. "Your Grace?"

He bowed. I noticed that he was very finely dressed in a doublet of deep wine-colored velvet. "Mistress Kelsden, the king wishes to speak with you."

My heart began to beat a little faster. What had prompted this invitation, I could not say. Certainly Tobyn and I had labored to make sure that His Majesty would have no reason to find fault with the gold we brought forth each night. And with no one to chaperone me, my benefactor...the man I loved...had managed to evade discovery. So why the summons now?

I knew any questions I asked would be ignored. Besides, I would discover the reason for this audience soon enough. After setting my embroidery down on the low table in front of the divan, I stood. "Of course," I said. "I am always at His Majesty's disposal."

Normally, the wry tone with which I delivered that particular statement would have made Lord Edmar's mouth twitch at least, even if he would not allow himself an outright smile. Now, though, he only nodded, and my heartbeat speeded up that much more. I had a suspicion that I might not care much for the motivation behind this audience the king had requested.

Attempting to delay would not help me, though. I went to the duke's side, and Rashelle opened the door so we both might exit. It was not until we had reached the end of the corridor and had begun to descend the staircase that Lord Edmar spoke.

"You are looking rather pale these days, Mistress Kelsden. Confinement does not seem to agree with you."

"I have not seen the sun for some time, Your Grace," I retorted. "I fear that His Majesty cares only that I produce enough gold for him, and not that I get any fresh air."

"Ah, well, that circumstance may change in the near future," he said darkly, and I frowned. Not that I was precisely overjoyed by my current situation, but his tone seemed to indicate it might soon take a turn for the worse.

In that unsettled state of mind, I went with him, not to the king's audience chamber, thank the gods, but to his royal suite. Whatever humiliation he intended to heap on me this time, at least it would not be in front of a crowd of amused, uncaring nobles.

The day outside was quite gray and lowering, and so a fire blazed in the massive hearth of gilded and carved oak. The servant who had let us into the suite bowed and returned to the door—in case someone else required entry, I supposed.

King Elsdon stood in front of the fire, his expression cheerier than I had seen it in some time. His pale blue eyes danced, and he hurried over to greet the duke and me.

"Ah, Mistress Kelsden, Lord Edmar. Very good. Spiced wine?"

I sent a mystified glance up at the duke, and his shoulders lifted ever so slightly in response. This unexpected good humor on the part of His Majesty did not put me at ease, but rather accomplished quite the opposite. But I knew I could not refuse the offer.

"Thank you, Your Majesty."

He gestured, and a footman stepped toward us bearing a tray with three silver goblets. The duke and I each took one, and King Elsdon helped himself to the one remaining. Duty fulfilled, the footman resumed his watchful position against the wall, empty tray tucked under his arm.

Awkwardly, I held my goblet, waiting for one of the other men to drink first. That seemed the safest thing to do. Should not the king have precedence in this, as in all other matters of etiquette?

Seeming to notice my unease, Lord Edmar said, "Thank you for the refreshment, Your Majesty."

King Elsdon nodded and helped himself to a healthy swallow. The duke lifted his own glass, eyes catching mine for an instant, as if to say that it was now all right for me to drink.

The silver of the goblet was warm against my hands. I took what reassurance from that I could, then allowed myself to sip at the liquid within. It was warm and rich and heavily spiced, not too sweet. The taste was pleasant enough, as was the heat that traced its way down my throat as I swallowed, and yet I could not allow myself to be too much at ease.

Once we had all drunk, the king turned toward me. "Mistress Kelsden, there is something I must needs say to you."

"Yes, Your Majesty?" To my relief, my voice did not shake at all. I told myself that perhaps he had had a change of heart. After all, he seemed quite jovial. It could be that he had finally realized the folly of his actions and wished to give me a friendly send-off.

That was a pleasant fiction, one I did not believe at all.

Beaming, he said, "I have been thinking a good deal on our situation, and I believe I have come upon an answer that will be advantageous for all concerned."

"You have, Your Majesty?"

"Yes. Indeed, I do not know why I did not think of it before, for it is such an elegant solution. I might have saved us all a good deal of wasted time." He paused then, fixing me with his pale eyes, and a shiver went down my spine, despite the warmth from the spiced wine I had just drunk.

"You, Annora, will become my wife, and the next queen of Purth."

Chapter Fourteen

I stared at him, thinking he must have gone mad. Or perhaps he had gone mad some time ago, and I was only now just noticing.

"Y-your Majesty?" I stammered. In that moment, I knew I wore an expression of dismay. Unfortunately, I could not think of how to remove it.

But the king was so caught up in his own cleverness that he did not seem to notice my distinct lack of enthusiasm. "Yes, of course," he said. "I do not know why I wasted valuable time attempting to convince my son that he should put away his wife and take you instead. If he wants that meaching milksop to be the mother of his sons—if she ever manages the task, that is—then so be it. I have been too long without a wife, and you will do very well."

I did not think I would do very well, no, not at all. Every fiber of my being shrank at the idea of being the king's wife.

Why, he was almost old enough to be my grandfather, let alone my father.

Of course I could not say any of these things out loud. Possibly it was treason for me to even be thinking them. But oh, gods, what could I do now? As Lorelis had said, the king always got his way in everything...or nearly everything. True, his scheme to have me marry his son had gone nowhere, but that was because Prince Harlin would have none of it, and the ambassador from Farendon had made it clear that his country's king would not react well to such ill treatment of his daughter. But in this terrible matter, the only players were King Elsdon and myself. I had no power, none at all, and so my protests would count for very little.

Because he was watching me, clearly expecting some kind of response, I swallowed and said, "This is...unexpected, Your Majesty. I understand the honor you are offering me, but how will the people react to your taking a commoner as your queen?"

He did not much like that question; his gray-frosted brows pulled together, and his jaw set. "It is not a question of how the people will react, for I care little for that. However, I have already anticipated this problem. I will grant you a title—you will be the new Countess of Wellinsdale. Once that is done, no one dare protest that your rank is insufficient for a king's wife."

Oh, dear gods, what now? I had heard that the king did have the power to create new titles if he so wished, but he had always been parsimonious with such largesse, and had handed out very few such titles during his tenure on the throne. Clearly, he intended to make a special exception in my case.

"I—I am honored, Your Majesty," I replied. What else could I say? All along I had thought I was trapped. Only in this moment, as I truly felt those golden chains descend upon me, did I realize that I had not understood what trapped actually meant.

I was definitely trapped now.

My present suite, it seemed, would not do for the newly created Countess of Wellinsdale and the king's affianced bride. I was taken to new apartments several floors higher and on the other side of the palace, where I looked down, not over the gardens, but the River Marden, which wound through the town. I supposed that many would think this the better view, what with the sweet-gum and goldleaf trees that lined its banks, all showing their autumn finery in blazing red and amber. As I looked at them, however, all I could think of was the inexorable passage of time, and how little would now be left to me, for the king had decreed that we should marry in three days. No doubt he would have pressed for the wedding to take place even sooner than that, but such affairs took time to plan and execute, even those that had been so hastily conceived.

Because he had found me before, I knew that Tobyn should have no trouble locating my new suite; indeed, one of his clients had probably already carried the tale of the king's precipitous engagement to him. No, the real problem was that my position as countess and soon-to-be queen meant that I did not have the luxury of solitude any longer. I had thought Rashelle burden enough, but now I had one lady's maid to attend to my wardrobe, and another to take care of my hair and bath, and both of them slept in a room adjoining my own. When I had protested to Lord Edmar that such arrangements meant I would be unable to spin any gold, he'd only smiled and said that the king did not mind my missing a few days, since after the wedding I would be given a chamber in his apartments where I could create as much gold as I liked.

Something in his manner had seemed almost mocking, and I said, "I suppose this pleases you, to see me made a puppet like this."

"No," he replied, but that hint of a smile lingered around the corners of his mouth. "It never pleases me to see a woman I want taken by another. But the king has laid his claim on you now, and I would certainly never attempt to stand in his way." Head tilted to one side, he added, "Do you now regret refusing me? I believe you had some concern as to my age, but His Majesty is a good fifteen years my senior."

"I know," I said, nettled. Had not that loathsome notion been rattling around in my head ever since the king made his outrageous proposal? The king would reach sixty in a few more years, a number which made the duke's forty and two far less repulsive. "But as for regret, my only true regret is that my father could not manage his compulsions at the dice table. Were it not for that, none of this would have happened in the first place."

"True." A pause, and then the duke went on, "I have heard he is overjoyed by this news. Not merely by your elevation to countess, and soon queen, but also by the knowledge that no member of the royal family—which he will soon be, by marriage—may be prosecuted for debt. That should be very convenient for him." He gave me a scornful little bow and went out after delivering his remark, leaving me seething.

That all may have been true. At any rate, I was already angry with my father, so a bit of extra pique did not matter one way or another. What bothered me the most, though, was that I had no one to comfort me in this, no one I could talk to. Dinnertime had not yet arrived, and so many hours must pass before Tobyn could possibly risk coming to see me.

At least the king did not expect me to sit in state with him at supper. No, it seemed he would rather wait to display me as his queen, to keep me away from court until my position was absolutely unassailable. In the meantime, ever since the formal announcement had been made, my suite had been filled with dressmakers and their assistants, and I had been stuck as full of pins as a hedgehog in one interminable fitting after another.

I had also been given something of a companion, for lack of a better word. In the wake of the dressmakers came a very grand lady perhaps some fifteen years or so older than I, or even more. I found it difficult to tell for certain, as her face had been expertly painted, and her figure, in its gown of bronze-toned damask, as slender as my own.

This lady introduced herself to me as Shelenna, Duchess of Ballinsvane, saying, "My husband and His Majesty are old friends, and so he thought it best that I come to see you, to help guide you through the few next days. No doubt this is all quite tumultuous, and you are still trying to take it all in."

Her pronouncement was nothing more than the truth, and so I nodded.

"Very good. I have already given instructions to the dress-makers, and so they know what is required. But I thought I might look at the jewelry His Majesty has given you, and see what else might be needed."

I began to get up from the divan where we sat so I might fetch the little casket of jewels that had been given to me for my use. At once the duchess laid her hand on my arm.

"No, my dear. It is not for you to perform such a task. Have that girl over there"—she flicked a hand at the elder of my two maidservants, the one named Felinda—"bring it to us."

Felinda, who was somewhat younger than Rashelle and far less composed, jumped slightly, then hurried to do as the duchess had bidden her. The box sat on the top shelf of the wardrobe in my bedchamber, and so she required some time to retrieve it, given that this apartment was so much larger than the last one I had occupied.

While we waited for her, the duchess turned and appeared to look me over from head to toe. "Well," she said frankly, "I can see why His Majesty would be so impetuous in making you his bride, for you are quite the beauty, aren't you?"

Hot blood rushed to my cheeks, but I managed to say, "Thank you, Your Grace."

"None of that," she replied at once. "We are equals, Annora. That is, we are equals in this moment. In a few days' time, you will be queen, and then I must address you as 'Your Majesty,' unless you give me leave to use your name."

Truly, the thought of anyone, let alone this elegant and intimidating lady, addressing me as "Your Majesty" was quite enough to send chills over me once again. I did not want to be queen. Not King Elsdon's queen now, nor Prince Harlin's in the future. The very thought of the king kissing me, let alone....

Somehow I managed to prevent myself from shuddering. No matter what else happened, I had to make this Lady Shelenna and everyone else around me think that I was quite happy to be marrying the king. After all, young women were married off to older men all the time. Most people would not think anything so strange about the situation, except perhaps that enough attractive girls of my age or thereabout already existed in the peerage, and so the king's choice of a mere merchant's daughter might seem somewhat odd.

"Of course...Shelenna," I said, hoping that she had not heard the way I hesitated before saying her name. "I do thank you for your guidance."

She waved a hand. Garnets and topaz winked from her fingers. Her hair was a rich russet shade, quite unusual, as were her amber eyes. Perhaps those auburn locks of hers had been enhanced a bit, perhaps not. But no one could argue that she was not a very striking woman.

Felinda appeared then, holding the small brass-bound box that contained the jewelry the king had given me to wear. In it as well was the pendant Tobyn had created. I had not put it on this morning, although most days it lay snugged in the hollow of my throat, a constant reminder of his regard for me. Why I had not worn it today, I could not say for sure, except that it did not quite go with the dove-gray gown I wore, with its trimming of silver.

Before I could reach for the box, the duchess snagged it from Felinda's fingers. "Thank you," she said, then turned toward me, effectively dismissing the serving girl. Felinda retreated to a corner, although not before having to dodge one of the dressmakers, who seemed to have appeared from nowhere, a bolt of deep green and gold damask clutched in her arms.

"What think you of this, my lady?" the woman asked, freeing a length from the bolt so I might see the way the colors of the silk shifted as she ran a hand under the fabric.

"It's lovely," I began.

But Shelenna broke in, saying, "I am not sure that particular shade of gold will do well with her ladyship's complexion. Something not quite so brassy, I think."

The dressmaker bobbed her head and retreated, and I refrained from letting out a sigh. Really, what difference did it make if one particular gown made me look a little sallow? Although I did not yet know how I would manage it, I was determined that this wedding would not take place, which meant I doubted I'd ever wear any of these gowns. I could only hope that they might be gifted to some other women of the court, so all that fabric and work should not be wasted.

Lowering her voice, the duchess went on, "You do not need to approve everything they bring to you. I understand that it may be overwhelming to you to have all these choices, but you will be the queen of Purth. You must always keep in mind that your appearance will reflect on the king as well, and so you must be impeccable."

I nodded.

"Well, then," she went on, "let us see what you have here. Judging by the size of this box, I can tell that you will need a much larger jewelry wardrobe, but we must begin somewhere."

With that she lifted the lid and set it down on the low table in front of the divan, then began arranging the pieces on the tabletop as well. Truly, they did look rather impressive laid out like that; once Tobyn had given me the ruby pendant, I had not paid much attention to the jewels the king had lent me for my use. Now, though, I realized there were sapphires and garnets and pearls, and hanging ear drops of golden filigree.

"These can do for a start," the duchess said, "but they are rather meager for a countess, let alone a queen."

To my eyes, it seemed that uncounted riches lay before me. I knew I did not have much experience with such things, however, and so I only nodded.

Then she drew out Tobyn's pendant. Her eyes widened, and she said, "But this is Master Slade's work, is it not?"

"Who?" I asked, my tone all innocence.

"Master Slade. He is a goldsmith here in the city, and does wondrous work. I have a few of his pieces myself. But I had not thought that the king had gifted Lady Ilendra with any of Master Slade's work."

"Lady Ilendra?" I repeated. I had not heard that name before.

At once the duchess shook her head. "Perhaps I should not have spoken of her. But soon you and the king will have no secrets from one another, so...."

In that I most sincerely hoped she was wrong. I had many secrets I wished to keep from the king, chief among them the true identity of the man who had made the pendant which now lay in the Lady Shelenna's hand. But of course I could not say such a thing to her, and so I only lifted an inquiring eyebrow.

"His mistress, my dear. Oh, there was really nothing all that improper about it, since after all he did not take up with Ilendra until some years after the queen had passed away. Since you were staying in the suite that had been Ilendra's, I suppose His Majesty thought you might as well have the use of her jewels, too."

To be sure, I had had a strange moment here and there when I'd stopped to think that I slept in the same bed that had once belonged to the king's mistress. But I had told myself that was some time ago, and of course they had changed the bedding since. I did think it strange that she had not taken her jewels with her when she left the palace, though. I said as much to the duchess, who shrugged.

"Oh, she took some, I think. What she left behind were the pieces she did not care for, I suppose. It does surprise me that she would have left this piece behind, however. But she was quite fair, and perhaps she thought it did not suit her coloring very well."

All that seemed very strange to me. Although the pendant Tobyn had made was far more beautiful, still the other items in the collection were lovely, far more elegant and expensive than anything I had ever imagined wearing. "What happened to her?"

Something in my tone must have alarmed the duchess, for she said hastily, "Why, nothing at all, Annora. That is, the king would not marry her, and she knew she did not have many years left before she would have difficulty finding a husband. And so she set her sights on the Earl of Ronnisleth, and after she wed him, they left the capital. They do not often come to court, which I think should not surprise anyone."

Those who were used to such behavior would not be surprised, I supposed. True, the world of the king's court had always seemed as far removed from me and my life as the very stars in the sky. It was obvious enough to me that they were far more worldly about such matters than I. My parents had always impressed on me that a woman's virtue was her greatest treasure. This Ilendra did not seem to care that she had given it over to the king, and the man she had married must not have cared, either. Or perhaps such matters were different when the king himself was involved. There were so many things about court life I did not know or understand, and in that moment I was not sure I wished to.

"Oh," I responded, my tone flat.

Apparently misjudging my reaction, the duchess said, "You must not be jealous, for of course that was several years before he met you."

I opened my mouth to correct her misconception, then decided it would be better if I said nothing. For if the duchess thought I suffered from jealousy over the king's past affairs, then she would most likely believe I had some feelings for him. I must do what I could to let that lie survive and flourish, for only by fooling everyone around me would I buy the time necessary to free myself from this hideous predicament.

"Yes, of course," I said, with the faintest of sighs.

Her eyes narrowed slightly, and then she gave a slight nod, as if pleased by my response. In that moment, I felt sure that she had been sent here to be as much a spy as a friend and confidant.

Once his pride in his cleverness had begun to wear off, the king had probably realized that my response to his proposal—if one could even call it that, since no question had actually been asked of me—lacked somewhat in enthusiasm.

"Anyway," she went on, tone brisk again, "I don't recall ever seeing Ilendra wearing a pendant such as this one, and I am sure I would have noticed."

That I did believe; even on my short acquaintance with her, I could tell that the Lady Shelenna had eyes like a hawk. "Perhaps it was not hers, but somehow got mixed in with the items she left behind?"

The duchess nodded reluctantly. "That seems the most likely explanation, although one would think that if anyone had such a piece go missing, they would have commented on it. Ah, well, some mysteries are never fully explained. It is a lovely bauble, though, and we will have to see if Master Slade can make you matching ring and earrings, and a diadem as well, so you have an entire parure. At the moment, that pendant looks somewhat lonely with nothing to match it."

Again, I could but nod. I had worn the pendant with the gold filigree ear drops in the collection, and certainly had thought nothing lacking. But then, I had very little experience of the styles and tastes of court, let alone the wealth required to support them.

One by one, she began to put all the pieces of jewelry back in the box, then fastened the lid on it. After calling Felinda back over to return the jewel box to its place in my wardrobe, the duchess rose, glinting skirts falling gracefully around her as she did so.

"It is a start, but there is nothing here that would be suitable for you to wear on your wedding day. Since we settled on the pale blush brocade for your gown, perhaps pearls? I will speak to His Majesty and request that we would like to see if any of the late queen's pieces might work."

"Oh, no," I blurted out. "I could not possibly wear anything of hers." Bad enough that I should be forced to marry King Elsdon, but to do so while wearing jewels that had belonged to his late wife? My mind recoiled at the thought.

The duchess gave me a curious look. "Whyever not? It is fitting that you should wear them. After all, you yourself will be the queen very soon."

"I—I would not wish to do anything disrespectful—"

"There is nothing disrespectful in the idea at all. Queen Nerissa has been gone these five years, and she certainly has no more need of those earrings and necklaces and diadems. Truly, it is no more than you deserve, Annora. You will be the queen. Never forget that."

After uttering that foreboding pronouncement, she took herself off, leaving me to contemplate my fate. Yes, if Tobyn and I could not come up with some sort of plan, I would be the queen.

And may the gods have mercy on me.

CHAPTER FIFTEEN

Although I dined alone that night, the experience was far different from eating off a tray in the salon in my previous suite. Here there was a separate dining chamber, albeit a rather small one, with a table that seated six. Felinda and her companion, a girl barely my age named Vianna, brought my supper to me course by course, although the food was barely lukewarm by the time I got it. These new apartments must be farther from the palace's kitchen. Not that it mattered much, as I could barely choke down a few forkfuls of the roast pheasant and the braised root vegetables. I knew I must eat something to keep my strength up, but my appetite had quite deserted me.

At least my two serving girls were too cowed being in the presence of the future queen to make any sort of comment on my barely touched plates. In silence they gathered up the uneaten food and took it away. I experienced a pang of guilt at such waste, although I knew I most likely would have made myself ill if I had attempted to force any more food down.

Then it was time for them to help me out of the heavy gown I wore, the boned stays and thick linen petticoats. Felinda braided my hair while Vianna put away my garments and shoes, and then at last it was time for me to retire for the night.

I told them to leave a candle burning on the bedside table, explaining that it would help me to feel more comfortable in my new surroundings. They only nodded and went out, closing the door behind them. I could not feel alone then, though, not truly, for I knew they would only be going to their own chamber next to mine. As far as I could tell, I would have no reason to get up in the night, for my spinning wheel had not even been brought to me here. Where it was being kept, I did not know. Perhaps the king had already had it removed to his own suite, or perhaps it still waited for me down in the apartments I had occupied until this morning. Either way, there was no study here where Tobyn might come to me.

Since there was little else I could do, I plumped up the pillows and rested my head against them. They smelled faintly of lavender, soothing and sweet. In that moment I realized how truly weary I was, how the stresses of the day had worn upon me. I had drunk very little wine with my dinner, knowing that I must stay awake until Tobyn arrived, and yet I still felt my eyelids beginning to droop, the dark blurriness of sleep encroaching at the edges of my vision.

No, I told myself. You must not fall asleep. He will be here. He will.

And then I was gone.

A gentle touch on my hand, a brush of lips against my cheek. I sat upright with a gasp, then relaxed slightly when I saw Tobyn's familiar hooded form sitting in the chair next to my bed.

"You are very beautiful when you sleep," he whispered.

"You found me."

He nodded. "As I've said before, news travels quickly. The story of your betrothal to the king was all over the town like wildfire. After that, it wasn't so very difficult to discover where you'd been brought." Reaching out, he wrapped gloved fingers around my hand nearest him where it rested on the coverlet. "Annora, how do you fare?"

"How do I fare?" I shook my head. "Better now that you are here, but still I cannot help but think that I have fallen into some terrible nightmare, one from which I cannot awake."

"It is a nightmare." His fingers tightened on mine. "I never thought the king would push matters so far."

"Well, now that he has, is there anything we can do about it?"

For a long moment, Tobyn said nothing. Indeed, he hesitated so long that I feared he was about to tell me we could do nothing, that I must resign myself to my fate.

But then he spoke, saying, "I am trying to decide what the safest course of action might be. For of course we can do nothing openly. And I *have* tried—I have attempted to see if I can somehow increase the strength of the spell I use to travel from place to place in an instant, to see if I could manage to bring you with me. As an experiment, I tried to see if it would work while I was carrying my neighbor's dog."

Despite everything, I had to smother a laugh at that revelation. "And the dog cooperated?"

"Of course, for I had a fine ham bone as a bribe. But it did not work—the spell, that is. While holding the dog, I could do nothing more than simply stand there. As soon as I put the dog down, I was able to travel from my workshop to the attic two stories up. And as many times as I tried, that outcome never changed."

"Well, then," I murmured, keeping my voice low, even though I wanted to groan in frustration, "we will have to try something else."

"And what would that be?" Tobyn replied, voice hushed as well. "I can come and go in this manner, but I cannot spirit you away. Your maids sleep in the room next to yours, and four men stand guard outside your door. And I very much doubt His Majesty will allow you to venture outside the palace until this abomination of a wedding takes place, so there is no stratagem I could attempt to get you away while you were out in public."

Phrased in such a manner, the situation did seem hopeless. Once again I had that sensation of time ticking away, even as the walls of my suite seemed to close in on me. And somewhere within the palace the king sat like a spider in the center of his web, biding his time until his prey was so tightly wrapped in silk that she could not possibly get away.

My throat tightened, and I swallowed. I could not allow myself to weep. Not now, when I must stay as strong as I could.

For if I allowed myself to despair, then I truly would have surrendered to my fate.

"I don't know what we can do," I whispered. "But all is not lost. Not yet. The wedding will not take place until the evening of the day after tomorrow. There is still time."

"Time?" he said bitterly. "Time is rushing away from us, Annora. And I fear I can do nothing to stop it."

I had no answer. Instead, I pulled him toward me, heard the bed creak as he settled on its edge. Our lips met, despairing, hungry. I clung to him, feeling the strength of his arms as they tightened around me, sensing the heavy pounding of his heart. How I wanted him in that moment! Beyond reason, beyond caring. All I could think of was the weight of his body on mine, the need burning in the very center of my being, a need I could scarcely identify, save that its only fulfillment lay in Tobyn Slade.

But then, with the one rational part of my mind that still remained to me, I heard a soft footstep outside my door, and a questioning voice say, "My lady?"

In an instant, Tobyn was moving away from me. For the barest instant he paused next to the bed, as if still contemplating tearing me from it, even though he knew he could do nothing to take me away from this place. And then he was gone, shadow fading into shadow, gone as if he had never been there at all.

A moment later, the door opened, and I saw Felinda's head poke in. What she thought, seeing me pressed up against my pillows, face flushed and chest heaving, I had no idea.

As her wide blue eyes met mine in the candlelight, I managed to say, "A nightmare. That is all."

"Truly, my lady? For I thought—"

"Thought what?" I said, tone sharp.

"Obviously, it was nothing, my lady, but—"

"Oh, do spit it out, Felinda," I broke in. Never had I spoken to a servant in such a way before, but my nerves had been stretched taut as bowstrings.

Her hands knotted in the sleep chemise of heavy linen she wore. Clearly, she had not even paused to draw on a dressing gown. "I thought I heard a man's voice."

My heart pounded away even harder, but I made myself say, "You must have been dreaming, Felinda. For you can see that no one is here."

She glanced around the obviously empty chamber and nodded. "Of course, my lady. It is as you say—it must have been a dream. I am so sorry to have awakened you."

From the slight tremor in her voice, I could tell she was terrified of being reprimanded, of perhaps being sent away to a different position within the palace, if not dismissed outright. This had to have been a step up for her, to be one of the attendants of the future queen. Voice softening, I said, "It is fine, Felinda. You were only doing your duty. But as you can see, I am safe, and quite alone. You may go back to sleep now."

"Yes, my lady." She dropped a curtsey, one that was half-obscured by the door. "Thank you, my lady."

Then she shut the door, and I let myself fall back against the pillows, a breath of relief escaping my lips.

That had been too close. And as I lay there, Tobyn's absence like a physical pain, I could not allow myself to think of what would happen after the king had made me his wife.

The next day passed in much the same fashion as the one before it, my chambers a managed chaos of dressmakers coming and going, of having to stand still while enough garments for any ten ladies were pinned and fitted to me, then taken away to be stitched. How in the world they expected to have any of this done in time, I had no idea, but then I realized the only gown I truly needed come the next day was the wedding dress, and it had already been constructed. They must have worked all night on it, but the dressmakers had already moved on to embroidering the bodice and the sleeves with silver thread and tiny pearls in cream and the softest pink.

Lady Shelenna also came by with the promised jewels from the late Queen Nerissa's trove. Despite my overall wretchedness, I could not help but be impressed by the riches revealed to me when the duchess had Felinda and Vianna bring out what seemed like uncounted jewels, each one richer than the next. Taking my murmured responses to each piece as assent, the countess decided on a heavy necklace of silver and pink sea pearls, with matching earrings and diadem.

"The king will not be able to take his eyes off you," she said in delight, once I had clasped the necklace around my throat to determine whether the length would suit.

In response, I could only manage a wan smile. I doubted very much whether the king cared what I looked like, as long as I was safely trapped as his wife and could continue to spin as much gold as he needed. And what on earth would I do if he demanded to watch as I worked? So far I had managed to avoid such a terrible request, but once I was his wife, I did not think I would be able to so easily hide in prevarications and manufactured strictures as to what constituted an optimal environment in which to spin my gold.

"I hope my appearance will please him," I replied.

"Of course it shall. How could it not? True, the late queen was quite a pretty woman in her youth, or so I was told, but I am sure that you far outshine her." The duchess paused then, peering at me closely with her amber eyes. "Annora, is all well with you?"

"Why, of course. Perhaps I did not sleep as well as I had hoped, but I blame that on sleeping in a strange bed. I am sure tonight I will fare much better." That was a plausible lie. I had to hope that Lady Shelenna would not see anything else in my shadowed eyes and somewhat wan appearance.

But she did not nod, or tell me, "Of course," or make any other response that would have set my heart at ease. Instead, she continued to study my face, then said gently, "My dear, there is nothing wrong with feeling...anxious. It is no small thing to marry the king, and of course you are very young and do not know much of the world, do you?"

I shook my head. At the same time, I found myself praying that she would not attempt to give me the sort of talk a mother might deliver to a daughter on the eve of her wedding day. For one thing, Lady Shelenna and I had shared only a very brief acquaintance, and hearing of such matters from her would be bad enough without having to contemplate sharing such intimacies with the king, a man nearly forty years my senior.

Somehow I managed not to shudder at the thought. After drawing in a breath, I said, "All this has been rather overwhelming. But I am ready to do my duty by the king and my country."

That reply made her smile, and even chuckle slightly. "You are not going off to war, you know. Yes, the king is a good deal older than you, but I never heard that the late queen was disappointed in her marriage, and certainly Lady Ilendra was content with her lot as the king's mistress, until she realized that he truly did not intend to ever marry her. I think that you will be far happier than you believe."

Once again I had to repress a shiver. No, I most certainly could not begin to imagine the king as a lover, especially not after I knew what it was like to taste Tobyn's kisses, to find myself melting in his embrace. However, I could not tell the duchess of such things. I could only hope that she would see any reluctance on my part as maidenly modesty.

"That is good to hear," I said. "For truly, although the king has always treated me with great honor, still I must confess to being somewhat apprehensive, for there is such a great span that separates our ages."

She patted my hand. Today she wore flashing topaz to match the gown she wore, which was the color of dark, warm honey. "I would think less of you if you were not experiencing such apprehension. It is only natural. But you will find that the king will do very well by you."

Because he has already proven himself to be so very honorable, I thought bitterly. *To keep me locked up at his whim, then attempt to force me to marry his son, and finally take me for himself when no other alternative presented itself. Yes, I am sure he will be quite the doting husband.*

Of course I did not say any of that. I smiled, murmured that of course she was correct in all her judgments, and guided the conversation to the jewels before us, and the gowns that would soon fill my wardrobe.

I could only pray that I would never have the chance to wear any of them, that somehow Tobyn and I would come upon the means to get me away from here. We had to. My mind would simply not allow itself to contemplate a future with me as the queen of Purth.

That night I did happen upon a desperate plan, although I knew that Tobyn would most likely have none of it. But I was increasingly approaching my wit's end, and knew I did not have many escapes available to me. I also worried that perhaps he would not come at all, not after Felinda had almost discovered us the evening before.

Still, I could give no sign of the misgivings that plagued me. Once again my maids prepared me for sleep, and once again I bade them good night after insisting that the candle next to my bed should remain lit. I pulled the covers up to me and waited, praying to every god who might be listening that Tobyn would not forsake me.

For truly, what did we share, save an attachment of only a little more than a week? He had never even come out and told me that he loved me. His actions seemed to indicate that he did, but I was, as I had confessed to Lady Shelenna, very inexperienced. He was the only man I had ever kissed. Perhaps I was confusing these strange—but pleasant—reactions in my body with the actuality of being in love. If that were true, it would make sense for him to abandon me now. I was a pleasant diversion, but when that diversion was weighed against the very real threat of reprisals from the king, should we be caught....

The shadows moved then, and one of them was Tobyn. He stepped toward my bed, hands out, and I immediately pushed back the covers and went to him, let him fold me into his arms.

"Thank the gods," I whispered, and he took me by the shoulders so he could gaze down into my face.

"What, did you think I would not come to you?" he asked, his voice also a whisper.

"I don't—I feared—"

By way of reply, he bent and kissed me, bringing the sweetness of his mouth to mine. In that moment, I realized how foolish my fears had been, how I had allowed my worry and doubt to tarnish the love I knew we shared. By then the roughness of the scarring at the side of his mouth had become as familiar to me as the sound of his voice. I did not care that he was not perfect, because then I knew he was truly my Tobyn.

"I'm sorry," I murmured, after he finally broke the kiss.

"Don't be, my darling. You have been alone here, with no support. Why, has your father even come to see you?"

"No," I replied, realizing that his absence these past few days was rather odd. Surely His Majesty would have allowed a father to visit his daughter once the news of her triumphant engagement had spread. "No, I fear he has not. Although I doubt that would have been a very pleasant conversation, so perhaps that is why he has stayed away."

"It is precisely why," Tobyn said, voice a grim mutter. "Far better for him to appear at the ceremony, all beaming pride, than to face the wrath of the daughter who would never have been in this situation in the first place, were it not for his own weakness."

Since that seemed a fairly accurate description of my current state of mind, I could only nod. Then I said, "Tobyn, I have thought of a way to stop all this."

He went still then, arms tightening on my shoulders. "How? For there are just as many guards tonight, and your maids still sleep next door. And certainly there is no chance of your leaving the palace tomorrow, not with your wedding taking place that same night."

"I know." Here it was. I would have to make the outrageous suggestion, and hope he would not think I had finally gone mad. But it did seem to me the only way. And perhaps the experience would not be all that unpleasant....

I reached up and pressed my hands against his chest, feeling the warmth of his wool cloak, the strength of the body beneath it. "The king will not marry me if I am not—not pure. So if we are together, you and I...then he cannot make me his wife."

Tobyn's response was immediate. "Are you mad, Annora?" he demanded in a harsh whisper. "Do you truly believe that I would take you in such a way, with no honor, no respect, only doing that which must be done so the king cannot have you?"

"It would be a gesture of the utmost respect," I retorted. "Seeing as doing so would keep me safe from the king's clutches." My fingers closed on the opening of his cloak, the heavy fabric scratching against my skin. "Is it—is it that you do not want me after all? I had thought, from the way you kissed me—"

That sentence was cut off by his mouth descending on mine, tasting me, forcing me into silence. My body heated, for I wore nothing but the lace-trimmed chemise I had put on to sleep in, and my breasts were pressed up against him, his thigh hard against mine.

"I do want you," he said, the words rough. "All the gods only know how much I want you. But as my wife, as the woman I want to spend the rest of my days with. Not in a hurried tumble whose only purpose is to prevent the king from taking you himself."

Joy rushed through me in a warm wave. So he did want to marry me. Perhaps he had held off from speaking of love and marriage because he still had not quite reconciled his own beliefs about his scarred face and form with my obvious need for him.

"But that 'tumble' is the only thing which might keep us together," I pointed out quietly. "I will admit that I am inexperienced, and therefore don't completely understand what is it that I am asking of you, but better that we have our tumble now so you may show me the proper respect due a wife at a later date. Otherwise, there will be no later date. Don't you see?"

My voice had raised on those last few syllables, and I cut myself off there, lest we give ourselves away. Up until that point, we had been speaking in whispers and soft murmurs, for I was still all too aware of how Felinda had almost discovered us the night before.

A long silence. Tobyn stood unmoving as I held onto his cloak and gazed imploringly up into his face. Or rather, into the shadows where his face should be. A little shiver went over me then. If I was able to convince him to do this, then I would see him at last. He could not keep that cloak on the whole time, could he?

"My love," he said at last. "This is not how I imagined us being together for the first time. I had hoped to ask you to marry me, and then there would have been no impediment to our being together. No impediment except this face of mine."

"I already told you, I do not care about that."

"You say that, Annora."

"I say it because I mean it. Just as I am saying that we should be together now. You can pretend I am your wife, if that will make you feel better about the whole thing. And you have already as much as asked me to marry you. So yes, Tobyn Slade, I will be your wife. Let me be your wife in body now, and I can be that in name later, once I have been freed."

For the longest moment, he hesitated. I sensed the war he fought within himself in every tense muscle of his body. Then his arms slipped under me, lifting me from the carpeted floor so he might carry me to the bed. Despite the fierceness of his embrace earlier, he lowered me with exquisite care to the mattress, then bent to kiss me on the mouth again before his lips traveled to my throat, moving ever lower, igniting such a fire within me that I wondered why I did not burst into flame then and there.

And he was kissing the bare skin of my chest where the neckline of the chemise parted, featherlight touches of flesh to flesh. My back arched as I moved up to meet him, my hands seeking the clasp that held the cloak at his throat so I might release it, free him from the shroud he hid himself within.

But even as my fingers closed on the cool metal, the door to my bedchamber banged open, and I heard Felinda gasp, "So there was someone in here!"

All heat within me was replaced by icy fear. Tall figures crowded the room, two of them grasping Tobyn by the arms and yanking him roughly away from me. A third man lowered a pale cloth over his hood and pulled it taut against Tobyn's mouth, effectively gagging him.

Gagging him? But why...?

So he cannot cast the spell that would send him forth from this chamber, my mind told me coolly. True, I had never heard him actually say any of his spells out loud, but once or twice I had overheard the softest of whispers, as if those syllables had escaped his lips as he mouthed the words to himself.

And how was it they knew that he could even use such a spell?

From behind the guards that flanked Tobyn, a man and a woman stepped forward. Candlelight glistened on skirts of dark honey, and I looked up into Lady Shelenna's face. She wore a smile of triumph, and glanced up at her companion. Shocked, I looked from her to the man who stood at her shoulder, and realized he was none other than Lord Edmar.

"You see?" said the duchess. "I knew she was hiding something."

The duke nodded grimly. "Take him away," he ordered the guards, who hustled a struggling Tobyn out of the room. Then his gaze fixed on me, and his mouth tightened even further. "And you, Annora...I believe the king would like to have a few words with you."

CHAPTER SIXTEEN

Perhaps the king did want to speak with me, but it appeared that he intended to do so on his own time. After Tobyn was taken away, both Lord Edmar and Lady Shelenna departed, but not before I saw them order a pair of burly-looking guards to stand watch outside my bedroom door. What difference that would make, I had no idea. It wasn't as if I could have gotten past the four who guarded the entrance to the suite itself.

They would have done better, I thought bitterly, *to have posted someone at my window, to ensure that I did not fling myself from it.*

For despair rose in my breast, threatening to drown me. All my thoughts were for Tobyn. Where had they taken him? What sort of punishment would he face, for the high crime of attempting to defile the king's affianced bride?

I did not know. But I doubted they would be gentle.

The hours passed, and I fell into an exhausted slumber, one in which I was tormented by nightmares of being chased through the halls of the castle until my legs threatened to give way beneath me. Sometimes my tormentor was the king himself, sometimes Lord Edmar. During one particularly harrowing episode, my pursuer wore my father's own face.

Needless to say, I did not get much rest.

Felinda and Vianna came to prepare me the next morning, both of them silent and avoiding my gaze. Just as well, because I had never in my life wanted to reach out and shake someone as I did Felinda. Perhaps she truly believed she was merely doing her duty. But in that moment, I could only think of how she had ruined my life.

Tobyn's life.

At least I would not have to wear that hated wedding gown, hanging in pale rose-colored splendor from the door of my wardrobe. Still, the two maidservants dressed me in one of my finer dresses, the crimson one with the golden trim, although the pendant Tobyn had made for me was conspicuously missing from my jewel box. Had Felinda or Vianna taken it, or had perhaps the duchess slipped it into her bag when I was not watching? Clearly, she had guessed at some connection between Tobyn and me, although how she had managed to put the clues together, I had no idea.

Not that it mattered now. We had both been caught, and now I must go to meet my fate.

The guards who had been standing outside the door to my suite moved to flank me as I exited. None of them gave any direction as to where we were going. Not that I needed it. I knew this would be no scolding in the king's royal apartments.

He would want to make sure I was humiliated in front of as many unfriendly eyes as possible.

I was marched down several levels to the audience chamber, which, as I had feared, was packed with twice the number of people who had been there during my former sojourn to that room. Indeed, the place was so crowded that some of the onlookers had actually spilled out the doors and into the wide hallway that led to the chamber.

A host of curious, unsympathetic faces watched my passage down the aisle to the front of the room, where the king sat on his throne. To his right was Prince Harlin, who appeared more bewildered than anything else, and behind the prince stood his wife. She studiously avoided my gaze as I glanced at her. No doubt she was praying that I would make no mention of the conversation we had shared a few days earlier.

But then I saw Tobyn, who knelt in the open area before the dais, two guards standing beside him. They had not removed his cloak; the hood still dropped low, concealing his face. I would have been glad they had allowed him that small dignity, except I knew they had not done so out of the kindness of their hearts.

The king stood. Glacial blue eyes fixed on me. "Annora Kelsden."

I could do nothing but move forward at his command. When I was a few feet from the dais, I stopped. I did not curtsey, for I owed this man no honor. "Your Majesty," I said coldly.

A muscle in his cheek twitched. "You are very bold, Annora, for someone who would so openly disrespect your king, the man you were to marry."

"That marriage was arranged through no choice of my own, as you well know, Your Majesty."

The hall filled with shocked murmurs at my audacious reply, but I ignored them. Surely no one present actually believed I truly wished to wed someone of the king's advanced years, no matter what his station.

"And so you saw no reason to be faithful?" He descended the steps of the dais and stopped a few feet away from me. This close, I could see the pouches under his eyes, the broken veins that framed them. It did not seem as if he had spent a much more restful night than I.

"I was being faithful," I retorted. "To the man I love."

That remark made him set his jaw. Eyes glittering, he said, "Indeed? That sorry specimen over there?" His gaze flicked in Tobyn's direction and then returned to me. "Do you even know what it was you fancied yourself in love with?"

"*He,*" I said, "is Tobyn Slade, a master goldsmith. His station is similar to mine, so why should I not have bestowed my heart upon him? Surely it is a much more logical match, especially since he is only a decade older than I, not almost four."

"So I suppose you have seen his face?"

"I—" Here I could lie...except it seemed as if the king was anticipating my answer, waiting for it, so he could spring the trap he had set. So I said simply, "No, Your Majesty, I have not. I would hope that I am not such a shallow woman as to give my heart to someone based purely on his appearance, rather than the truth in his heart and soul."

"Ah. That is very noble, to be sure. But I think perhaps you should see what it is that you have been letting into your bedchamber every night."

The king gave a curt nod at the guards who stood next to Tobyn. Only then did I notice that the heavy silver clasp which usually held his cloak shut was missing. Because of that lack, it was easy enough for one of the men to grasp a handful of the heavy black wool and jerk it backward, revealing Tobyn's face.

For one long, agonizing moment, I could only stand there and stare, even as the watching courtiers gasped. He had warned me that he had been scarred badly by the pox, and so I had not been expecting perfection. Far from it. But the ruin I saw now could not have been caused by that fell disease. One half of his face was pulled and twisted, livid with scar tissue. It continued to his mouth on that same side, which explained the roughness I felt whenever we kissed, and even traveled down his neck.

Despairing green eyes met mine. As I forced myself to look at him, I realized that the more or less unharmed side of his countenance would have been considered handsome, with the fine strong brow and nose, the heavy dark fringe of lashes around his eyes. His hair, too, was thick and black, although it seemed some of it grew patchily on the same side of his head where his face was scarred.

So much worse than what the pox could have done to him...and yet I found I did not care. I was able to look into his eyes, to finally see him. And when our gazes locked, I smiled. I would not speak the words, not in front of the entire court, but I would mouth them, so he would know that the ruin of his face mattered nothing to me.

I love you.

The king saw those mouthed words, however, and his features twisted in fury. "He is a monster, Annora. Not only his face, but his entire being. How think you that he got those scars?"

I shook my head, for indeed, I could not begin to puzzle out what might have happened to him. A house fire, perhaps, when he was young?

"Ah, well, you would have been only a child when it happened, and perhaps your parents shielded you from the story." King Elsdon turned from me toward Tobyn, asking, "Shall I tell her the tale, or shall you, Master Slade?"

Tobyn's scarred mouth pulled into a flat line. "Perhaps you should have the telling, Your Majesty, since you appear to take such pleasure in it."

"How very accommodating of you." Once again the king shifted back toward me. "You see, Annora, this man you profess to love was born with the foul witch-blood running in his veins. Luckily for the good people of Bodenskell, he was not overly careful about concealing his powers—liked to amuse the children in his neighborhood by making coins disappear and reappear. The silly street trick of a conjurer, most people thought. But my investigators found him to be possessed of true magical powers. He was brought to trial and found guilty. And you know the penalty for being mage-born."

"Burning at the stake," I whispered. Of course. That terrible punishment would explain his scars. But how had he managed to survive?

"Precisely," the king replied. "Only we did not understand the true extent of his powers, and so he was able to make his escape, even as the flames licked at him and almost consumed him. My agents hunted the kingdom for him, and yet there was no trace to be found of this terrible user of magic who had festered at the heart of my realm like a cancer. Now, of course, we know that he went to live a quiet life as a goldsmith, hoping that no one would ever discover who...what...he truly was. The story of the pox was a convenient one, for it came to Bodenskell not long after his burning, and enough were left scarred by it that no one would question his desire to conceal his face."

And he had been discovered, because of me. If he had not come to my aid, Tobyn would have remained anonymous, hidden and safe. In that moment, my heart seemed as if it were being squeezed in a vise, so wracked was I with guilt. If I had known what he risked, I would never have allowed him to help me, would never have let matters between us progress as they did.

But, as my mother once said, eggs cannot be put back into their shells. I had no idea how either of us would ever escape now, not when we were surrounded on all sides by guards and the members of King Elsdon's court. For the first time, I noticed Lord Edmar, saw how close the Lady Shelenna stood to him.

Perhaps a little too close. For just the briefest second, I saw him sweep an indulgent glance down at her, and her mouth curved in reply. I guessed that the nondescript-looking but richly dressed man on her other side must be her husband; he watched the goings-on with avid dark eyes, and if he noted anything of the connection between the duke and his wife, he gave no sign of it. Some people truly could not see past the tips of their noses.

Had the Lord Edmar and Lady Shelenna colluded to expose my relationship with Tobyn? I could not see how they had even begun to guess, but as the king waved peremptorily in the duchess's direction and said, "Your Grace, if you would step forward," I had a feeling I would soon find out.

She moved toward the king and curtseyed with a graceful rustle of her silken skirts. While His Majesty was occupied with looking at her, I risked a glance over at Tobyn. He had not moved, still stood there with his head high, jaw clenched. I could only imagine what it must cost him to stand there and pretend to ignore the stares of the courtiers, the whispering behind fans and handkerchiefs. For the briefest second, his eyes flickered toward mine.

My lips formed a single word. *Go.*

For I knew he could escape now, just as he had escaped the flames some ten years ago. They had removed his gag, so he could speak the words of the spell if he wished to. Indeed, I wondered why he had not.

The faintest shake of his head. One gloved hand moved up and touched his breast near his heart for a scant second before he let it fall to his side once more. I knew then that he would not escape, even if it was within his power.

He would not leave me.

No doubt the king had counted on such loyalty, else he would most assuredly have kept Tobyn gagged. Hatred burned within me, but I knew I could not give in to it. I must keep my head about me, no matter what happened.

"I would thank you for your service to this realm," King Elsdon said to Lady Shelenna. She bowed her head, that same secretive smile playing about her lips. And to think I had believed her to be, if not a friend, then at least friendly. That more than anything else showed me how little I knew about life at court, and how its private pathways to power functioned.

"I only did what anyone else in my position might have done, Your Majesty," she replied. "Indeed, I am just grateful that my suspicion proved to be correct."

"It was quite the insight, all the same," the king said. He was smiling now as well, secure in his power, gloating over how he had managed to capture the hated user of magic once again. And I doubted that Tobyn would be able to make an escape a second time. Still with that smile on his face, King Elsdon glanced over at me and went on, "You see, Annora, when your lover made you a gift of that pendant, he sealed your doom, for Master Slade's work is quite distinctive, and Her Grace here recognized it at once. She also realized that my late wife never had such a piece in her collection, and neither had I ever given one to the Lady Ilendra, whose apartments and jewels you first used when you came to the palace. And so she had to wonder, whence came such a thing? She approached me with the question, for she thought that perhaps I had given it to you directly in the last few days, but I had not given it to you, and neither had I ever commissioned such a piece."

"It sounds like quite the investigation," I remarked past the dryness in my throat. As much as I wanted to look over at Tobyn and somehow communicate to him that it was all right, that I did not blame him for giving himself away when he had only wished to give me something beautiful, I knew I dared not.

"Quite." The king approached me and then paused to pull something from the inner pocket of his doublet. Dangling from his fingers was the pendant Tobyn had made, the ruby winking at me like a baleful crimson eye. "It is beautiful work, I will grant you that. And something that could only have come from the hand of Master Slade, the goldsmith all the ladies of my court rave about. Such a secretive man, it turns out, who goes about in a cloak and hood at all times, no matter what the weather. He claims to stay hidden because of his pox scars, but even the worst-scarred folk show their faces now and then, especially when the weather is warm. So why should Master Slade be any different?"

I remained silent. My soul rebelled at looking into the king's gloating face, and so I made myself stare stonily past him, to the dais where Prince Harlin still sat, his wife at his shoulder. To my surprise, I saw no condemnation on the prince's face, no echo of his father's poorly hidden triumph. If anything, Prince Harlin appeared almost sad, as if he took no pleasure in Tobyn's humiliation, or my anguish. Unfortunately, I knew that the prince's feelings counted for very little with the king.

My continued silence seemed to discomfit him not at all. He puffed out his chest and continued, still in the same loud, carrying tone, "Even more curious, it turned out that this Master Slade was the one who retained a certain lawyer to sue the High Court to let Mistress Kelsden free. Master Jamsden had provided his services to Master Slade on more than one occasion, but he had no connection to Mistress Kelsden here... until Master Slade hired him to defend this poor innocent girl, this young woman who had committed no crime, save having a profligate father. But it turns out you were not quite so innocent, were you, Annora?"

Again I said nothing. We might have been in his court, but it most certainly was not a court of law. Nothing I said or did now would make one whit of difference. But the king must put on his show, and so it seemed my best policy now was to greet all of his utterances with stony silence.

If he was nonplussed by my lack of response, he gave no sign of it. This time he did not even bother to look at me, but stepped forward so he might directly address the courtiers surrounding us. They seemed to be listening, entranced, for I had no doubt they hadn't had gossip this juicy to devour for many a month...if ever.

"And so it turns out that this Master Slade has known Mistress Kelsden for some time. In exchange for her favors, he produced the gold that kept her gambling father solvent, for if it were not for this sorcerer's intervention, the entire family would have been on the street many months ago."

"That is a lie!" Tobyn burst out, at last breaking his silence.

"You dare to call the king a liar?" Lord Edmar demanded. He stepped forward, grey eyes glinting like steel.

"I call things what they are," Tobyn said. His own eyes blazed green fire, and I had no doubt he wished in that moment his magical skills were of a more martial nature than simply conjuring gold and gems from the very air itself, or making himself disappear and appear at will. "And he does lie in this. He lies most damnably. I had never even met Mistress Kelsden before this last seven-day."

The duke raised an eyebrow, and a mocking smile touched his lips. "You expect us to believe that, when it is only your gold that would have kept her family solvent?"

"It was not Master Slade's gold," I broke in, "but rather my father raiding the dowry which should have been mine and my sister's. That is what kept food on our table and clothes on our backs. I know you are determined to believe the very worst, but I speak the truth in this. Just as I will say now that Master Slade came to my aid expecting nothing in return, his only thought to protect me from a king so blinded by his lust for gold that he would overlook all decency, all law and notions of what is right and wrong, just so he could fill his miserable coffers!"

At this outburst, the king began to splutter—no doubt attempting to find his voice so he could protest his innocence—but Lord Edmar still only smiled.

"So the magician expected nothing, even from a young woman as beautiful as you? What, pray, was he doing in your bedchamber last night, if all he wanted was the noble feeling of having helped someone in need?"

Oh, they would twist this any way they wanted, no matter what Tobyn or I said. And I would not speak of how we had come to love one another, not in front of this crowd of greedy, unsympathetic faces.

As I wracked my brains for a reply that would be both suitably biting and yet reveal nothing, Lady Shelenna spoke up.

"What is this talk of gold?" she inquired. "I must confess that I do not quite understand the connection. Yes, this Master Slade must have gold to create the jewels he fashions for the ladies of the court, but I do not think that is what you meant."

The king's lips compressed. I could see that even now, with his captured sorcerer on display like a prized buck he had just hunted down, he did not wish to divulge the true secret of Tobyn's powers.

"Yes, tell her, Your Majesty," I said, with a curl of my lip and lift of my eyebrow that would have done Lord Edmar proud.

Not that he appeared particularly proud in that moment. He frowned, and cast an uneasy glance at the king. It seemed our good duke had no more desire to reveal the source of the gold I had mentioned than the king himself did.

"He speaks of this gold," Tobyn said loudly. A negligent flick of his hand, and a pile of gold coins appeared at Lady Shelenna's feet.

"Gods!" she exclaimed. Quite abandoning her dignity, she stooped down and gathered up several of the coins, then turned them over in her hand, inspecting them closely. "But—but these are real. Or is this some sort of terrible illusion?"

"No illusion at all, my lady," he replied. "You could spend those coins anywhere in Purth, and fear no repercussions."

The crowd murmured again, the sound taking on a restless edge I did not like. Surely Tobyn had known what he was doing when he revealed that particular facet of his gift, and yet....

Lady Shelenna's amber eyes glowed. Great duchess she might be, but it seemed that even she was not immune to the lure of wealth so easily produced. Although she did not lose control so much that she bent to gather of the rest of the coins Tobyn had produced from thin air, she did place the ones she currently held in the reticule which hung from her waist.

He went on, scarred face still as a mask, "Just as you could take the golden thread Mistress Kelsden and I spun each night, Your Majesty, and melt it down into ingots or crowns or whatever else pleased you. That gold did not disappear. That gold was intended to buy her freedom, not make her your slave."

"Ah, but it is you who should have been the slave, is it not?" the king replied, his pale eyes taking on that greedy glint I knew too well. "You should have spoken up the first time you were caught, and bought your own life with the gold you could create. But you would not have been a slave, not at all. You would have been given an honored place in my court, just as I wanted to make Annora my queen."

Tobyn appeared singularly unmoved by this argument. "A cage is still a cage, whether its bars are made of gold or no. I would rather have a life as a free man, scarred as I am, than be your puppet. Especially since you have proven over and over again that nothing is enough for you. You can never be satisfied, because the hole you seek to fill is within you."

"Silence!" King Elsdon thundered. I shrank, even though the command had not been directed at me. Veins bulged on his brow, and his breast rose and fell as he pulled in short, angry breaths. "I had thought to burn you a second time, and make sure the deed was done properly, but now I know you will serve me far better as a living man."

"I will never serve you," Tobyn said calmly. "My gift is mine to use as it pleases me. I rule it, and not the other way around."

The king's hand descended on me, gripping painfully as his fingers bit into my upper arm. "Oh, yes, you will, Master Slade. For if you do not, I will use your lady love as I please. And I do not think you will care for that at all."

I tasted bile at the back of my throat. For of course I knew that Tobyn would never allow such a thing, would rather spend all his days producing such riches that King Elsdon would be as wealthy as the fabled rulers of old, whose very castles themselves had been built of gold.

But my lover shook his head, saying, "I would be very careful if I were you, Your Majesty. For I do not think you understand how close you are to your own doom."

The king laughed. "You speak fine words, Master Slade, but I see the truth of it now. Your magic is useful, true, but if you possessed the means to blast me from this earth, as it is said the mages of old could do, then you would have done so already. Your threats mean nothing."

"Ah, but they do. It is just that you do not have the wit to understand those threats." Tobyn paused then, and, to my surprise, he did not look at me, but rather up at the dais, where Prince Harlin sat and his princess stood behind him, both of them tense, pale. "I regret this, my prince. Believe that."

Harlin rose. "Master Slade—"

But Tobyn had already turned back toward the king. "There is no room in your heart for anything but gold. And so gold it shall be." He made a curious gesture with one hand, as if cupping his hand around an object the size of an apple.

Or a heart.

My hand flew to my mouth, even as King Elsdon's eyes began to bulge. He made a choking noise, one hand reaching for his chest, and then he slumped onto the polished stone floor of the audience chamber, pale eyes staring unblinking at the painted and gilded ceiling overhead.

Prince Harlin was on his feet at once, rushing to kneel at his father's side. "What have you done?"

"What needed to be done," Tobyn replied. Curiously, there was no triumph in his scarred face, only a sort of resignation. "I hope you are ready to be king, Your Highness."

And then Lord Edmar was striding toward Tobyn, countenance twisted with rage. His hand rested on the hilt of the long dagger he wore at his hip, the only weapon allowed at court.

"I would not," Tobyn said. "For do not think I cannot do to you what I did to the king." He shifted so he faced the crowd of courtiers, all of them this time apparently shocked into silence. "Or to any of you, if you seek to stop me."

Moving almost as one, they stepped backward, and a grim smile touched his lopsided mouth. "That is what I thought." Then he paused and looked over at me. In those green eyes there was hope, but also worry, as if he feared I would be so shocked by what he had done that I would turn on him as well.

I knew I would not. He would not have killed the king if he had been allowed any other option. How could I reject him, when King Elsdon had, as Tobyn warned, brought his doom upon himself?

"Shall we go, my love?" Tobyn asked, and I went and put my hand in his.

"Yes," I said. "We should go."

CHAPTER SEVENTEEN

Despite my fears, the crowd did let us through. Perhaps if all the guards and those of the men who were armed had rushed us all at once, they might have prevailed, since I had no clear idea of precisely how this strange and deadly facet of Tobyn's gift even worked. But since it seemed clear enough to me that none of them wished to be the first to bear his assault, we were able to walk through the throng and out the doors of the audience chamber, through the corridors of the palace and the curiously empty courtyard before it, and from thence to the very streets of Bodenskell itself.

A fresh breeze blew off the river, and I marveled at the scent of water and earth and damp leaves on the wind after so many days spent inside. We moved quickly, putting as much distance between us and the palace as possible. Yes, we had been allowed to leave unmolested, but what if Prince Harlin overcame his shock and sent his guards after us?

Tobyn held my hand, fingers tight around mine. I understood why, for this was his first sojourn out of doors without the protection of his cloak. I caught furtive glances sent in our direction, and murmurs from some of the street vendors as they watched from their stalls, but no one said anything to us directly.

"Where now?" I asked quietly. "To your home?"

"Yes, but only to gather up a few things and then be gone. I do not think we need to fear pursuit from the prince, but neither do I think we should linger."

"Why do you think he will not seek us out? Surely he must do something to find justice for his father, if only to make it clear that he did not collude with you in this thing."

Tobyn guided me down a side street, one that arced away from the palace and wound gently uphill. "Because he will not risk his men against such a dangerous one as myself...or at least, that is the story he will tell. And who will argue against that, when most people these days only know of mages as terrible bogeymen, fearsome enemies who could kill you with a single glance?"

I nodded, for I knew what he told me was true. Indeed, I had thought the same thing...until I met Tobyn, and understood what an honorable man he was.

Still walking briskly, he continued, "In truth, I think the prince knew that his father needed to be put down, rather the way one would a mad dog, although I am not sure he is quite ready to admit such a thing to himself. But the king would have hungered for more and more gold, and the more he had, the greater his madness would have grown. Such hungers can never be assuaged, and in the end, he could have endangered the entire kingdom by looking outward and wishing to use his newfound wealth and power to expand the borders of this land. You do not think the king of Farendon or the Hierarch of Keshiaar would have taken such incursions lightly, do you?"

Indeed, I had not followed the course of the king's greed to its logical conclusion, but if Tobyn was correct in his estimations, then he had just saved, not only the two of us, but perhaps a great many more Purthian lives. "I doubt not," I replied. "What I cannot understand is how someone can be the king of a great land, and yet still not be satisfied with his lot."

"It is a rare gift to be content with what one has," Tobyn said, "whether one's lot is to be king of Purth, or a goatherd. Prince Harlin has that quality, and this kingdom will be the better for it." He stopped in front of a sturdy-looking house, three stories tall, half-timbered and newly lime-washed. "Here we are."

It looked to be a fine home, but I wondered how we would get in, since I knew the king's guards must have taken any keys or other valuables from Tobyn when they captured him. However, I had not stopped to consider all the ramifications of his gift. He held out his hand, and in the next moment a fine silver key sat in his palm. Within the minute, he had the door unlocked, and we both stood inside the front room.

Within was much the same as without, the furnishings heavy and good quality without being ornate. The air was chill, though, the large stone hearth empty and cold. I wondered what it would be like with a fire blazing in it. But I would never know. We had only stopped here briefly, and must needs be on our way as soon as we could.

I followed Tobyn into a study of sorts, with a goodly number of books on the shelves and a large desk covered in papers. He seemed to have already decided what he would take with him, for he plucked three volumes from their resting places on the bookshelves and set them on the desk.

"My satchel is upstairs in my bedchamber," he said. "I will fetch that, along with some spare clothing."

"And we will go to my father's house after this?"

He hesitated, then said, "If we must."

"Of course we must," I replied. "For I have some things of my own I would like to retrieve, and I would never forgive myself if I left without saying goodbye to my sister." The thought of that impending farewell sent a pang through me, and tears suddenly stung my eyes. Could I say goodbye to Iselda, and leave her all alone here? It seemed such a cruel thing to do. "Tobyn, where *are* we going, anyway?"

"To North Eredor, for there I will not have to fear persecution because of my gifts."

North Eredor. Our destination might as well be over the very edge of the earth itself. And yet I knew he was right, that we must go someplace where we would not have to constantly look over our shoulders. "I suppose it would be foolish to take Iselda with us."

At once he came to me and took my hands in his. "My darling, I have no brothers and sisters of my own, and yet I can imagine what a terrible thing it must be to leave your sister behind. But would you really drag her halfway across the continent to a strange new place? At least here she will be in familiar surroundings."

I could not argue with that, although I did not think she would find my father's company to be particularly reassuring, nor compelling. "I know, Tobyn," I said quietly. Then I slanted him a look through my lashes. Those scars he wore were terrible to behold, but they were not him. And even now I thought I was beginning to be used to them, to look past the surface damage to the strong, fine bones of the face underneath. "Is that truly your name?" I added. "For I would have thought you would not dare to use the same name after your escape from the king's fire."

"That is my name," he replied. "'Tobyn' is common enough—I was named for my grandfather. But no, 'Slade' is a name that I assumed. Rathskell is my family name, and I suppose I may take it up once again, now that my identity is no longer a secret."

"Rathskell," I murmured. I rather liked the sound of it, and thought I should do very well as Annora Rathskell.

Tobyn must have heard some approval in my voice, for he pulled me toward him, his mouth touching mine. Despite everything, that familiar awakening heat moved through me. I could not allow myself to succumb to it, however. We still had much to attend to.

After a few seconds, I pulled away, although I did so gently, and made sure I wore a smile as I looked up at him. "You will distract me, Master Rathskell," I said in tones of mock sternness. "And we still have much to do."

"Ah, that is true enough." A rueful lift of his shoulders, and he went on, "I will only be a moment, and then we can go on to your father's house."

He moved away from me then, going out the door of his study. A few seconds later, I heard his footsteps, light and quick, as he headed up the stairs. Since I had nothing else to occupy me, I took a quick glance at the three books he had chosen from the many volumes that lined the walls. One was a volume of various maps of the continent, another a book on its flora and fauna, with many fine engraved illustrations. The third one was titled Tales of the Age of Magic, which sounded much more intriguing. Perhaps, once we had settled somewhere, Tobyn would read something of it to me.

I realized I would not have to worry about a comfortable situation, even in the wilds of North Eredor. Tobyn's gift ensured that we would always have enough to support ourselves, and he had already shown that he understood the wisdom in being comfortable without being ostentatious. His scarred face would most likely attract attention, but I had to hope that as people became accustomed to him, his disfigurement would matter less and less.

The front door banged open then, and I startled, turning away from the modest stack of books on Tobyn's desk. Heavy feet sounded on the wood floor, coming closer. I knew that could not be him, for he had gone upstairs. Frantically, I glanced around the room, but it had only the one door, and the window was quite firmly latched.

In the next moment, Prince Harlin entered the study, with four soldiers flanking him. Behind them, I glimpsed at least five or six more; it was difficult to tell, since several of them crowded the doorway, blocking my view.

So much for Tobyn's assertion that the prince would not offer any pursuit. My heart pounded in my chest, and a thrill of cold fear flowed through my veins, but I kept my voice steady as I said, "Your Highness."

His expression appeared bleak to me, mouth hard and brows pulled together, and yet I saw no real sorrow in his face, no redness in his eyes. What he did now, he did out of duty, I guessed, and not because he truly grieved over his father's passing.

"Where is he?" the prince asked harshly.

I knotted my shaking fingers in the heavy silk of my skirts. "He is not here. He went to fetch some supplies—"

"You're lying."

Well, of course I was. Did Prince Harlin truly think that after everything Tobyn and I had been through, I would give him up so easily?

But then there was some commotion out in the main room, and in the next moment, two of the guards hauled Tobyn into the study. He carried a satchel that he had not yet latched, and the rough treatment caused him to drop it, spilling clothes that had been neatly folded onto the floor.

Despite that, he straightened as best he could, and fixed the prince with a blazing green stare. "Do you really think it necessary to carry out this farce?"

"Farce?" Prince Harlin returned, eyes narrowing.

"You think it necessary to bring me to justice. Believe me, justice has already been served this day."

By the way the prince's gaze flickered from Tobyn to the men who held him, and back again, I guessed that he did not entirely disagree with that statement. He hesitated, then said, "Guards, leave us."

One of them began to protest. "Your Majesty—"

"You heard me."

At once the man subsided, bowing his head in resignation, then backed out of the room, his companions following him. The last one out shut the door, but not before he sent Tobyn such a black look that I very much feared he would ensure we never left this house alive.

"Better," Tobyn said. "Now we may speak like reasonable men."

"There is nothing reasonable about this situation, and you know it," Prince—King—Harlin replied. His men had already begun to address him as "Your Majesty," and so I realized I should think of him in that way as well.

Tobyn shrugged. I could see the way he glanced over at me, though, see the worry in his eyes. For even if Harlin understood that his father needed to be stopped, that did not mean he would do the merciful thing and let us go.

"Perhaps not," Tobyn said, his tone almost too casual. "And I know that you have been put in a difficult situation. Imprison me if you must, but please, let Annora go free."

The new king paused for a long moment. Indecision seemed to be printed on every plane of his face, every line of his body. I knew then that he did not wish to punish us, but thought he must, so as not to appear weak.

"No," he said at length. "I am not my father, but having you nearby would be too much of a temptation, I think. The ease with which you could fill our kingdom's coffers is not something I could ignore forever. But I cannot let you go. I would be forever known as the man who did nothing to avenge the murder of his father."

I winced at those harsh words. Yes, the king was dead, and by Tobyn's hand, but I could not think of his death as murder. Was it murder to kill someone before he killed you?

"Then don't let me go," Tobyn said. "Kill me instead."

I let out a shocked sound, and Harlin's eyes widened.

"Are you mad?"

"Not at all." Tobyn gestured toward the long dagger the new king wore at his belt. "Very well, I didn't mean that you should actually kill me. Only create the illusion of it, and tell your men that you have avenged your father. Cut my arm with that dagger, and make sure it is well-bloodied. Then you can tell the guards that I turned into a puff of foul green mist as I died, or some such thing. Otherwise, they would wish to see the evidence, I suppose."

Harlin was shaking his head, while I could only bite back my own protests. The thought of Tobyn allowing himself to be wounded in such a way bothered me deeply, and yet I was forced to admit that such a macabre deception was better than the alternative.

"And what of the lady?"

Tobyn smiled. "Escort her to her father's house, for she is not a mage, nor guilty of any crime. Surely no one could have any issue with that."

"I suppose it might work...."

"It will. I can take myself away, and since it will be obvious that I never left this room, what can the soldiers think, except that it happened as you described it?"

Again one of those long, considering silences. The new king glanced toward the door, then over at Tobyn and back again. At last he nodded. "Very well. I think that is the best plan." He paused, then added, "And I do have your word that you will be well gone from Bodenskell?"

"From Bodenskell, and Purth itself. You need not fear that anyone will discover our subterfuge."

Another nod, and then Harlin drew his long dagger from its sheath. Tone almost kind, he said, "You may wish to turn your head, my lady."

"No," I said stoutly, although I hoped I would not put the lie to my own words, and faint when I saw him cut my lover's arm. "If he is willing to do this for me, then the least I can do is be here to share his pain."

Something like approval flickered in the new king's eyes. "If that is what you wish."

As we were speaking, Tobyn had removed the glove from his left hand, and was beginning to push back his sleeve. For the first time, I could see the terrible scarring on his arm, although his hand appeared relatively untouched.

Harlin noticed it, as well, for he seemed to wince, then steadied himself as he held up his dagger. "This is going to hurt."

"I rather expect so," Tobyn replied. "But believe me, I am well-acquainted with pain."

Lips tightening, the new king grasped Tobyn's wrist with his free hand, then quickly drew the dagger across the exposed flesh of my beloved's forearm. Blood welled up quickly, coating the blade. I bit back a sound of dismay, realizing that we had nothing to staunch the wound. But then my gaze fell on the clothes spilling from Tobyn's dropped satchel, and I bent down and grabbed the first thing I could find, a shirt of fine linen.

"It would be my best shirt," he said in resigned tones. "Very well."

I gave him a reproving look as I hurried over to him and wrapped the shirt around his arm. Harlin stepped away, gazing down at the blood on his dagger.

"Is it sufficient, do you think?" Tobyn asked.

"Yes," the new king said slowly. "I rather think it is." He hesitated, "And you will...still be able to depart from this place, even wounded?"

"Of course." Tobyn turned toward me. "Go with him, Annora, and have him bring you to your father's house. I will meet you there."

Before I could reply, he had bent and gathered up his satchel. In the next instant, he was gone. I blinked, and Harlin startled as well. True, I had seen Tobyn come and go in this mysterious fashion before, but always at night, always with the shadows to soften the reality of his abrupt disappearances. Seeing it like this, in daylight, was more than a little unsettling.

The new king seemed to think so as well. He shook his head, as if to clear it of that unnatural vision, then said, "Come, my lady. Let me take you to your father's house."

CHAPTER EIGHTEEN

As my royal escort and I approached my family's home, with its walls of warm brick and climbing ivy shocked into bright hues of crimson and scarlet by the frost, I could not help staring. For there in front of the house stood a carriage, and attached to that carriage was a pair of fine bay horses, their breath puffing out into the chilly autumn air. I knew it could be no one from the royal household, not considering my current companions, but I could think of no one who owned such a fine equipage who would deign to visit my father's house.

All of us stopped there. I had shared the mount of the king's captain, but I slid out of the saddle then as gracefully as I could and approached Harlin where he waited on his handsome black gelding.

"It seems your family has company, my lady," he said. "But I must leave you here, and go to the palace with the news of the sorcerer's 'death.' Will you be quite all right?"

"Yes, Your Majesty," I replied. Lowering my voice, I added, "After all, he will be here to meet me soon, and then I will be very well indeed."

A brisk nod. "Very good. Go on, then."

I curtseyed as deeply as I could, hoping that he would look past the clumsiness of the gesture and see the sincerity in it. For it had been within his power to imprison the both of us, if he so wished, and yet he had shown us mercy quite unlooked-for. He smiled down at me, then raised a hand. The entire troop wheeled about and headed back toward the palace, leaving me alone.

As I glanced toward the front door, it came to me then that I had no key. I would have to knock. Fitting, I supposed, when I considered that very soon this would not be my home at all.

I rapped on the door. A long pause, during which I wondered if anyone intended to answer it at all, and then Darinne stood there, face flushed, tendrils of greying hair escaping the tight knot of hair she wore at the base of her neck.

When her gaze fell upon me, her eyes seemed as if they intended to pop out of her head. "My lady Annora!"

"Hello, Darinne," I said coolly. "It seems I have lost my key. May I come in?"

"'May you come in'?" she repeated, sounding breathless. "Why on earth would you not? This is your home after all."

"I would speak to my father and my sister."

"They're—they're in the main salon," Darinne replied. "With company."

Her news did not surprise me, considering the smart carriage that waited outside the house. I gazed at Darinne expectantly, thinking she would elaborate on the identity of the visitor or visitors, but it seemed my sudden appearance had quite discommoded her.

"Well, then," I said, "I'm afraid I will just have to intrude."

I brushed past her and continued into the house, heading toward the downstairs salon, the only room really fit to receive visitors. As I approached, I heard voices—my father's, and that of a woman, somehow sharp with annoyance, and vaguely familiar.

"...quite beyond the pale, Benedic. The gods only know what has happened to Annora, but if you think I will stand idly by and see Iselda suffer anything close to the same fate—"

In that moment, I stepped into the salon. The woman speaking faced away from the door, but I knew her even so, from the mass of heavily looped and braided mahogany-brown hair, the same shade as my mother's, and mine.

"Aunt Lyselle?" I said in some incredulity.

At once she turned around toward me. Her hand went to her mouth, even as I glanced past her to see my father standing by the hearth, arms crossed and face flushed with anger. And there on the divan was my sister Iselda, who was somehow managing to look both discomfited and thrilled at the same time.

Well, this is an adventure worthy of your storybooks, sister, I thought then. I had no chance for further speech, however, for my aunt came toward me at once and drew me into her arms.

"Oh, my dear Annora, I had feared you lost forever!"

"Not precisely, Aunt Lyselle. However, I thought it better to remove myself from the court immediately." I deemed it best in that moment to leave Tobyn out of the conversation. He had said he would meet me here, but I did not know precisely when. Of course he wouldn't materialize in the salon in front of everyone. He was far too circumspect for that. Perhaps he was even now waiting for me upstairs.

My aunt's eyes widened. "How is it that you managed to get away? For I heard the worst—of—of sorcery, of—" Words seemed to fail her, and she plucked a lace-edged kerchief from her bodice and waved it in the air, as if the drift of perfume that came from it might help to restore her nerves somewhat.

"The court does love its gossip," I said airily. "I cannot tell you everything, dear aunt, for your own safety. But at least be heartened that I am well, even if I must be leaving soon."

"Leaving?" Iselda piped up, even as my father said, tone rough with anger,

"And good riddance, for you have brought down such calamity upon this house that the name of Kelsden will never recover!"

"Indeed?" I said, my voice cold as the River Marden when it froze in the winter. "I think it more accurate to say that you were the first to bring down that calamity, and everything I did afterward was only an attempt to survive it."

"Peace," my aunt said, holding up her hands, which sparkled with gems that would have done the Lady Shelenna proud. "Done is done, and we must all live with the consequences. If you feel you must leave after everything that has happened, my dear Annora, I cannot fault you for your decision. I think it most wise, in fact." Her gaze shifted back to my father. "Indeed, I was just telling your father that I did not think it a good situation for Iselda to remain here any longer, and I would take her back to my home with me."

My eyes widened, even as I acknowledged the wisdom of such an action. Aunt Lyselle had three daughters of her own, the eldest only a little older than my sister. At my aunt's grand country estate, Iselda could escape her father's iniquity, as well as her sister's notoriety. And with the wealth and title of my uncle the baron to shield her, she might have a very good start in society, once all of today's terrible events were in the past and the gossips had moved on to another story.

Well, true, moving past the killing of a king in front of his entire court might take longer than it would some more trifling matter. But I must hope for the best.

"I think that sounds like a most excellent idea," I said. "What think you, Iselda?"

She was silent for a moment, seeming to consider my words. Then, golden head cocked to one side, she said, "At first I was not sure, because I would be missing you, but if you are to go away, then I really have no reason to stay in Bodenskell."

My father winced at those words, but I could not feel any pity for him. He had never shown Iselda any particular affection or regard, so why should he be surprised now that she did not feel any true connection to him?

"Then it is settled." Aunt Lyselle fixed my father with a stern look, one that dared him to defy her. But he, witnessing the collapse of his family before his eyes, did not seem to have any arguments to offer. Indeed, as I watched, I saw how his gaze was fixed, not on any of us, but on the cut-glass decanter of brandy that sat on one of the side tables. No doubt he would pour himself a strong measure as soon as we were all safely out of his sight. "Iselda, go pack your things, for I wish to return home as soon as possible."

With a nod, my sister pushed herself off the divan and hurried out of the salon, giving me a knowing glance as she passed. That look told me she expected to be told all the details of my sojourn at the palace before she left. While I could not tell her everything, I did resolve to let her know as much as I could. I owed her that much.

Once she was gone, I said quietly, "Thank you, Aunt Lyselle. For that was my one worry about leaving—that she should have no one to properly care for her."

My father winced again, but Lyselle affected not to notice. I had no doubt that she did, for her sharp green eyes missed very little. However, she had clearly decided that she would waste no more thought on my father's feelings, not when he so clearly had no regard for those of anyone else, least of all his daughters.

"I think she will do very well," my aunt said. "It will be better for her, to be surrounded by girls close to her own age, and not to always have her nose in a book. And you, Benedic—do not think that with both your daughters gone, you may continue to raid my late sister's dowry. I will be enlisting legal help on Iselda's behalf in the very near future, so you should begin thinking now of how you will fund your carousing from here on out."

"I know a most excellent attorney here in the city, if you do not have any local contacts," I put in, not bothering to keep the amusement out of my voice. No doubt Master Jamsden would find my sister's cause a very worthy one.

Aunt Lyselle appeared startled that I had made such an offer, but then she smiled and nodded. "That would be most excellent, Annora, for I must confess that I have spent most of my time in the country and do not know much of the business-people here in town."

"You would help her in this!" my father thundered. Once upon a time, being addressed in that tone would have made me shrink away, but I had faced down the king, and so now my father did not frighten me any longer. "In taking away my last means of support? Have you no family feelings at all?"

"I have feelings for my sister," I said calmly. "That dowry is hers. Where I am going, I shall have no need of it."

For the first time, my aunt appeared somewhat hesitant. "Yes, Annora, you have said that, but where are you going? Surely you cannot be thinking of setting forth on your own?"

I hesitated. "I will not be alone," I replied, thinking I should give her something of the truth. "I would not say more on that subject. Only know that I will be quite safe and protected. As to where I am going...." I let the words die away, then lifted my shoulders. "I think perhaps it is best if you do not know that."

My father's lip curled. "You need not be so mysterious, Annora. Do you not think the word has already spread about who you have been consorting with? Abandoning your father to be with that foul sorcerer?"

I did flinch at those words, for I had been hoping the gossip had not gotten quite this far. But no doubt the tale had already begun to run through the city, even as Tobyn and I went to his house to retrieve his belongings.

To my surprise, Lyselle waved her handkerchief and said, "As far as I can tell, the people of Purth should be thanking that 'foul sorcerer,' for Elsdon seemed to be going quite out of his mind. Why, he threatened to dishonor your daughter, right there in front of everyone! Any father hearing that should have been asking for his blood, king or no."

"You were there?" I asked, quite shocked by her declaration.

"Yes, I had made one last trip into town before winter settled in, and of course if one is in town, one must go to court. I had heard nothing of how the king was holding you in the palace, Annora, for of course that is not the sort of thing a person wishes to get about. And we are so isolated up there in Daleskeld. But when I came to town, I heard how the king was planning to marry a young woman with the same name as my niece, which I thought somewhat strange, although of course 'Annora' is not that uncommon in this part of the realm. But then the wedding was called off, but the king still wanted everyone present, and...." She trailed off then, shaking her head. "Never in my life had I expected to see anything like what I witnessed earlier this afternoon, but it was clear enough what had to be done. I had often said to the baron that this land would be a far better place if Prince Harlin sat on the throne, and now we will be able to see for ourselves. So I suppose it is all very regrettable, but on the other hand, I think that your sorcerer has rather done Purth a public service."

My father looked very nearly apoplectic at that statement. "Public service? Are you mad?"

"No, but I fear His Majesty was," she said calmly. "But that is neither here nor there. I am sure you will wish to get your things, Annora. Do not worry about your father—I will make sure he does not interfere."

And though his eyes bulged and his cheeks flushed an even darker red, he did nothing to stop me from smiling at her and then leaving the room. I went up the stairs to the little sunlit chamber that had been mine ever since I was old enough to be out of the cradle, with its narrow bed of carved oak and the tarnished mirror that hung on one wall.

For a long moment, I stood there, surveying those familiar surroundings, committing them to memory, since I knew I would never see them again. And as I stood there, Tobyn appeared by the window, light glowing around his dark form, for it seemed he had acquired a new cloak sometime after he disappeared from his study.

I ran to him then and threw my arms around him, and he held me close, then bent and kissed me, over and over. It was as if we both had to reassure ourselves that the other person was real, that we were here together and ready to face whatever came next.

At last we drew apart, however, and I said, "Truly, I am not sure what to take with me."

He took my hand, then kissed it gently. "Only the necessities, my love. Your warmest dresses, and a good sturdy cloak. It is cold in the northlands, even this early in Octevre. And remember that we can purchase anything you might lack."

Those words reassured me, and I retrieved the sturdy leather satchel that had once been my mother's from its resting place on the floor of my wardrobe. I had never before had cause to use it, for I had never gone visiting, but now I filled it with undergarments and chemises and my warmest, plainest gowns.

"I fear I will be somewhat conspicuous in this," I said then, running a finger over the embroidered damask of my sleeve, for of course I still wore the rich court dress I had donned earlier that day.

"Then change your gown."

I lifted an eyebrow at him, and he added hastily,

"While I wait outside your door."

Chuckling, I said, "I fear I will need something of your help, for this gown laces up the back, and I cannot manage it myself."

"Annora—"

"It was your idea, Tobyn, was it not?"

Without replying, he came to me and reached for the lacings at the back of my gown. One tug, and I felt them loosen. He pulled a bit more, and suddenly the dress began to slip down my shoulders. I quickly caught it, saying, "That will do very well. Now it is probably better if you wait outside."

He moved with such haste that I wanted to laugh again, and then shut the door behind him. I made short work of slipping out of the gown, which I then folded and placed on my bed, and pulled one of the dresses I had already packed from the satchel and stepped into it. Because both Iselda and I had to dress ourselves, we made sure our gowns were made with side lacings, and so I was able to get myself modestly attired in very short order.

The whole time, though, I had been thinking of Tobyn's fingers pulling at the laces of the first gown, and what it would be like when we were alone together, and he could do that very thing all over again, at a time when he would not have to stop....

I shivered, then shoved the discarded court gown into my satchel and buckled it closed. When I opened the door, it was to see Tobyn standing there, and Iselda looking up at him with a quizzical expression on her face.

"Are you the one who is taking my sister away?" she asked.

Although I could not see his face, I guessed that he smiled. "I would not say that I am taking her away, but rather that we are about to go on a journey together."

She seemed to consider those words for a moment. Then she sent him one of those direct looks I knew all too well. "Why do you wear that cloak when you are indoors? Do you easily take a chill?"

He hesitated, and I saw the hood shift slightly in my direction, as if asking for my opinion as to how he should answer.

"That is your decision, Tobyn," I said. "But it is better if she knows the truth, I think."

"The truth about what?" she inquired. I noticed then that she held a satchel of her own, far smaller and more battered than mine. Where on earth had she found it? Perhaps it had been a discard of my father's; Iselda often liked to give throwaways a home, declaring that they had not yet outlived their usefulness.

"About this," Tobyn said quietly as he reached up to push back his hood.

Iselda's eyes widened. But I noticed she did not flinch. Instead, she frowned slightly, as if attempting to determine what could have caused the scars on his face. "Was it a fire?" she asked at last.

"Yes, it was. You see keenly, my lady Iselda."

A pink flush spread over her cheeks. "Well, it is only that Grimsby—Grimsby is our cook—has a scar on his arm rather like that, from hot oil, only his is not quite so bad. Was it a very terrible fire?"

"I fear it was." Clearly, he wished to speak no more on the subject, for he glanced at me and said, "Several streets over is a livery stable. I had thought to go there and see if I can acquire some horses for us. Shall I do that, while you say your goodbyes to your family?"

How had he known that I desired some privacy to make my farewells? It was not that I did not love him, or want him near, but neither did I want him to witness my grief at leaving my sister and see anything in it of regret for going with him. They were two entirely separate matters, although they both lived in my heart.

"That sounds like a very good plan," I said. "Thank you, Master Slade."

He nodded at both of us and went down the stairs, while Iselda and I lingered on the landing. After a brief pause, she said, "He does not look very much like a handsome prince."

"That is because he is not one."

She let out a sigh. "I suppose not. I had just thought that you must have a handsome prince one day because you are so very beautiful."

"No, dearest. I think it is up to you to find your own handsome prince, if that is what you think you want."

"At least there is more chance of that now I am going to live with Aunt Lyselle. A baroness must have a prince around from time to time, don't you think?"

Her expression was so serious that I smothered the smile which had begun to form on my lips. "I would think that is a possibility, yes."

Iselda fell silent for a moment, her gaze fixed on the staircase Tobyn had descended just a few moments earlier. "It is all right that he is not handsome."

"Well, I am glad you think so. What made you come to that conclusion?"

Her hazel eyes, so like mine, were wide and guileless. "Why, because he loves you so."

Bluster he might, but my father could do nothing to stop any of us, not with Tobyn appearing suddenly like a harbinger of doom in his black cloak, and not with my aunt fixing him with a narrow-eyed stare that promised all manner of repercussions if he should attempt to stand in our way. In the end, I hugged her and thanked her for taking Iselda into her household, and I hugged my sister rather longer and told her to be good, and to make Aunt Lyselle proud of her.

"Of course I will," Iselda responded. "But if I don't make her proud, how will you ever know?"

"I have my ways," I said, and kissed her.

She laughed and shook her head, and then the footman shut the door of the carriage behind her. After he got back up on his perch, the coach began to rattle away over the cobbled streets.

"Come, my love," Tobyn said quietly, taking me by the hand and leading me over to the horses he had just purchased. They were not nearly as fine as the blood bays drawing my aunt's carriage, but they seemed sturdy and strong enough, and probably better suited for an overland journey of many leagues.

My father had already retreated into the house, slamming the door behind him. All of us had pointedly ignored that display, although I couldn't help experiencing a pang as I caught a brief look at him as he pulled the curtains of his study shut, blocking out any last glimpse he might have had of his wayward daughter.

I allowed Tobyn to boost me up into the saddle, praying all the while that I could manage the feat without looking horribly awkward. When I was younger and had visited my aunt's estates in the summer, her grooms had taught me the rudiments of riding, but I was sorely out of practice. Well, I would get plenty of practice on the journey to North Eredor.

Tobyn mounted his own horse once he was sure I sat more or less securely in my saddle. His movements were far more graceful than mine, and it seemed he knew something of horses as well, for they both moved down the street at his direction, once he made a small chirruping sound and guided his mount in the direction that would lead to Bodenskell's northern gate.

By then it was quite late in the afternoon, and the sun had already begun to dip down behind the forests that bordered the eastern edge of the capital city. A look of concern must have passed over my face, for Tobyn said quickly, "I thought it best to be beyond the city gates come nightfall. There is a town only an hour's ride to the north, and I have heard it has several good inns. We will stop there and set out again in the morning."

That news did reassure me somewhat. "And we will stay there...as husband and wife?" For certainly it made more sense to share one room, rather than to take two.

"We will stay however you wish."

His tone was neutral. It seemed that he still had not completely accepted my desire for him. "That is how I wish. And perhaps...."

"Perhaps?"

Gathering my courage, I said, "Perhaps we will not get there so late that we cannot find a priest. If we do, then we truly can be husband and wife...assuming that is your wish."

"'My wish'?" he repeated with some incredulity. "Annora, you know that is my fondest wish."

"Then let us make it so."

We rode more quickly after that, and in time came to the town he had spoken of, a pretty little place with buildings of stone and wood, nestled in a pleasant valley where the River Marden cut through. And after asking several of the townspeople we came across, we did find a priest. He seemed somewhat startled by our urgency—or perhaps was somewhat annoyed that we had sought him out just as he was about to sit down to his evening meal—but he did perform the ceremony for us, with his exasperated wife standing as witness. We made sure to give the priest an extra silver coin for his trouble, although I was not sure that was enough to mollify his wife over her cold dinner.

And then we went to the town's finest inn, and took its finest room for the night, and had our own little feast of venison stew, washed down with the strong local red wine. After that, we were alone in our room, the two of us gazing at each other, neither wishing to be the one to speak first.

At last I said, "Perhaps I should be grateful that this gown laces on the side." I pulled at the cords, and it came loose enough so that it fell to the floor in a puddle of green linen, leaving me standing there in my chemise.

Tobyn had already taken off his cloak, since we'd barred the door behind us. His green eyes glinted with desire in the light from the candles in their sconces on the wall, but he did not move. "Annora—"

I stepped out of the folds of my discarded dress and went to him, fingers working at the buttons on his doublet. He did not stop me, and shrugged out of it once it was completely unfastened. But when I went to tug at the ties that held his shirt closed at his throat, his hand closed on mine. "Annora, you must know—"

His intention seemed clear enough to me. Even in the uncertain candlelight, I could see the scarring on the hand that held my fingers so tightly. I wondered that it should be scarred, when the other was quite unblemished. "It is all right, Tobyn," I whispered. "Whatever that fire did to you...I do not care. Unless it was so bad that...." I had to break off then. My knowledge of such matters was meager at best, but I had heard whispers of how sometimes a man could not be a true husband to his wife.

"No," he said at once, his words calming my fears. "No, it was not that bad. I can still...love you."

"Then show me, Tobyn," I replied, still clinging to his shirt. "Show me, my husband."

That seemed to be the only encouragement he required, for he gathered me in his arms and took me to the bed. Our mouths met, even as our hands worked to remove our remaining pieces of clothing and fling them to the floor. And then it was his skin against mine, and yes, he was scarred, but I did not care, because that was part of who he'd become. The king could not destroy him. Instead, he had only made the man I loved that much stronger.

Two bodies became one, perfect, whole. He healed me, and I healed him, and we fell asleep in one another's arms.

We would wake with the dawn, and go on to forge one life together, shining, golden, and bright.

THE END

CPSIA information can be obtained at www.ICGtesting.com
Printed in the USA
LVOW06s0010131215

466452LV00002B/442/P